# PRAISE FOR *U*

# Books by Nelle L'Amour

### Unforgettable

*Unforgettable Book 1*
*Unforgettable Book 2*
*Unforgettable Book 3*

### Seduced by the Park Avenue Billionaire

*Strangers on a Train*
*Derailed*
*Final Destination*
*Seduced by the Billionaire Boxed Set*

### An Erotic Love Story

*Undying Love*

### Gloria

*Gloria's Secret*
*Gloria's Revenge*
*Gloria's Forever*
*Gloria's Secret: The Trilogy*

### THAT MAN Series

*THAT MAN 1*
*THAT MAN 2*
*THAT MAN 3*
*THAT MAN 4*
*THAT MAN 5*

### Writing under E.L. Sarnoff

*Dewitched: The Untold Story of the Evil Queen*
*Unhitched: The Untold Story of the Evil Queen*

# Unforgettable
# Book 1

# Unforgettable

BOOK ONE

NELLE L'AMOUR

NICHOLS CANYON PRESS
Los Angeles, CA USA

Unforgettable Book 1
By Nelle L'Amour

Cover by Arijana Karcic, Cover It! Designs
Proofreading by Mary Jo Toth
Formatting by BB eBooks

# Dedication

*In memory of my Daddy.*
*You'll always be unforgettable.*

*"A remembrance of things past is not necessarily one of things as they were."*

—Marcel Proust, *In Search of Lost Time*

# Unforgettable
# Book 1

## *Prologue*

## *Zoey*

*Twenty years earlier*

*M*ama. She's beautiful. As beautiful as a princess. She has long, wavy red hair that dances in the wind. And whenever she waltzes around our house, singing so pretty, her hair prances too. She reminds me of Ariel, The Little Mermaid. Except my mama never ever swims.

After I saw that movie with Mama, I asked her why she won't swim. She told me she once almost drowned in the ocean when she was a little girl. Like my mama, I'm afraid of the water. Even Papa, when he was alive, couldn't get me to go in. I miss Papa and so does Mama.

Especially on days like today. I'm five! I'm a big girl now, says Mama. For my special birthday, she's taken me to the Santa Monica Pier. I may be afraid of the big bad ocean, but I love the pier. And so does Mama. So many fun rides! And games to play too! And guess what! Now that I'm a big girl, I can finally go on the ginormous rollercoaster. Yippee! Mama and I sit together, and holding on to her floppy straw hat, she screams as much as me. *Whoosh*! It's so fast! So much fun!

"Pretty please. One more time," I beg when it's over. One smoochie and she lets me do it again. I wish my cousin Jeffrey was here too, but Mama told me he came down with the flu and had to stay home with Auntie Jo.

"Mama, I'm hungry," I say after we hop off the ride.

"Me too, baby girl. Let's get some corn dogs."

"YAY!" I love corn dogs.

Mama buys two corn dogs from a food stand, one for me and one for her. "C'mon, let's look for dolphins while we eat them." She takes my hand and we walk over to the edge of the pier. The blue-gray ocean is below us. I know that color from my Crayola box. We watch the high as the sky waves roll in. Mama tells me the water's very rough today.

I take a big bite of my corn dog and then ask Mama, "Do you think we'll see a dolphin?"

She smiles. "Of course, my precious girl. They'll dance for your birthday. But I want you to hold my hand and not lean in too close to the railing."

I giggle. "Mama, I won't fall in!"

She squeezes my hand. Mama's beautiful hands are soft like velvet. And they're magical too. They make me feel safe and fix all my boo-boos.

I keep my eyes out for some dolphins. The sun is so bright it hurts them. Squinting, all I see are lots of squawking sea gulls.

In the background, I hear music. There's a concert going on. They always do concerts on the pier in the Spring. I know that song! It's Mama's favorite. "Unforgettable." She sang it all the time after Papa died. It reminds her of him. Mama smiles and sings along. I love the way she sings. She sounds like an angel.

In the middle of the song, a creepy man walks up next to me. He's got an eyepatch like a pirate and a cigarette in his mouth. I thought people weren't allowed to smoke on the pier. He blows out a puff and I cough. I want to tell him to put it out, but he scares me. I move closer to Mama and hope the man will get in trouble. If Uncle Pete were here, he'd arrest him and put him in jail.

I frown. "Mama, the dolphins are hiding today. Let's do one more ride."

"Patience, sweet girl." Mama always says patience has its virtues, but I don't know what she means by that.

I beg again for another ride and even say the magic word, "please." Then, just after I take the last bite of my corn dog, I see one, leaping out of the water. And then, another and another! "Look, Mama! Dolphins!" Jumping up and down, I point at them.

But Mama doesn't hear me. She's slumped over the railing. She's got an ouchie! And she's bleeding! A whole big bunch!

She whispers my name. The blood is spreading all over the back of her pretty sundress. Why won't it stop? I must help her!

"Mama! Mama!" I tug on her. But I can't get her to budge.

I turn to the yucky man for help.

"Mister—"

A loud grunt and then he falls to the ground. Face up. There's blood all around him. Everywhere! His shirt is all red. His eyes are still open, but I think he's dead. I scream so loud my throat hurts. And then I see him. A scary man with a gun! He fires it one more time—at me—and then he runs away. He disappears into the crowd, but I'll *never* forget his ugly face.

I turn back around. Oh no! Mama she's gone! Spinning, I search everywhere for her and then I look down. I scream again. Louder.

"Mama!" She's fallen into the angry ocean. It tosses her. Around and around and around. She's drowning!

"Mama!" I cry out again, tears falling.

An arm reaches out to me. Her lips mouth three words: "I love you." Then, her eyes close and she goes under.

"Mama! Mama!" I sob. "Someone help my mama! PLEASE!"

The pier is so noisy nobody hears me. She's floating now. On her back, her hat by her side. Her coral hair is spread out like a sea fan. And there's a little smile on her face. Maybe she's all better.

"Mama! Can you hear me?" I shout out, hope in my voice. "Wake up! Pl—"

Before I can say the magic word, a gigantic wave crashes over her peaceful body. With a roar, it carries her away.

"Mama, come back!" I no longer see her. Or will I ever.

My tears salt the sea.

The words of Mama's favorite song drift into my ears.

I'm crying so loud I can hardly hear them.

But I know this moment will always be unforgettable.

# *Brandon*

*Two weeks earlier*

FUCK.
CLUNK.
SMACK.
BLACK.

# Chapter 1

## *Brandon*

Beeping sounds clog my ears.

A chorus of muddled whispers surrounds me.

My eyelids flutter.

A woman's urgent voice: "Quick. Get this! He's waking up."

I peel my eyes open, one by one. Slowly. Painfully. As if they've been super glued shut. The bright light burns my retinas. Everything's a blur. A haze of bodies scuttles about me. I blink several times. My vision becomes clearer, and then I'm blinded by the flash of a camera. *Click. Click. Click.* I blink again until I stop seeing spots. A new lens assaults me. What's a hand-held camera doing in my face?

"Get in tighter," orders the woman, her voice growing shrill. "I want a close-up."

A pair of lips comes crashing down on mine before

I can get my mouth to move. They hold me prisoner while camera flashes bombard me and the hand-held camera captures the unexpected kiss. The fierce lips pull away, but the camera in my face stays put.

"Get that away from me!" I croak, barely able to free my tongue from my desert-dry palate. My voice is a rasp and my throat sore as hell.

I swat at the cameraman with my hand that's not hooked up to all kinds of freaky, beeping machines. Reality hits me hard. I'm in a hospital. And the pain hits harder. I've got a headache the size of Texas. Unable to deter my harasser, I throw the bedcovers over my head.

"We've got enough." That woman's authoritative voice again. "We'll edit in post."

Hesitantly, I lower the covers from my face. A stunning, willowy blonde with cat-green eyes hovers over me. Her billowy scarlet lips are parted in a pout and then they break into a wide toothy smile. The cameraman follows her.

She brushes her manicured hand along my forehead. "Darling, you're awake. Finally. Smile for the cameras." She mugs for the cameras while I rub the back of my scalp. A large scab brushes against the pads of my fingertips along with a bump as big as a walnut. I wince.

"That's a wrap," calls out a craggy man with a ponytail. "We'll pick it up when he blows out of this joint." My eyes fix on the small crew as they pack up their equipment and file out of the room. The attractive woman stays behind and lowers herself onto the edge of my bed. She cranks her body so she's facing me.

"Who are you?" My voice is still strangled.

She flashes a ring with a diamond the size of a bullet in my eyes. The bling blinds me. I blink again.

She hesitates for a beat and then purses her full lips. "Your fiancée."

A golf-ball sized lump lands in my parched throat. "Excuse me?"

She flings her full head of platinum hair. "Come on, now. You know who I am."

"What's your name?" I manage in my disoriented state.

Her feline eyes narrow. "Are you playing games with me, Brandon?"

She called me Brandon. Yeah, that's my name. Brandon Taylor. I remember that. But I have no clue who this woman is, yet she claims we're engaged.

With a groan, I sit up slowly. It's an effort. My body feels like it's been rammed by a bulldozer. Every muscle aches. And my head's still pounding. I take in my surroundings. I'm in a sleek all-white suite with wall-to-wall flower arrangements. Their overbearing sweet smell assaults my senses. A wave of nausea sweeps over me.

"Can I have some water?" I ask, hoping the liquid

will assuage the sickening feeling and knock some sense into me.

"Of course, darling." The woman reaches for a sippy cup on the stand alongside my bed and hands it to me. I take a long sip through the straw. The cool beverage feels good. As it courses down my throat, it quenches my thirst. I take a few more sips and place the cup on my lap. To be more precise, on my cock. It's soft as a pillow, but thank God, it's still there. I remember my cock better than I remember my name. It's a big, hard fucking machine. Or at least it once was. The drop dead gorgeous woman beside me, who says she's my fiancée, does nothing to stir it. Not even one teeny-weeny testicular tingle. I shudder. I may be in big trouble.

"So tell me your name."

"Katrina. Katrina Moore. Does it ring a bell?"

Her tone sounds like she's testing me. I shake my aching head.

"Are you sure?"

It doesn't ring anything, including my balls. My attention is diverted by a stocky man bursting through the open door.

"Hey, my boy. You're awake!" He strides up to me and pats me on my back.

I gaze up at him. Tanned, teeth perfect and pearly white. Hair bottle-brown and greased back. Expensive Italian twill suit and flashy gold jewelry. Forty. Maybe fifty? Yet another unfamiliar face.

"And who are you?"

He shoots Katrina a questioning look. His left eye twitches. "Is he fucking kidding?"

She shakes her head. "I don't think so."

They hold each other's gazes as if they're silently communicating, and then the strange man casts his eyes back on me.

"I'm your manager. Scott Turner."

I have a fiancée. And now I have a manager?

"What do you manage?"

"Jeez, Brand-man. Your career."

"My career?" Reality to Brandon. Come in for fuck's sake.

The woman named Katrina interjects. "He seriously doesn't seem to remember a thing."

My so-called manager furrows his dark brows. "He's bullshitting us."

Rage surges inside me. "I'm not bullshitting anyone. I don't even know how I got here."

With a smile, Katrina defends me. "Trust me, Scotty-Wotty, he's not acting. He's really lost his mind."

Unconvinced, Scott twists his thin lips. "Does *Kurt Kussler* mean anything to you?"

"Who's he?"

"He's the character you play on TV. The number one rated show that's made you Hollywood's highest paid actor. And every woman's wet dream."

I'm an actor? A Hollywood heartthrob? All I know is right now I'm a nut job. "So, how did I get here?" My voice falters.

"You seriously don't remember what happened?"

"Not a clue."

Shifting, Katrina fiddles with her engagement ring. "Scott, I think it'd be better if he heard it from you."

Scott's expression darkens and then it relaxes. "You were struck by a car. It was a hit and run. You're lucky I called it in. I saved your ass. You suffered a skull fracture, underwent surgery, and have been in a coma for two weeks. It's been headline news. All over the Internet and TMZ. And don't get me started on Twitter. You've got more followers than Justin Bieber."

*Justin Bieber? TMZ?* Digesting his words, I stroke my jaw. A bristly beard scrapes my hand. I must look like a caveman.

Katrina cups my other hand, the one with all the IVs. "You had me so worried. I've been by your side praying you'd recover." She plants a hot kiss on my cheek. It does nothing to arouse me. More worry washes over me as she runs her fingers through my hair.

"Darling, we're going to have to get you cleaned up and into shape. You should be just fine by the time the wedding is televised."

Impulsively, I yank my hand from hers. "What are you talking about?"

Her face lights up. "We're getting married and the whole world is going to watch. On a special edition of my reality show, *America's It Girl*. My ratings are going to go through the roof."

A sinking feeling sets in. I don't remember a god-damn thing. And you know what, maybe I don't want to.

# Chapter 2

## *Brandon*

The next three days in the hospital are ones I'll remember. I get my first taste of fame, and I'm not sure I like it. Once word gets out that I'm alive and well (except for my memory loss), every nurse, attendant, and doctor stops by my suite on Cedar's VIP floor for my autograph. It's like a circus. My hand is so sore I may need a sling.

Katrina shows up every day, in one designer outfit after another, and sits with me for an hour or so. Now that I'm out of my coma and on the road to recovery, she's got better things to do. Like shop and work out. And, of course, plan for our wedding.

Each time she visits, she brings along a slew of tabloids to jog my memory. I *am* headline news. The front page of last week's *Enquirer* is plastered with a photo of me in my coma all hooked up to gizmos and monitors and my teary-eyed fiancée by my bedside. Or should I say deathbed. The all-caps headline: "DOOMS-DAY FOR BRATRINA!" *Bratrina?* What bonehead came up with that? I cringe.

Older issues from last month feature photos of Katrina and me in happier times . . . out to dinner . . . at a movie premier . . . at the beach. I read the articles and study the pictures. We look and sound like the hottest couple in Hollywood. But no matter how hard I search my brain, I can't remember a damn thing. *Nada. Zippo. Zilch.*

"How did we meet?" I ask my fiancée on my third day of being conscious. Despite her goddess-like beauty and come-ons, America's It Girl still doesn't do a thing for me. Not even a little rise.

Sitting nearby on an armchair and thumbing through one of the tabloids, she looks up and rolls her eyes. I'm not sure if she's frustrated with my memory loss or pissed off for the interruption.

"Through Scott. He's my manager too. He hooked us up at the Chateau Marmont. Remember?"

A hint of sarcasm underscores her last word. I shake my head no. "And how long have we been together?" Despite all the articles I've read, the details of our relationship are sparse.

Crossing her long, toned bare legs, she quirks a small but seductive smile. "Almost two months. It was love at first sight. The minute we fucked our brains out, we couldn't be apart."

So, I fucked my way into her heart. But why can't I feel anything for her there or elsewhere? Amnesia sucks dick.

"And when did I propose to you?" My eyes soak in her engagement ring with its sparkling mega-sized marquise diamond. Must have cost a bloody fortune, but I have no recollection of buying it. Scott, who handles all my finances, must have a record of it somewhere.

"Just before the accident." She holds up the *Star* magazine she's reading. A close-up photo of her, looking tearful, her ring in full view, dominates the front page. Headline: "Tragedy Strikes after Brandon Pops the Big Question!" I glimpse the publication date. If my calculations are right, it came out the Monday after my accident.

I snatch the newspaper from her and flip through it until I get to the cover story. Photos of Bratrina grace the pages. I quickly peruse the article. So, I proposed to her over a romantic meal at my Hollywood Hills house the night before the accident and purchased the gazillion carat ring at Tiffany's. I have no memory of the event or, for that matter, of my house. I'm eager to see it. And to get out of this antiseptic hellhole where a doctor or nurse is either fawning over me or poking me every fifteen minutes for my vitals. I'm feeling pretty good. And now that I've shaved, look almost back to normal.

"And what happened after I proposed to you?"

"Take a guess, Brandy-Poo."

*Brandy-Poo?* The sound of it gives me mental diarrhea. I don't recall anyone ever calling me that in my entire life. Or at least what I can remember of it.

"We toasted with champagne?"

She throws back her platinum mane and laughs. "Don't be ridiculous. We fucked our brains out. Right on your terrace."

She scoots in closer and cups her hand over my crotch. And then squeezes it.

"I can't wait to get some of you. It's been a while."

I go wide-eyed as she yanks down my cover. I'm clad in a hospital gown with nothing underneath. She hikes it up and there it is parked like a car. My enormous Rolls Royce of a cock.

Katrina licks her full upper lip. "Remember me?" she purrs as if she's talking to my stationary organ. Without moving a muscle, I watch as she wraps her long fingers around the shaft. My goddamn cock just lies there as if it's still in a comatose state. Brain to cock: Wake up. Nothing. There's no connection. She begins to pump it with long, hard, vigorous strokes, but my cock doesn't respond. It's like the battery is dead. Frustrated, she strokes harder, faster. Not a peep from Mr. Willy no matter how much I will it to attention.

"Jesus, Brandon!" Katrina grumbles, pumping so

hard it hurts. "What the hell is wrong with you?"

I must say I'm a little worried myself. Scratch that. I'm friggin' freaking. My pulse leaps into overdrive, and one of the monitors I'm still hooked up to starts beeping madly. Where's a damn doctor when you really need one?

"I-I don't know," I stutter, gazing down at my pathetic limp dick. "Maybe it's all the pain meds I'm on."

Katrina abruptly releases her hand. "Probably. I'm going to have a little chat with your doctors. The only pill you need is Viagra."

My cock sags. Amnesia is bad enough. But erectile dysfunction?

Kill me now. I might as well be dead.

# Chapter 3

## *Brandon*

At the end of the long, frustrating week, I'm finally released from the hospital. The doctors have told me I have a classic case of retrograde amnesia—a common side effect of the traumatic brain injury I sustained from the accident I can't remember. While it likely won't be permanent, they cannot determine how long it'll last. It could be weeks. Months. Even years. What's important is that I stimulate myself with people and things from the past. My biggest concern: will they stimulate my cock? I haven't even been able to wank myself off. My libido, thanks to the amnesia, is in limbo.

My house is a sprawling glass and concrete contemporary that sits high atop a private road in the Hollywood Hills. The views from the ubiquitous floor-to-ceiling windows are spectacular; I'm able to see all the way from the Pacific Ocean to downtown LA. They also overlook a spacious backyard, which boasts an Olympic-sized pool and a guesthouse. A three-car garage is attached to the main house and lined up inside it are a sleek black Lamborghini, a vintage green Jag, and a monster red Hummer. To say I'm awed by my wealth would be an understatement.

I roam the expansive one-story house, taking in my surroundings and hoping something will stimulate my memory while Katrina goes to the kitchen to make lunch. It's decorated with slick, oversized Italian furniture, mixing rich woods with leather. Photos of me are everywhere. Many of them sexy poses, with my chiseled chest exposed. A large framed picture hanging on a wall captures my attention. It's a blow-up of a recent cover of *People Magazine*. The headline: "Brandon Taylor: Sexiest Man Alive!" With my perfectly mussed up ebony hair, those piercing violet eyes, that cocky smile, and my strong stubble-lined jaw, I look pretty damn hot, if I must say so myself. A troubling thought flashes into my head. Yikes. Maybe I'm gay. That's why I can't get it up for Katrina. Nah. None of those good-looking docs at the hospital did a thing for me. And I can't remember doing it with another guy. The unsettling thought goes away.

Katrina returns with a tray of gourmet sandwiches along with two flutes of champagne. Today, she's clad in tight-ass jeans, a turtleneck halter, and sky-high mules that make her look like a total Amazon. Her bountiful boobs stay as still as mountains as she saunters my way.

"Your doctor says you need to eat and rest to get your strength back," she says, setting the tray on the coffee table.

I can't argue with her. At the reminder of my ordeal, I inwardly shudder. According to Katrina and my doctors, I was almost *People Magazine's* "Sexiest Man Dead!" I'm still weak and have lost some weight. Maybe a little R&R will help restore my memory. And potency. The cock is like a muscle, right? I remember reading somewhere that muscles have memory. Well, score one for me. I've remembered something. But why won't my cock do the same?

Katrina reaches for the two flutes of champagne and hands one to me. "To us," she toasts, holding up her glass. I clink mine against it. The ping resounds in my ears.

"I only drink Cristal," my companion says as she lifts the crystal glass to her lips. They look much fuller than they did a couple of days ago. I follow her actions and take a sip of the chilled bubbly. The cool sparkling liquid sails down my throat and triggers another memory. I'd rather be drinking a beer.

"Katrina, do we have any beer? A Heineken by chance?"

She rolls her feline green eyes. "Darling, beer is a

four-letter word reserved for peasants. We're royalty. How can you not love the world's finest champagne?"

Stuck with the champagne, I take a seat on the over-sized u-shaped couch. Setting her flute back down on the tray, my fiancée follows me, except she straddles my long legs and sits on my lap. Her toned arms fold around my neck. Her tits skim my chest, and through my cotton T-shirt, I can feel her plastic-hard nipples. I have no desire to touch them or see what lies beneath her top. The scent of her cloying floral perfume wafts in the air and nauseates me.

"Does it feel good to be home?" she purrs before nuzzling my neck. Goosebumps pop along my skin, but that's all that's rising. Her mouth moves to my lips and she kisses me fiercely. Biting my lower lip, she forces me to part my mouth and her tongue darts inside. She takes the lead, swishing it around. Nothing's familiar. My eyes stay wide open while awaiting some feeling of arousal. *Nada.* Not even a little buzz.

She breaks away. Her manicured forefinger traces my wet lips.

"Do you like the way I taste?" she breathes into my mouth.

"Yeah," I lie. She doesn't taste good. A hint of tobacco mixes with mint and champagne. Is she a smoker? She shoves the finger into my mouth, adding a salty layer of flavor.

While I force myself to suck her finger, she works

the button and fly of my jeans. Successfully, she frees my soft cock. My unblinking eyes stay trained on her as she grips the thick length in her hand and goes down on the wide crown. Her lips wrap around it and then she trails her mouth down the shaft. Her tongue licks the underside as she comes back up. Moving her hand to the base, she squeezes my cock, pumping it hard as her mouth, in tandem, glides up and down. I finally feel the beginnings of a hard-on, but just as fast as it swells, it completely deflates. Frustrated, Katrina lets go of my cock and sits back up. Her eyes flare with fury.

"Brandon, what is wrong with you? I spoke to your doctor and he said there should be no problem. Especially with the Viagra."

"I don't know." Screw the Viagra. I do know. I don't like the way she tastes or the way she smells. And her sharp teeth scraped so hard against my shaft I must have teeth marks.

"Fuck you!" She jumps off my lap and, to my shock, flings her glass of champagne across the room. The glass hits the massive stone fireplace and shatters into shards.

*Temper much?*

"You're mental," she rants. "You need help."

And she needs anger management. Before I can respond, the doorbell chimes. Literally saved by the bell, I leap up from the couch to open the front door.

It's Scott. I've asked him to come over so I can

review my finances and recent expenses. Dressed in a three-piece gray suit, he's carrying a briefcase. He follows me into the living room where Katrina is cleaning up the mess she made. Her eyes connect with his and a smile crosses her face.

"Oh, hi, Scott. You're just in time for lunch. Want some champagne?"

Scott declines, but helps himself to one of the fancy sandwiches. Chomping into it, he lowers himself into one of my overstuffed side chairs. After setting down his half-eaten sandwich on the tray, he raises his briefcase to his lap and pulls out a thick file. "Your expenses over the last month," he says, handing it to me.

Out of the corner of my eye, I see Katrina sashay out of the living room, carrying the shards of glass on a plate. "I'll be right back," she calls out as she heads in the direction of the kitchen. She sure knows how to move her tight, perfect-shaped ass.

Once she's out of sight, I open the file. Skipping over the pages and pages of hospital charges, which my insurance will cover, I start with the month before the accident. Man. I'm quite the big spender. Restaurant after expensive restaurant. Thousands and thousands dropped at Barneys. Numerous exorbitant charges at a florist I never heard of. A couple of trips to Vegas at the pricey Venetian.

"I like to gamble?" I ask Scott, stopping to look up

at him.

His left eye twitches. He's got some kind of weird eye tic. "Yeah. You're a big gambler."

News to me.

"And what about all these florist and Barneys charges?"

Scott smiles. "After meeting Katrina, you couldn't stop buying her extravagant flowers and clothes. I've never seen anyone as smitten as you." He takes another bite of the sandwich. "Katrina showed me the love letters you sent with your gifts. I swear, man, you're a regular Shakespeare."

I find it disconcerting that my fiancée would share something so personal with him. But then again, they must be close. Maybe she saved them. Reading them might help jar my memory and my amorous feelings toward her. With this thought in mind, I go back to scanning the multitude of expenses. Another entry jolts me—a hefty one hundred thousand dollar check made out to the Bella Stadler Academy of Acting. My eyes flutter. Bella Stadler . . . the name rings a bell. I ask Scott about it.

"Don't you remember, Brandon? She was your acting coach. You give to her school annually. You're a big supporter."

Tugging at my bottom lip with my thumb, I dwell on her name, a memory trying to break through. It's futile. I move on. A few minutes later I find what I've been looking for. A whopping one point two million dollar charge at Tiffany's. Made on the day of my accident. Katrina's engagement ring.

"Did I buy Katrina's ring just before the accident?" I'm a little surprised I didn't give her one over our engagement dinner the night before.

"After you proposed and she said yes, you wanted her to pick it out. I was there when you phoned in the charge. You were practically creaming your pants."

"Wish I were doing that now," I mumble under my breath before regretting I said anything at all about my condition.

Scott lets out a little laugh before clearing his throat. "Equipment trouble?"

None of your damn business, even though you're my business manager is what I want to say, but I bite down on my tongue. Instead, I ask to see more of my statements. Without probing further, Scott reaches into the briefcase and hands me another thick file.

"This is your portfolio. You're worth a billion dollars. You can thank me."

Holy crap. I am. Or at least close to that I estimate as I leaf through page after page of my investments. I own a shitload of stocks and bonds along with a boatload of real estate around the world. This house alone is worth seven million dollars.

My wealth eats at me. A wave of anxiety courses through me. A new worry. "Scott, I need to ask you something."

"Shoot," he says, taking the last big bite of his sandwich.

"Do I have a pre-nup?"

He laughs back his mouthful of food. "Are you kidding me?"

My stomach twists. "What do you mean?"

"What I simply mean is you don't have one. I tried to talk you into one, but you outright refused. Said you didn't need one. That you had no plans to get a divorce. And even if you did, you'd want to do the fair thing."

"Shit." The word escapes my mouth.

"Man, don't worry about it. Hey, in the worst-case scenario, if you have to give her half, you'll still be worth close to five hundred mill. That's not too shabby."

A good point. I suppose I'm doing the right thing.

Katrina steps back into the living room. She looks spruced up, a fresh coat of crimson lipstick lining her lush lips. "What are you boys talking about?" she asks coyly.

I quickly close the folder. "Just some business stuff. Nothing terribly important."

She plucks out a piece of lettuce from one of the sandwiches and nibbles on it like a rabbit. "Well, I'm going to leave you two alone to talk business. I've got to meet with my stylist to get my wardrobe together for this week's show and then head over to Monique's for my first wedding dress fitting. And then I have my spin class followed by yoga. And after that, I'm heading over to Posh for my regular mani-pedi, facial, and massage."

Man. She knows how to fill her days. This girl's high maintenance.

Scott blows her an air kiss. "Bye, babe. Try not to spend too much of my client's money."

Before disappearing, Katrina winks at him. "Very funny."

Not really. My money is not yet hers to spend. I polish off my sandwich once she's gone. A sports car peeling out of my driveway sounds in my ear.

Scott kicks back, plunking his feet on the coffee table. "Do you mind if I have a smoke?"

I don't object. I watch as he pulls out a pack of Camel Lights from his breast pocket and lights up a cigarette with a gold monogrammed lighter. He inhales and then exhales, the smoke wafting in the air.

I cough and then my heart jumps. I suddenly re-member something about myself. I hate cigarettes. The smell. The taste. Even the look and feel of them. The taste of Katrina drifts back into my head. I hope she's not a smoker. There's no way I can live with one.

Scott's nasal voice cuts into my thoughts. "I brought something else over—the latest *Kurt Kussler* script." He pulls it out of his briefcase.

"They've had you missing in action to cover for

you," he says as he hands it to me. "Everyone's looking forward to having you back."

I glance down at the episode title and shudder. "The Return of the Living Dead." And then a bolt of trepidation zaps me. With my memory so out of whack, I wonder: can I still act?

*Chapter 4*

# Brandon

I should spend the rest of the afternoon resting, but I'm restless. I wander around my house, searching for anything that'll give me a clue about myself. My past. At least what's happened over the last ten years of my life. My memories of my childhood and teenage years are intact, including my parents' demise—that fiery car crash that consumed them both. I shiver, thinking my life almost ended in a similar way.

Frustrated, I go to my office and boot up my computer. The first thing I do is check my emails. There's a ton of them in my inbox from names I don't recognize, except those of a few big stars. I go through them quickly. All basically the same. People from all over the world sending their prayers and love, wishing me a speedy recovery. My heart swells with unexpected emotion. I can't believe how many people care about me. I'm overwhelmed. I'll respond to each of them later. Right now, I have something more important to do.

I google my name. Wow! A whopping 244,000,000 results! To my astonishment, my hospital departure is already headline news. A PerezHilton.com entry posted a few hours ago—"Bratrina Going Home at Last! When Will They Set the Date?"—glares in my eyes. Seriously, *Bratrina?* I can't stand that name. And it includes a totally embarrassing photo of Katrina wheeling me out of Cedars. I cringe and jump down to the Wikipedia biography.

My eyes don't blink as I scroll down the page and absorb what's written about me.

Born: December 12, 1984 in Oceanside, California.

Parents: Edward and Phyllis, deceased.

Siblings: None.

Other family members: None.

I read on. I learn that I always wanted to be an actor and when my parents perished in that tragic car crash when I was seventeen, I took my small inheritance and split for Los Angeles where I studied at the renowned Bella Stadler Academy of Acting. While working as a lifeguard in Venice Beach and doing small theater bits, I was spotted by top Hollywood talent manager, Scott

Turner, who's been with me ever since.

Credits: A list of minor roles beginning at age twenty is followed by my breakout hit, *Kurt Kussler.*

Romantic Involvements: This section takes up half a page. In addition to Katrina, I've been linked to a slew of actresses and supermodels, most of whose names aren't familiar to me. The list goes on and on. I'm a fucking player. And now I can't fucking get it up.

Awards: Twice nominated for an Emmy Award for my portrayal of ex-CIA agent, Kurt Kussler. Recently nominated for a Golden Globe. My stomach tightens. I may be a good actor. Have I lost it? Will I disappoint?

Now that I know the basics about myself, I click on several more gossipy sites, including E! Online, TMZ, and more of Perez Hilton. The long and the short of it . . . this is who I am: Professionally: Dedicated. Talented. A-list Actor. Personally: Arrogant. Self-centered. Pompous. Player.

I've read enough. I've got it. Whether I like it or not. Now, onto my fiancée. I google her name. She has almost as many results. There's a Wiki bio and a short IMDb piece, but most of the entries are from online social registries and tabloids that are filled with news of our engagement and her vigil while I was in the hospital. The number of google images is countless, running the gamut from glamorous award shows and galas to endless selfies and paparazzi pics, including several with me. To my amazement, she's never caught wearing the same thing twice.

Katrina Moore comes from money. An only child, she was born and raised in Beverly Hills. She attended Buckley, an elite private school, and then went to live abroad for several years after graduating. Her mother, Enid, is a celebrated event planner and her father, Clayton, is a real-estate tycoon. However, a year ago, he got busted for tax evasion and a Ponzi scheme and was sentenced to serve five years at a white-collar penitentiary. The Moores were forced to sell their house and subsequently divorced.

Katrina is famous for being famous. She's invited to every A-list Hollywood party, and she's a muse to several major fashion designers. Using her clout, she developed a reality TV show called *America's It Girl,* which she subsequently sold to a fledging cable network—Celebrity-TV (CTV). While the show initially enjoyed moderate success, ratings have lately floundered. There's lots of talk about the show being canceled after only a year on the air, the producers and network equally fed up with Katrina's spoiled brat behavior both on the screen and off it. She is notorious for her partying ways and her difficulty to work with on the set.

I wonder what attracted me to her and led me to choose her over all the other women I've dated. Yes, she's stunning, but all my liaisons have been. What made her "the one?" Do we have a lot in common? Was the sex that great? As I'm about to read about her romantic involvements, my doorbell rings. I hurry to the front door.

With one eye, I peer through the peephole. A stocky, dark-haired man flashing a badge meets my gaze.

"Detective Pete Billings. LAPD. Open up."

My heart beats double time. What does he want? And how did he get onto my gated property? I swing open the unlocked door.

"What can I do for you?" My voice is shaky but cordial.

"Can I come in?"

"Sure," I say, ushering him into my house. He follows me into the living room with a loud shuffle of his feet. Wearing a rumpled trench coat, the ruddy-complexioned investigator looks to be in his fifties though his full head of unruly slate hair defies his age. His keen dark gray eyes take in everything.

"Can I get you something to drink? A soda? Water? Or a beer?" I ask, hoping I have some of each. He doesn't seem the champagne type.

"No thanks," he says, loosening the belt of his worn tan coat. "I just want to ask you some questions about your accident." His sharp eyes wander around the room. "Nice place you have here. And I just want to tell you I'm a big fan of your show. Never miss an episode. Record them all. My wife loves it too."

"Thanks." Inside, I'm cringing. I seriously have no clue what my series *Kurt Kussler* is about. Later today, I'll do more research, try to find a couple of episodes online, and read the latest script. I'm grateful the detective doesn't dwell on the show and cuts right to the chase.

"Mind if I have a seat?" Without waiting for a reply, he plops down on the chair Scott was sitting in. I return to my spot on the couch.

"Do you remember anything about your accident?"

I debate whether to tell him about my amnesia. In the end, my gut tells me to tell the truth. At least partially. "Sorry, I don't. I've blocked it out."

The detective nods understandingly. "I've seen that happen a lot. Post-traumatic stress. But I want you to dig deep. A color. A shape. An odor. Anything come to mind?"

I squeeze my eyes shut. All I see is red-hot blackness while the lingering, putrid smell of smoke assails me.

"Nada," I tell the detective as I reopen my eyes.

"You a smoker?" The detective casts his gaze down at the ashtray with the remains of Scott's cigarette butt.

"No. My manager was here earlier. He smokes."

"Scott Turner?"

"Yeah." I wonder how he knows his name. On second thought, he's a detective. A sleuth. He knows this kind of stuff.

He cocks a bushy brow. "Are you on good terms with him?"

"I suppose." In retrospect, that sounds dumb.

"Did he exhibit any form of strange behavior before your accident?"

I search my mind, but it's just one big blank. I can't even remember my history with Scott. All I know is what he's told me and what I've read. He's had my back since the beginning of my career and made me a fortune. And I guess I owe him my life since he called in my accident.

I shake my head and reiterate that I don't remember a damn thing.

"What about your fiancée?"

"You mean, Katrina Moore?"

"Yes. Is there anything you can tell me about her?"

"She's been with me almost 24/7 since my accident." Being a detective, he must know as much about her as I do. Maybe more.

"That's some ring you got her."

"Yeah," I say hesitantly. He's probably seen pictures of it in the tabloids or online.

The detective reaches into his coat pocket. "We found this at the scene of the crime."

"Crime?" My muscles tense.

"Yes. We're dealing with a hit and run."

When he uncurls his stubby fingers, a small zip lock bag is in his palm. He removes the contents—a heart-shaped iridescent green pendant. About the size of a dime, the surface is badly scratched and the edges are chipped.

"What's that?" I ask, glaring at it.

"I took it to a jeweler. It's a piece of Murano glass from Venice. It could be part of a pair of earrings or cufflinks. Or it could have fallen off a bracelet or necklace. Does it look familiar to you?"

I study the object. It means nothing to me. I shake my head no.

"That's too bad." Returning the mysterious glass heart to the bag, the detective stands and shoves the evidence back in his coat pocket. "If you remember anything, give me a call." He hands me a business card.

"Oh, one last thing." His hand slides beneath his trench coat, and for the first time, I glimpse his holster and gun. Like the coat, the brown leather holster shows signs of age. A bulky envelope is tucked under the frayed strap. He slips it out and unfastens the clasp.

My eyes widen as he slides out the contents. A DVD boxed set of *Kurt Kussler*, Seasons 1-4. I'm on the cover, looking smug and pointing my right thumb and index finger like a gun.

"Would you mind signing this? It's for the missus. She's madly in love with you." He pauses. "She's been too embarrassed to ask my daughter to ask you."

His daughter must be someone who works on the show. I laugh lightly. "Sure. No problem." My eyes dart around the room for a pen. The burly detective comes to the rescue and hands me one.

"Thanks. What's her name?"

"Jo. J-O. She'd really appreciate it if you wrote your signature line."

Shit. I have no clue what it is. I nervously twirl the pen between my fingers.

"I have so many," I say nonchalantly. Guess what? I *am* a good actor.

"You know . . . 'Get it. Got it? Good.'"

*"To Jo . . . Get it. Got it? Good,"* I say aloud with macho attitude, enunciating each word I inscribe on the cover.

"Wow. That's just how you say it on TV," says the awed detective while I sign my name with an *xo*. My bold signature comes easily to me as if I've been writing it my whole life. A bolt of optimism shoots through me. Maybe my memory is coming back.

"Thanks," says the grateful detective as I hand him back the DVD set. "My wife is going to pee in her panties."

I laugh again. This time loudly. I escort Detective Billings to the front door. Just before he leaves, he asks me one last question.

"I forgot to ask you. Do you have any enemies who would want to harm you?"

The question makes me uneasy. I search my muddled mind. "None that I can think of."

"A disgruntled fan? An ex-girlfriend? A former assistant?"

I shake my head though from what I know about myself, I probably did piss off some ex-assistants. Enough to drive one of them to try and kill me?

The detective shoots me a crooked smile "Don't forget—no pun intended—to call me if you remember anything."

Fingering his card, I assure him I will.

I want to remember everything.

But right now, I want to find out everything there is about my alter ego, *Kurt Kussler.*

After taking a long, hot shower, I spend the rest of the afternoon googling *Kurt Kussler* and screening episodes of my TV series, starting with the first season. I found DVDs of them on my bookshelf. I'm totally engrossed. It's an awesome show.

The rundown: Kurt Kussler is a top CIA agent who's been hunting a notorious terrorist. The bad guy's code name: The Locust. Kurt tracks him down and, in a showdown in Beirut, kills The Locust's beloved brother, Ahmed. The Locust lusts for revenge. And at the end of Season 1, he kills Kurt's beautiful pregnant wife Alisha by blowing up her car as she turns on the ignition. Kurt, who witnesses the murder, has a breakdown and leaves the CIA. But with the help of his assistant, Melanie, a fellow ex-CIA'er, he recovers and becomes a vigilante, hell-bent on eliminating his wife's elusive assassin . . . who's equally determined on eradicating him. The deadly cat and mouse game begins. And so do the stellar ratings.

The character I play is intense. Almost insane. On a mission to right the Mob-style execution of his wife, he takes out the baddest of badass bad guys with brutal force, no holds barred. Not to sound boastful, I'm a dammed good actor. Every word I deliver is memorable and I can really kick butt. The supporting cast is terrific too, especially Kellie Fox, the quirky redheaded actress with the retro cat-eye glasses, who plays the merce-nary's best friend and assistant, Melanie. Knowing enough about the show and my character, I dive right into the script Scott brought over. It's a page-turner, and I find myself mouthing the words of my lines. I *am* Kurt Kussler.

Halfway into it, I hear a car pull into my driveway. I spring up from the couch and peek out the window. Who the hell is that? My front door unlocks.

*Chapter 5*

## *Zoey*

"Freeze!" Brandon barks. "What are you doing here?"

Jeez. He's in a good mood. Just kidding. I've been away for almost three weeks, and this is how he treats me? Okay. I didn't expect him to run over to me in movie-time slow-mo and hug me, but I expected a little warmth. Something along the lines of "Hi. I'm so glad to see you." Wishful thinking. Once an asshole. Always an asshole. Though a damn gorgeous one.

I stop dead in my tracks and soak him in. He looks fresh out of a shower. Just the way he did the first time I met him. His damp inky hair is perfectly uncombed, and a thick towel is wrapped around his toned torso, hanging sexily low on his hips. How could anyone look so ridiculously gorgeous after spending so much time in a hospital? Alright, he's pale and a little thinner, but the weight loss only accentuates the definition of his lean, finely honed muscles. My breath hitches in my throat as my eyes travel from his devastating face to his broad chiseled chest, past his rippled abs and that perfect pelvic V, and then down his long, muscular legs to his perfectly formed bare toes. Every sculpted feature and limb sends a rush of tingles to my core. He's still the epitome of pure masculine perfection. My legs turn to jelly. I'm not prepared for the panty-melting impact he has on me. I maintain a poker face, not letting him know how much he affects me. I've become a master of my emotions and reactions.

His long-lashed violet eyes laser into me. "Answer my question or I'll call the police."

His harsh, unexpected words sober me. Did he lose his mind in the hospital? Sustain some kind of head injury? I mean, he's always been mental, but this is insane. My eyes meet his fiery gaze.

"Hel-lo-O. It's me. Zoey Hart. Your assistant. Re-member?"

Cocking his head, he looks at me confoundedly. "Huh?"

"You know. Your go-to girl. Go-To-Zo." Maybe he doesn't recognize me because I've lost a little weight. On second thought, fat chance.

"How did you get past the gate?"

"Do I look like the type who would jump it?" My sarcasm is lost on him. "Duh! I have the security code."

His dense brows furrow. "How long have you been working for me?"

He's got to be kidding. Maybe he's just putting me on. "To be exact, two years, two months, and two days." *Over two insufferable years.*

His eyes blink pensively. "Really?" The word is infused with doubt and surprise.

"Are you okay?" I ask.

"Kinda. I guess you know I had an accident."

"Yeah." The horrific memory flashes into my head. To be honest, I haven't stopped reliving it. The bloodshed . . . his touch . . . the sirens . . . my words. For the second time in my life, death stared me in the face. A chill passes through me.

"Why didn't you come visit me at the hospital?" His tone sharpens.

"Believe me, I wanted to." *Oh, God did I. More than you'll ever know*. "But your lovely manager Scott forced me to take a paid vacation for as long as you were there. He told me that if I didn't obey his orders, he had the authority to fire me. I didn't want to lose my job." *Or you.* "So I did as he asked."

Digesting my words, Brandon tugs at his lower lip with his thumb. He always does that when he's thinking. It's so damn sexy. My cheeks heat. I want to jump out of my skin. Jump him.

"Where were you?"

"He sent me to a retreat with no connections to the

outside world."

Brandon purses his lips. "I see. How did you know I was back home?"

"From one of the women who checked in this morning. That's all she could talk about. Your release was all over the news and Internet. As soon as I found out, I packed my bag and checked out." I pause. "Oh, and by the way, I called Scott from my car and told him I was coming back."

Brandon's jaw tightens. "Did he tell you I have amnesia?"

*What?* My eyes widen and my blood pounds in my ear. I blurt out an angry "no." I'm so pissed Scott didn't tell me I could kill him, but then again, I shouldn't be so startled. The man despises me, and let me tell you, it's mutual. *Slimeball!* Well, at least, that explains my boss's strange behavior. I wonder if he's forgotten what an asshole he is. That would be refreshing.

His voice cuts into my deviant thoughts. He apologizes for threatening to have me arrested and then asks me to join him for a drink in the kitchen to catch up. It's not an invitation but rather an order. The amnesia has clearly not changed his bossy personality. Being his employee, I give in to his request but tell him I can't stay long. I have a lot of catching up of my own to do. Including responding to the zillion tweets he got from fans while he was in the hospital. At the kitchen island, I sit cattycorner to him, drinking a bottled water, while he nurses a Scotch. My eyes stay on him. God, he's gorgeous! I'm sure he hasn't forgotten that.

"So refresh my memory, Zoey, and tell me, what exactly do you do for me?"

Ha! What exactly *don't* I do for him would be a more apropos question. Let's see . . . where should I start? After a big gulp of the water, I begin.

"I maintain your daily schedule, your Facebook fan page, and respond to your tweets, which, by the way, exceeded five million from fans around the world while you were in the hospital."

"Wow." He actually seems quite surprised. "What else do you handle?"

I spit out the rest of the list. "I get your Starbucks coffee every morning, make your travel and restaurant reservations, prepare your lunch, send out your two hundred pairs of jeans for laundering and take care of your dry-cleaning, stock your refrigerator, order your supplies, coordinate things with your entourage, and even help you with your lines. Oh, yeah. I almost forgot. I give you massages. I'm a certified massage therapist. That's one of the reasons you hired me."

His eyes dart to my hands, lingering on them. His eyes flutter as if he's trying to remember them. And then he twists his luscious lips.

"How did you end up working for me?"

"I got the job through an agency that specializes in placing personal assistants with celebrities and VIPs."

"What's it like to work for me?"

The words tumble out of my mouth. "You're a conceited, egotistical, arrogant asshole."

His brows jump to his forehead. "Hmm. If I'm a total jerk, why do you work for me?"

The truth. Well, almost. "I need a job, and you pay me decently, plus you give me room and board along with a car allowance. It sure as hell beats being holed up in a dark, claustrophobic massage room." I add in one other reason. "And despite what you may be thinking, I actually really like my job." *And could look at you all day long.*

He studies me. I can feel his eyes raking over my body.

"How old are you?"

I think that question is banned by some equal opportunity employment act, but I tell him anyway. "Twenty-four."

"Have I ever fucked you?"

*What?* That out-of-the-blue question takes me aback. Every muscle in my plus-size body tenses while my ovaries do a somersault. I somehow manage not to fall off my stool and find my voice.

"Your cock is the one thing I don't handle." I rebound nicely. "Unless you count all the times I've booked a hotel room for you and your hook-ups." *And dreamed about it.*

My eyes flick to the bulge between his legs and then

quickly return to his pensive face. I feel myself flush and my awareness only heightens the sensation.

"Do I share my social life with you?"

"Uh . . . no. I just know what I read online and in gossip magazines."

A short silence and then he breaks it after a chug of his drink. "Do you know my fiancée, Katrina Moore?"

At her name, my blood curdles and my chest clenches. I gulp my bottled water and swallow it over the rising lump in my throat.

"I've met her a couple times," I stammer. Two times too many. The second encounter flashes into my mind—at the hospital after Brandon came out of surgery. The bitch was with Scott and she told me three was a crowd. Especially with a heifer like me. Her insult stung me, and if the tears from Brandon's life-or-death condition weren't enough, I shed another round and fled. In retrospect, I wish I hadn't. It was just too much.

Brandon's voice hurls me out of the painful memory. "What do you think of her?"

Mama always told me if you have nothing nice to say don't say it all. But growing up with my uncle and his family, I learned to speak my mind. So, this is hard. I take a deep breath. "She's okay." *Fucking stuck up bitch. I hate her guts!* "I guess I owe you a congratulations."

"Thanks." Brandon's voice is distant. He polishes

off his Scotch, and I take a last sip of the water. A blue feeling washes over me.

"Well, if you'll excuse me, I'm going to settle back into my quarters. I'll have your Starbucks for you first thing in the morning—right after your swim."

"I like to swim in the morning?"

"You never miss a day."

"That's good to know. Can I help you with your bags?"

Well, that's a first. It's just a simple roller bag that's in the trunk of my car, so I politely decline.

Brandon's eyes stay on me as I hop off the stool. "Good night, Zoey. I hope you can help me piece together the last ten years of my life."

Silently, I pray and hope they include me.

# Chapter 6

## Zoey

It's good to be back home. Three weeks at that new age spa was unbearable. It was closer to being in prison. Cell phone and computer usage was banned, and even if you managed to sneak some time with your devices, there was no cellular or Internet access. I bunked in a small room no bigger than a jail cell, and there was no air conditioning in the hundred-degree desert heat. And I'm the kind of person who's always hot to begin with. I almost died doing hot yoga. I couldn't even cool off in the pool since I'm not a swimmer. And don't get me started on the food. The food Nazis forced me to do a cleanse. All I ate—or should I say drank—was vile-tasting green juice that looked like Nickelodeon slime. I learned a new four-letter word. KALE. I hate the way it tastes and hope I never see another one of those monster-ugly leaves ever again. Ugh! Cabbage with a bad perm.

Next to my "spa" accommodations, the furnished guesthouse I reside in is a palace. It sits on the edge of Brandon's property just off the pool. With a bedroom, living room, and kitchenette, it's small but functional. Mimicking Brandon's main residence, the contemporary furniture is high-end Italian stuff—not exactly my taste, which leans toward funky, but I can't complain since I live here rent-free. Plus, the multiple windows offer a view of the city that so many would kill for. On a clear day, I can see all the way to the ocean. As I stash away my garments, the sky darkens and the timed lights of the city kiss it a gentle goodnight. Twinkling like stars, they never cease to amaze me.

Just as I unpack my last bra, my cell phone pings. Sure enough. It's a text from the slave driver. I haven't been back for more than ten minutes and he's already bugging me. So much for wishful thinking. Nope. Nothing's changed. Scrunching my face, I read it.

*I'm hungry. Pick up a burger and fries.*

Fucking great. I was looking forward to curling up in bed and watching some TV before getting some work done, but now I have to run out to service his majesty. And it's not like I can just go down the hill to close-by McDonald's. Mr. Taylor is very particular about his burgers—and in fact, just about everything. The only burgers he'll eat are from In-N-Out, so I have to schlep all the way down Sunset in rush hour traffic to get him what his heart desires. But wait! Maybe he doesn't remember what he likes and I can go to McDonald's. I almost give in to temptation but in the end decide weathering his bad temper isn't worth it.

If battling the insane traffic is not enough, the drive-thru line at In-N-Out is thirty cars deep. Moving at the speed of a slow freight train, it takes me forty long minutes to get my order, and by the time I get to the pick-up window, I'm famished. I ask for another cheeseburger with everything on it but then change my mind. Thanks to the spa, I've lost some weight (the one and only benefit), and I'm determined to keep it off. So instead, I force myself to order a Protein Burger—a measly hamburger that's wrapped up in a lettuce leaf and not sandwiched between one of those delicious toasted buns. My stomach rumbles. Trying to be thin sucks.

"What took you so long?" snaps Brandon as I strut into his living room. Now wearing perfectly ripped jeans and a white tee, he's sitting on the couch fiddling with the remote.

"Can you show a little appreciation, please?" I snap back at him before handing him the bag with his burger and fries. "I got you a cheeseburger exactly how you like it with ketchup and grilled onions."

Without thanking me, he reaches into the bag. I watch his toned biceps flex as he bites into his burger.

*Bite me, asshole.*

With my burger bag in hand, I march off.

"Where are you going?" he asks before I've taken two steps.

"To my living quarters. If you don't mind, I'd like to eat my dinner in solitude." *And in peace and quiet.*

He grabs a couple of fries. "That's not going to work. We need to make this a working meal. I have a lot of catching up to do. Now take a seat."

"Are you going to pay me overtime?"

"Yes." His voice borders on a growl. "Now, please take a seat."

Well, at least he said please. I search for a good place to sit, the farther away from him the better. I head toward a corner chair. His voice stops me in my tracks.

"No. I want you to sit next to me. There's a lot to go over."

*Grrr.* Reluctantly, I meander back to the couch and plop down on the leather cushion beside him, curling up in a cross-legged position. He stretches his long legs out on the coffee table in front of us. My knee brushes against his rock-hard thigh and my eyes glimpse the sizeable package between his legs. It's quite a chunk of meat. My hunger consumes me. I take a bite of my pathetic burger.

"What exactly do you have in mind?" I ask after swallowing. The Protein Burger isn't as bad as I thought. It's pretty juicy.

"I thought we'd screen some episodes of my show,

mainly from this past season."

My insides light up. I love *Kurt Kussler* and could totally binge on it. I've been watching the series since the day it premiered. I've seen every episode a dozen times and, with my crazy memory, know many of them by heart. When I found out from the job recruiter that I'd be working for the superstar, I practically drove my car off a cliff. I should have. Little did I know at the time what I had in store.

"Sure," I say casually, masking my excitement as he presses the remote with one of his long tapered fingers. Just like the rest of him, his hands are beautiful, sculpted works of art. The action-packed opening credit sequence set to the pulsing theme song instantly plays on the built-in big screen TV. A fast-paced montage of memorable clips culled from various episodes, each ending with Kurt in a sexy pose. Kurt Kussler is hot. So scorching hot. My heartbeat speeds up and a heat wave melts my entire being. I feel like the deconstructing Wicked Witch of the West. All hot molten liquid.

Brandon presses a button on the remote and the opening credits speed up.

"What are you doing?" I yell.

"Fast forwarding. We don't need to waste time."

"Stop! I love the opening credits." I snatch the remote from him and slow down the credits to normal speed just in time to see Kurt do his signature line at the end. Lunging, he aims his big gun straight ahead and says:

"Get it. Got it? Good." I say the words with him.

Brandon gives me an odd look as Kurt pulls the trigger and a loud BOOM! fills the room. I gasp. There's something about Kurt holding that big gun and looking directly into the camera with those fierce violet eyes that makes my heart ricochet out of my chest every time.

"Are you okay?" asks my companion.

Is it *that* obvious I'm totally in love with Kurt Kussler? Just like every woman in the world. "Yes," I pant out and then chomp into my burger to satisfy my carnal craving.

"Have some fries," he orders after I gulp it down. He holds out the bag.

Without losing eye contact with the TV, I lose my willpower and dig in. God, they're good. Crispy and lightly salted. Worth every sinful calorie.

The opening credits segue right into the episode. Holy moly! It's one of my favorites. The one in which Kurt doesn't know he's standing right next to The Locust, Alisha's killer.

Every inch of me clenches while my eyes stay glued to the TV. Oh God! The way he swaggers in those tight jeans! Snarls his lush lips! Smolders his violet eyes! Every word that comes out of Kurt's mouth sets my body on fire. The suspense is killing me. I gasp when the disguised assassin almost runs him off a cliff. Kurt can't die! And then toward the end, up comes my favorite scene of all—a flashback to Kurt and Alisha's nuptials. The perfect church wedding, the beautiful, happy couple surrounded by loved ones. My heart pounds madly. I just hope the sound of the TV drowns it out so Brandon doesn't hear it. I glance at him. He's into it as much as I am. I can tell by the intense, unblinking expression on his face. I return my attention to the TV. Thanks to my eidetic memory, I know every line.

The Pastor: "Do you, Kurt Kussler, promise to love and cherish this woman for better or worse, for richer or poorer, in sickness and in health, until death do you part?"

Kurt: "I do, sir. I will love, cherish, *and* protect her forever."

Oh my God! The passion in his sultry voice! The love and lust in his eyes!

The pastor asks Alisha the same question. She holds Kurt in her impassioned gaze, whispers her vow, and finally says, "until death do us part."

I softly say the words with her. Tears well up in my eyes. Knowing the cruel fate that awaits Alisha, her vow gets me every single time. By the time they embrace (oh, what a kiss!), tears are streaming down my cheeks and I'm heaving.

Brandon turns to me. "Jeez Louise. What's the matter?"

My tear-stained lips are quivering. Words are trapped in my throat. Snot is dripping from my nose. I'm a blubbering mess.

Finally, I get my mouth to move. "It's so sad. I can't take it," I splutter as the show fades to black and the closing credits come on. "He's going to lose her!"

Brandon turns the TV off and hands me a paper napkin. "Here. Blow your nose."

I gratefully take the napkin from him and put it to my face. I honk into it.

"Thanks," I stammer, totally embarrassed.

"It's just make-believe."

I sniff. "I know, but still . . . "

Brandon's eyes don't leave mine. "You like my show?"

*Duh!* "I love it! I love you!" *Gah!* "I mean, I love *Kurt Kussler.*"

His brows lift. "Really?"

"Totally," I say convincingly, moving past my slip-up.

"What makes him appealing?"

He seriously doesn't know? He *must* have major brain damage. "Isn't it obvious?" I ask, my tears subsiding.

He draws in a sharp breath. "With this damn amnesia, nothing's obvious."

Obviously. So, I tell him.

"First of all, he's sexy as sin—"

He cuts me off. "You think *I'm* sexy—"

I cut him off. His pending question unnerves me. "No!" *Big fat liar.* "*Kurt's* sexy as sin."

The conceited egomaniac looks a little deflated. "What makes him sexy?"

"He may think with his cock like most men, but he's ruled by his heart."

Clueless Brandon screws up his face. "What do you mean by that?"

"He's damaged but so passionate. I mean, just look at his abiding love for his wife, Alisha. He won't stop until he finds her killer."

Brandon is all ears, listening intently. I continue.

"Every woman wants a Kurt Kussler to love, protect, and cherish her."

"Yes, don't we all." A sardonic breathy voice enters the room. I look up. My stomach churns. It's Katrina. The temperature in the room drops ten degrees as the willowy blonde stomps toward us in her gazillion dollar stilettos.

"Well, if it isn't little Miss Chubster."

My boiling blood heats my skin. "Hi. Nice to see you again too."

I remember the first time I met her. I thought she was here for a business meeting with Brandon and Scott. She acted like I was invisible and then had the nerve to tell me to take her Mercedes for a car wash. As if I were *her* servant. I told her to take a hike—no pun intended—and pissed her off royally. Until I started seeing pictures of them together online and in various tabloids, I had no idea they were romantically involved. And truthfully, knowing Brandon's reputation as a player, I thought it was just another casual hook-up. His latest conquest. You can only imagine my shock when I learned of their engagement—the news broke just hours after Brandon's horrible accident. It was bad enough that the gorgeous man I worshipped was lying in a coma but then to find out he was engaged sent my emotions into a tailspin. I cried for hours, knowing that even if he lived, I was losing him to America's It Girl.

Fraught with jealousy and loathing, I meet her predatory gaze.

She smirks and then snubs me. "Brandy-Poo, are you ready to go out with Mommy and me?"

Brandon's eyes blink several times. "What are you talking about?"

"Seriously, don't you know we have a reservation at The Ivy to go over wedding plans? We made it weeks ago."

Brandon looks perplexed. "I'm sorry. It's one of those things I don't remember." He turns to me. "Zoey, did you write it down somewhere or put it on my calendar?"

"This is the first time I'm hearing about it."

"Maybe, I forgot to tell her," mumbles Brandon in my defense.

Katrina huffs. "Honestly, darling, you really should look into getting a competent assistant. This one's a bigger waste of space than the space she occupies."

I'm seething. *Bitch!* I bite back my tongue. Katrina again ignores me and plants a kiss on Brandon's forehead.

"Well, darling, don't just sit there. Throw on a jacket. I don't want to keep Mommy waiting."

Slowly, Brandon stands up. His eyes penetrate mine. "Set some time in my schedule to review more episodes tomorrow."

"Sure," I murmur. I stay seated while Brandon dons an outrageously sexy leather bomber jacket. It's just what Kurt Kussler would wear.

Emptiness fills me as I watch Katrina shuffle Brandon out of the house. And then a wicked thought brightens my spirits. Maybe the bitch and the asshole deserve each other. My moment of satisfaction is fleeting. Who am I kidding? I wish it were me.

# Chapter 7

## *Brandon*

Located on nearby trendy Robertson, The Ivy is a bustling but charming restaurant that feels more like an eclectic cottage with its vintage floral décor and jugs of colorful fresh roses on every table. According to my fiancée, this is one of our favorite places to "see and be seen." It's a popular LA hangout with A-list celebrities, agents, and other movers and shakers. I, of course, don't remember ever being here.

Katrina's mother is already seated at a corner table in the front room. Upon sighting us, she waves a bony hand, the other curled around the base of a fluted glass. Holding my hand, chicly dressed Katrina leads me with long strides in her direction. All eyes on us, whispers of Bratrina stir the air.

Katrina rounds the table and gives her equally chic mother a double-cheek kiss. "Hello, Mommy."

"Darling, I'm so glad you could make it, and of course, this must be Brandon." Enid formally introduces herself and extends her hand.

I assume we've never met and shake it, careful not to crush it. I help Katrina into a chair across from her mother and then I slip into the one next to hers. Enid is effervescent.

"I hope you don't mind, but I ordered a bottle of champagne. Cristal, only the finest. I thought we'd start off the evening with a toast."

Like mother, like daughter. "Sure," I say, studying her cosmetically enhanced face. Her jet-black hair is pulled back in a tight chignon, her skin so taut it may split into puzzle pieces.

"Wonderful." She raises her glass and we follow suit. "To the most unforgettable wedding *ever!*"

We clink our glasses and then sip the bubbly. I'm not in the mood to drink champagne, but I go with the flow. Enid guzzles hers, then refills her glass.

"Why don't we order first and then we'll talk about the wedding. I have so many fabulous ideas, especially since the wedding is going to be televised."

I take another sip of the champagne and clear my throat. "Um, uh, excuse me, Enid. But can we talk about that? I was thinking something smaller, more inti—"

With a sharp turn of her head, Katrina cuts me off. "Brandon, there's absolutely nothing to discuss.

Everything's set. It's going to be a live televised event. Period. Millions of people around the world will see it on TV and on the Internet. It's going to make me a global name and send my ratings into the stratosphere."

This just doesn't sound like the kind of thing I'd agree to. I may be a very public TV star, but I'm a private kind of guy. That I do know about myself. My gaze stays on Katrina. "Did we *ever* discuss this?"

Throwing her head back, she lets out a haughty laugh. "Of course, darling. It was practically your idea. You were all over it. You were even the one that said, 'Eat your heart out, Kim Kardashian.'"

I don't even know who Kim Kardashian is. I'm growing frustrated with this amnesia thing. It's getting old fast and causing me one problem after another. I'm really not comfortable with the idea of getting married on TV, but this is clearly not the forum to challenge it. I'm not going to get anywhere with headstrong Katrina or her outspoken mother.

We order dinner from an apron-clad young waiter. Recognizing me immediately, his eyes light up. "Wow! You're Brandon Taylor. *Kurt Kussler* rocks!" He steps back from the table and imitates me. Aiming his fingers like a gun, he says, "Get it. Got it? Good."

I'm getting sick of hearing this line. I'm sure this dude is an aspiring actor, and in a breath, he confirms my hunch. "Hey, listen Mr. Taylor, I hope you don't mind. But can I give you my headshot before you leave and maybe you could show it to your producer and consider me for a guest-starring role? Even a cameo? I'm a method actor and studied at the Bella Stadler Academy. You won't be disappointed."

Bella Stadler. I studied with her too and have learned I'm a big supporter. But, in the back of my mind, I feel there's something more. It's like a memory is trying to knock down the door. *Think, Brandon, think.*

"Yes?" The waiter's eager voice interrupts my ability to concentrate.

"Sure," I tell him, feeling sorry for yet another hopeful in this town, waiting tables while waiting for a break.

The thankful waiter's face brightens and then he takes our orders. Having just eaten that giant burger, I'm not hungry and just order a small salad. Katrina and her mother each order a platter of poached asparagus (sauce on the side) and then decide to splurge on a shared shrimp cocktail. No wonder the two of them are whippet thin.

While we wait for the food to arrive, Enid starts in with her ideas for the wedding.

"You know, I really wanted to do it in Venice like George and Amal, but too many of my friends have travel plans to go to Italy over the summer."

"George who?"

She tuts. "George Clooney."

*What?* Forever bachelor George Clooney got married? Where have I been? I've really missed a lot. Enid rambles on while I bemoan my fate.

"I, however, came up with a perfect local venue. The Four Seasons Hotel. You'll get married in the divine garden and then we'll have the reception in the ballroom."

Katrina's face lights up, more animated than I've ever seen it. "Mommy, tell him the theme we've chosen."

"Theme?"

"Of course, darling. All my events have themes. And yours will be Cinderella—a celebration of my little girl finally marrying her Prince Charming. Happily ever after at last! I've already ordered dozens of pumpkins to carve and fill with exotic flowers along with gilded cages that we'll fill with little white mice as table centerpieces. And Monique is designing The. Most. Divine. Dress. Ever. Along with a pair of magnificent glass slippers. Katrina will be the envy of every woman in the world." She laughs lightly. "Even her own mother."

"Oh, Mommy," Katrina coos after taking another sip of champagne. "Tell him about the best part."

"The cake? It's going to be a six-foot high buttercream recreation of the Disney Magic Kingdom Castle."

"No, Mommy, I mean how we're going to get

there."

Enid dramatically throws up her hands and rolls back her eyes. "How could I forget? The two of you will be arriving at the hotel in a custom-made pumpkin carriage drawn by four white Arabian horses. Miniature replicas are accompanying the two thousand invitations I just sent out."

*What?* The invitations are out. There may be no turning back now. I gulp.

Enid gives me the once over. "We should talk about what you'll be wearing, Brandon."

I bet I'll be dressed in some ninny prince suit that looks like it comes straight out of the Disney store. I don't even want to know. "When is all this happening?" I ask, evading the subject.

Katrina chimes in. "Why in four months—at the end of May sweeps—Saturday, May twenty-third. It's going to send the ratings of my show into orbit. *America's It Girl* is going to become a universal sensation!"

One last question. "And who's flitting the bill for all this?"

Smiling coyly, Katrina answers. "Well, since the budget for my show is only $20,000 per episode and poor Daddy is in jail and can't even come to his own daughter's wedding, you are."

"I am?"

"Of course, darling. I discussed it all with our mutual business manager Scott while you were in a coma, and he agreed to everything. You'll never miss the ten million dollars."

Dinner arrives. Maybe, I would have been better off staying asleep in a coma. At least past our wedding date.

# Chapter 8

## Zoey

The only good thing about Brandon going out to dinner with Katrina is that I have some time to catch up on the gazillion tweets I have to respond to on his behalf. It's like every woman in the world wished him—*Get Well. I love you! <3*—while he was in the hospital. I send the same response back to each of his infatuated fans: *Thanks, baby! Feeling good. Luv you back! <3* I can only imagine their expressions when they get a tweet back. Total swoonsville!

I skip over the ones congratulating him about his engagement or asking when he's getting married. Don't know. Don't care. And the truth is I don't want to be reminded.

Two hours into tweeting, my iPhone pings. A text from Mr. Swoonworthy himself.

*Did u say u give massages?*

I reply.

*Yes.*

He responds.

*I want one now.*

Sheesh. It's almost ten o'clock. I was about to call it quits with the tweeting and get ready for bed. Maybe I should tell him to give himself a testicular massage and then jerk off. That'll probably have the same relaxation benefits. He sends me another text.

*Well . . . ???*

In my mind's eye, I can see the anger on his face. The furrowed brows, the pinched lips. Let him pout. I don't respond. He wastes no time texting me again.

*Do I need to fire u?*

GAH! He wouldn't. *He would!* Fucking spoiled asshole.

*FINE.* Shouty caps. I hope he gets the message. I'm not a happy camper.

Ten minutes later, I'm in his living room after schlepping over my massage table and my special aromatherapy oil. Brandon's on the couch reading what must be a *Kurt Kussler* script.

"Why aren't you ready?" I snap.

He looks up from his script. "Should I strip down?"

His words send goosebumps all over me. I've never

seen him in the buff though I've used my imagination when it comes to his ass and equipment. *Pure manly perfection!*

"No," I reply, trying to sound as calm as possible. "It's in my contract. I don't do you naked. You've got to put on some underwear."

"I don't do underwear."

My eyes unconsciously shift to his crotch. That big cock of his (at least I think it's big) is one zip away. I wonder how *really* big it is. Nine inches? Ten?

He interrupts my mental calculations. "Fine. I'll find a pair of boxers. I must own some."

"Perfect." I pause. "By the way, in case you don't remember, I only do vanilla massages." *Unfortunately.*

His brows shoot up. "What do you mean?"

"I'm not going to rub your cock and give you an orgasm."

His brows furrow. "That's too bad."

A flutter of heat stirs between my legs. "What do you mean by that?" After asking the question, I'm sorry I did.

He looks at me earnestly. "My cock's pretty stressed out."

No more questions. "Ask Katrina to de-stress it." My voice is thick with sarcasm.

His mouth twists. "Yeah, right."

I detect attitude. "By the way, how was your dinner with her mother?"

"Stressful. That's why I need a massage."

*Don't ask.* The less I know the better. "Get ready. I'll set up my massage table in the meantime."

Five minutes later, he's back, clad in adorable purple and white polka dot boxers that hang sexily low on his hips. My heart beating fast, I soak in his bare-chested body. My eyes travel down his gorgeous chiseled chest and land on his crotch. His cock is just a handful away. One could just reach inside the slit of his boxers and own it.

"Get on the table, face down," I tell him, trying to act professionally. These lewd thoughts are disturbing me. But it's hardly the first time I've had them.

He does as requested, setting his head on the headrest attachment. His long, muscular legs reach almost to the very end of the padded table. I admire his beautiful sculpted back and his broad swimmer's shoulders. The burning urge to run my hands over every glorious ridge and contour has my heart racing with anticipation.

"Good. I'll be right back. I'm going to put on some relaxing music. It'll help you loosen up."

I tread over to his sound system and make a selection. A vintage compilation of *Kenny G's Greatest Hits.* "Loving You" is first up. The sound of the saxophone is slow, smooth, and soothing. Pure perfection. On the way back to the table, I dim the lights and light a scented candle. The atmosphere is just right for a sensuous massage. *Or* a sensuous fuck.

"Are you ready?" I ask him when I return to the table.

"Yeah. More than ready."

"Are you cold? I can drape a sheet over you."

"No. I'm hot. Just get to it."

*Mr. Hot and Bossy. Ms. Hot and Bothered.* I bend down and reach into my tote bag for the bottle of aromatherapy oil I've brought along. Standing up, I squirt a generous amount on my hands. I place the bottle on the nearby coffee table before rubbing my palms to warm it.

I start with his neck and upper back. That's where most people feel the most tension. I press my strong, oiled-up hands on his taut flawless flesh and start to knead his muscles, making deep circular motions with my thumbs. My hands melt into his body.

He curses under his breath. "That feels amazing. Where'd you learn to do that?"

"I went to a special training school. I told you I'm a certified massage therapist."

"Mmm. What smells so good?"

"The oil I'm using. It's therapeutic. Inhaling it will help you relax faster."

As I continue to work his back, he takes in a deep breath through his nose and then lets it out with a sensual, drawn out sigh that makes my skin prickle. It's just like the sound of a man having his cock sucked.

"You're very knotted up," I say, working him harder and deeper.

"Tell me about it."

"Why?" I ask.

"A lot of reasons. The amnesia, the wedding, going back to work. Plus, I have some other major shit I'm dealing with. A crisis."

"You *do* have a lot stuff going on," I agree, wondering what his personal crisis is all about. Something other than his amnesia-induced identity issue?

Applying more pressure, I knead his knots, but they're not loosening up. "You're carrying a load of stress in your upper back. If it's okay by you, I need to straddle you so I can go deeper."

"Be my guest."

As the next instrumental piece starts up, I climb onto the table and mount him, my legs straddling his narrow hips. It's a good thing I'm wearing stretchy yoga pants. Not the most ass-flattering thing I own, but they're comfy and functional.

The sexy sound of the sax mingles with the soothing lavender scent of the massage oil as I press my fingers deep into his tissues and make circular motions. His skin feels like warm velvet and glistens from the sheen of the oil. My fingertips burn at the touch of his flesh. I'm working up a sweat. As I work him deeper and deeper, leaning into him and using my elbows, my breasts brush against his shimmering flesh. My nipples harden beneath my sports bra. His massage—or should

I say my massage?—is arousing me, sending pulsing sensations to my sex. With every rock of my hips, the cluster of nerves between my legs rubs against him, buzzing with my hunger for him. I'm a hot, wet mess. I suppress a moan of my own while he groans.

"Oh, yeah."

He sounds like a man on the verge of a major orgasm. His low, sexy rumble rouses me further, creating a tremor of excitement in my core. Making my way down his chiseled back, I have the sudden impulse to drag my tongue along the curve of his spine and taste him, then press my lips against his delicious skin and kiss him everywhere. My body is burning with lust. It takes all I have to concentrate on the massage.

"I feel so much better," he mumbles, his voice muffled.

And I feel flush with fever. Delirious with desire. I've gotten out all his knots, but now I'm the one who's tense, twisted, and on edge. Touching him has made me want to touch myself. And quell the pulsing ache between my thighs.

"Should I turn over?"

"Not yet," I breathe out, trying to compose myself. "I want to massage your feet."

I unstraddle him—far from a graceful move—and stagger to the end of the massage table. My heated body is still aflutter. "Bend your right leg."

He complies wordlessly. After squirting more of the

massage oil on my palms, I take his foot into my hands. Painfully aware of my body's sensations, I admire the length and shape of it—so elegant and manly, and the skin is soft, not calloused. I dig my thumbs deep into the sole, pressing hard against various pressure points.

He hisses.

Good. He's releasing stress. I rub and tug each of his beautiful toes. The truth: I'd rather be sucking them while bringing myself to a toe-curling orgasm with one of my talented hands.

"Jesus Christ," he murmurs while I squeeze his little toe.

Silently, I repeat my motions with his other foot. His moans and groans grow louder, and he cusses again under his breath. Foot massage, formally called reflexology, is very powerful. It's called reflexology because the nerves in your foot connect to all the nerves in your body. What you feel in your feet can be felt elsewhere. There's even one spot that connects to your genitals. Women, in particular, have reported achieving orgasms when that trigger spot is massaged.

I ask him to flip over. With a groan, he twists onto his back.

Kenny G's moving rendition of the *Titanic* theme song filters into my ears and my eyes widen. Make that pop out of their sockets. Holy smoke! His eyes closed, he's got a Titanic erection. I underestimated it. It's fucking monstrous! And it's straining against his boxers, begging to burst through the slit. My breath catches in my throat; my heart beats like a jackrabbit's. My pussy pulses madly. I've seen plenty of hard-ons, but nothing like this. I have a decision to make—let it sail or let it sink. I opt for neither.

The melody of the haunting song plays on. I've forgotten how much this song affects me. Auntie Jo and Pops took me to see the epic movie with Jeffrey opening day for my tenth birthday. Little did they know it would end with a drowning. Like Mama's. In the ocean no less. I bawled my eyes out and made myself sick. So sick I had to stay home from school the next day. The unsung lyrics play in my head:

*Every night in my dream*
*I see you, I feel you.*

A surge of emotion overwhelms me. Tears well up in my eyes. I think of Mama. I think of *him.*

My eyes stay locked on his colossal cock. I want to touch it. Hold it. Stroke it. Possess it. Fill the deep need that's stealing my breath.

Unable to control myself, my hand descends toward his mega erection. The heat of it, radiating right through the fabric of his boxers, draws me like a moth to a flame. I touch down lightly on it for a heart-stopping second. It stirs, and a soft, throaty "mmm" exits his lips. At the sound of the rumble, my hand jumps off as if it's been singed. A twinge of guilt is followed by a twitch of his dick.

"Brandon, we're done." I barely manage the words. The tangle of emotions I'm feeling is strangling me while the erotic sensations are debilitating me. I'm shaking all over, from my head to my toes. I can't go on like this.

His eyes blink open. He bolts up to a sitting position and faces me. His lids are hooded, his expression dazed and confused. "What do you mean?"

My eyes quickly shift from the outrageous bulge between his legs to his dreamy face, which looks even more beautiful in the warm glow of the flickering candle. His lush lips are slightly parted and his violet eyes flutter, adjusting to the light. My heart hammers painfully in my chest for the stunning man I can't have. Touching him has touched me in all the wrong places.

"I mean, time's up. In our contract, we agreed to a one-hour maximum massage." I glance down at my watch. It's way past eleven. "I've actually given you extra." *More than you'll ever know.*

"Oh," he mutters. "I don't remember that clause."

Thank goodness for his memory loss. He has no clue I'm bullshitting him. My contract actually calls for me to be at his beck and call 24/7—even on Sunday, my one day off. I'm at his command. But right now, I need to get away from him. Desperately. The combination of touching him physically and this melody touching me emotionally has wreaked havoc on my body. I feel lightheaded and weak, short of breath. I cling to the corners of the massage table, thinking I may faint.

"Brandon, I've got to go," I breathe out. "You need to get off the table."

Brandon repositions himself, draping his long legs over the edge. Unable to move, I stare at him, memorizing every beautiful feature that basks in the candlelight. The *Titanic* love song, still playing, tears at my heart, tears me apart. I fight back the tears that are threatening to spill.

"Zoey, help me off the table."

I don't move. I don't respond.

"Zoey . . ."

I will my unsteady legs to move. Every little step is an effort.

"Just stand up slowly," I tell him softly, face to face, almost eye to eye. I avert casting my gaze downward.

He stays put. His warm breath heats my cheeks. His gemstone eyes glisten and hold me captive.

"Are you okay? You look like you're about to cry."

"I think I'm allergic to that oil I used." I fake a little smile before a telltale tear escapes.

He tenderly brushes it away with this thumb. "Thank you, Zoey."

*A thank you?*

"You helped me with one of the issues I was dealing with." He looks down. "Enormously."

My eyes flick to his enormous erection. No way can Brandon Taylor, the sexiest man alive, be suffering from erectile dysfunction. He's sex on a stick.

Trembling, I look back up at him and mumble one word: "Sure."

"Do you want to share some wine with me?"

My heart skips a beat. He's never asked me to share anything except those fries earlier tonight. I glance down again at the mega-tent between his legs and decline. I don't trust myself. I don't trust him.

"Brandon, I think what you need is a hot bath."

His smoldering eyes stay glued on me. "Then, draw one for me." Another order.

"No." My voice is shaky. "I don't do baths."

"I suppose that clause is in your contract too?" A layer of sarcasm laces his voice.

"Correct." Another white lie, though personally I've never taken one since Mama's drowning.

Silence. The *Titanic* theme segues into "Going Home." My cue.

"Well, I'd better be going." While I put the bottle of oil back into my tote, he stays put on the massage table.

I move back to the table. I need to fold it up. Except he's still on it. His bulge hasn't budged either. "Um, uh, would you please—"

He cuts me off and clasps my hands in his. He raises them close to his lips, so close I can feel his warm breath skim my knuckles. Every nerve inside me is buzzing. His eyes stay on my hands and then they hold me fierce in his gaze.

"Zoey, your hands are magical. And they're beautiful."

"Thanks." My voice is so small I can barely hear myself. It doesn't help that my racing heart is pounding loudly. I'm sure he can hear it.

"That massage really helped me."

"I'm glad I could help." I learned in my massage classes about the power of touch. It can arouse feelings. Even bring back memories. In fact, just a single caress can become a symphony of passion, an unquenchable desire to possess.

"You've made me feel something I haven't felt for a long time."

My chest is tightening. And my heart's beating so hard it may burst right through my bra. I force myself not to look down at his straining erection. "Feeling is the gift of touch," I say softly.

Suddenly, his eyes flutter madly. Like he's having some kind of seizure.

"Brandon, are you okay?" I ask anxiously. Maybe it's associated with his head trauma.

A smile curls on his luscious lips. His violet eyes light up. "Yes! I've remembered something."

A sinking feeling eats at me. I've aroused both his cock and his memory. He remembers how much he loves Katrina.

"What?" I ask with hesitation.

"The day I hired you."

My eyes widen with surprise. "You do?"

"Yeah. Like it happened only yesterday. It was raining and you crashed your car into my garage."

I screw up my face. He's right! I've tried not to think about that little incident. Sometimes forgetting is better than remembering.

"I was a nervous wreck." *Just like I am now*. A hot wet bundle of nerves. I was in love with his character, Kurt Kussler, but I wasn't prepared for the shock of meeting Brandon Taylor in person. He was even more gorgeous than I'd imagined. The most gorgeous man I ever met.

Brandon chuckles. "You were quite amusing."

"I was?" My hands tremble in his.

"Yeah. When you got out of the car, you dropped your purse. All your tampons came flying out. I had to help you pick them up. If I recall correctly, they were the easy-to-insert brand."

Mortification races through me. I chew on my lip. That episode plays in my head like a scene out of a sitcom. Yeah, I was a total spaz. That's because I was shaking all over. And it didn't help having Mr. Gorgeous squatting next to me and trying to look up my skirt. Making me wetter than the pouring rain. And then our fingertips accidentally met, and it was as if a bolt of lightning had zapped me.

I'm not going to tell him about the effect he had on me. "I was freaked out. It wasn't exactly a joy ride driving up to your house in the pouring rain with all those narrow, winding, dimly lit streets and those crazy drivers whipping down them."

"I would imagine you're very good at them now."

"I'm very good at a lot of things, Mr. Taylor."

He smiles seductively. "I'd say you are. Are you sure you don't want to have some wine?"

The word "yes" is burning on the tip of my tongue, but just as I'm about to say it, his cell phone rings.

"Would you mind getting me my phone? It's on the coffee table."

He lets go of my hands. Wordlessly, I retrieve it and hand it to him. He hits answer.

"Hi, Katrina."

My stomach twists.

He listens intently and then says, "Love you too."

The three little words have a massive effect on me. The ache in my chest overtakes the ache between my thighs. It hurts to breathe. With an avalanche of tears forming behind my eyes, I pass on the wine.

"I've gotta go." I rush the words.

"No, Zo. Don't go!"

Leaving my massage table and a miffed Brandon behind, I hurry back to my little guesthouse. I don't even say goodnight.

# Chapter 9

## *Brandon*

Thank you, boner gods, Lords of the Universe, for restoring my potency. I wasn't sure I'd ever get it up again. I'd done some online research and it didn't look good. Lack of libido was a common aftereffect of a traumatic brain injury and could last longer than amnesia. While I'm not pleased the last ten years of my life are still stuck in some neverland, I'm ecstatic my cock's memory has come back. But now, I have a new problem.

Damn my assistant. She took off like the wind, leaving me horny as sin. My cock's so hard it hurts. And don't even get me started on my swollen balls. They're probably so sore because I haven't had an orgasm for ages. I still can't remember the last time I did.

In retrospect, I should have knocked down the door

of her guesthouse and given that girl what she deserved. A good spanking. Slapped some sense into that ripe ass of hers. Reminded her who's the boss. But instead, I'm doing what the cock tease told me to do—soaking my body in my whirlpool tub.

My cock sticks up in the waist-high water like a rocketing torpedo. I stare at it. It's big. Really big. Bigger than I remember. It belongs in a cock museum. Or *The Guinness Book of Records*—"The Monster of All Cocks." I could seriously be a porn star.

The jets of bubbles gurgle in my ears, and curls of steam shoot up from the hot, sudsy water. Yeah, thank God, I can get it up again. I was worried. Worried sick. While a big flaccid dick gives a man confidence, a big erect one gives a man power.

Except my smartass assistant gave me a serious case of blue balls. She knew exactly what she was doing. And I think she did it on purpose to show me she has bigger balls than me. From the minute she showed up, she's been fucking with my head. No pun intended. I don't need this. With my damn amnesia, my head's fucked up enough as it is.

My memory's coming back slowly but surely. So, now I remember what a monster boner feels like. Or should I say, a neglected one. My raging cock is mad as hell. Berating me. "I woke up. Now, asshole, *you* better wake up and take care of me."

Katrina's going straight to her condo after she and

her mother have cordials at the Polo Lounge. And that little minx assistant of mine would rather see me suffer than comply. Tomorrow, first thing in the morning, I'm going to ask Scott to bring over her contract. I bet wanking me off is written in stone. But then again, what does it matter? I'm engaged. For some reason, I keep forgetting this or at least wanting to forget.

My throbbing cock shouts out to me again. Christ. It's threatening to fall off. I have no choice. I've literally got to take matters into my own hands. Desperate for relief, I wrap my fingers around my thick shaft and begin to slide my hand up and down. Harder and faster. I shut my eyes tight and imagine *her* magic hands following mine, picking up speed, pumping me just right. Oh, yeah! So fucking good! And then she grips the base, squeezing it while her mouth descends on the crown. She parts her full lips and covers it. Sucking and humming. The erotic sounds in my head mix with the gurgling bubbles, creating a heady symphonic combination. She goes down on my length, taking me to the hilt, and in a heartbeat, she's bopping up and down in sync with my hand movements. I hear myself groan. She's bringing me to the edge. Pressure is building in my groin. My cock is pulsing. Ecstasy is just a few strokes away. "Come for me, Brandon." Her raspy voice sounds in my head, coaxing me to climax. I pump harder. Faster and more furiously. My breathing grows labored. Colors swirl behind my eyes and every muscle tenses with anticipation. Yes! I'm about to have an orgasm of epic proportions. Finally! But just as an eruption is about to rock my world, another voice interrupts my fantasy.

"Brandon, what are you doing?"

Katrina.

My cock sinks like the Titanic. I wince. The pain. The humiliation. It's like I've been attacked by a weapon of mass destruction.

I snap my eyes open. She glowers at me.

"Oh, so I'm not good enough for you?" With a fling of her head, she stalks off.

Jeez. You'd think she'd be happy to see my cock at attention. Take advantage. I mean, she's been begging me to take Viagra. Complaining about my ED. Shit. Maybe she's the source of it. The truth: It wasn't her hands and mouth I was fantasizing about.

They belonged to someone else. My infuriating assistant.

Zoey.

What the hell is wrong with me? I stare at my de-flated cock. I'm engaged to a woman who loves me and I'm fantasizing about another who loathes me. Maybe *I* am the biggest dick in the world.

# Chapter 10

## Zoey

Fighting back tears, I head straight to the bathroom. I rinse my oily hands and then shower. Letting the needles of water pound on me, I stay in longer than I should, given LA's current drought conditions. I need to wash him away. Get him out of my skin. After the lengthy shower, I towel dry myself and throw on my pajamas. Running a comb through my wet chestnut locks, I take a glimpse of myself in the mirror. My reflection makes me more depressed. I'm nothing like Katrina. I'm not supermodel beautiful nor will I ever be. At best, I'm cute with my button nose, big chocolate brown eyes, and my dimples—that is, if I ever smile again.

I look glum. The shower has done little to quell my emotional or physical pain. Giving Brandon massages has always been a struggle. When I touch him, I want to touch myself. I feel things in forbidden places. "Feeling," said one of my massage instructors, "is the other side of the coin for touch." But tonight was different. I aroused him. And he aroused me in another forbidden place. My heart. It was my own fault. I let myself get carried away by a fantasy. But now reality has set back in. I'm just his Plain-Jane assistant and always will be. Men like Brandon Taylor don't go for girls like me. I'm a far cry from his type. And besides, he's engaged . . . in love with someone else. America's It Girl, no less.

*Forget about him! Get him out of your head!* No matter how many times I've said these words both aloud and to myself, I can't. On the wall, facing my bed is a life-sized framed *Kurt Kussler* poster. Brandon—or should I say, Kurt in his signature pose—all six-feet-two of his superstar gorgeousness. His fingers, aimed like a gun, point at me. *Get it. Got it? Good.*

Brandon gave me the poster the first Christmas on the job. Please don't think it came with any meaning. It's what he gave to all his employees as well as fellow cast and crew members, and I was the one who had to get them gift-wrapped and delivered. All two hundred fifty of them. That was a bitch. And it wasn't easy to get Brandon to sign each and every one of them. In one of his bad moods, he stopped after the first fifty and made me forge his signature and sign the rest. I never bothered with mine.

So the poster's nothing special, yet it's special to

me. I wake up to it and go to sleep with it. Brandon's in my dreams every single night. Even before I close my eyes, he's in my mind, watching me finger myself to a state of delirious bliss.

Sitting up in my bed, I shift my vision to my hands. I study them. Brandon called them magical and beautiful. The truth is they are. They don't even look like they belong on my body. Unlike the rest of me, my fingers are long and slender. Elegant. I inherited them from Mama. They're definitely my best feature and the most useful. They've been many places.

My eyes return to the poster. My pulse quickens. My skin heats. How could one man affect me so much? The ache in my clit is greater than the ache in my heart. I can't take it or shake my basest desire.

Desperate, I thrust my hand beneath the waistband of my pajama bottoms to that place that's crying out to be touched. I stroke my sensitive tissues. They're so hot and wet. I close my eyes, but Brandon's beautiful face occupies the space in my head. What would it feel like if he touched me? Spreading my legs, I imagine his hand between them as my fingers move to my throbbing clit. I rub it vigorously, making ragged circles like a finger-painting child. My breathing grows heavy, my temperature rises, and my heartbeat accelerates. I circle harder, faster, and as I get closer to a climax, I break out into a sweat. Vibrations flood me. Behind my eyelids, violet lights strobe as I work myself more urgently. I fantasize his mouth all over my pussy, sucking, licking, flicking. Talking dirty to me. Telling me I'm sexy. Telling me: "You're mine." He plunges two fingers into me, his warm tongue still loving me, fucking me with relentless licks and flicks. And then in my head, I hear him whisper, "Come for me, baby," and I fall apart at his command. Shatter into a million little pieces. My whole body trembling with spasms, I collapse back against my pillow and keep my eyes closed and my hand beneath my pajamas until I catch my breath and my heartbeat calms down. Slowly, I remove my fingers from my still pulsating pussy and peel open my eyes. My magic hands can fix my aching clit, but they can't soothe my aching heart. Rage fills me.

Goddamn fucking poster. Jumping out of my bed, I march over to it and yank it off the wall. Mustering all my strength, I fling it across the room. It crashes on the hardwood floor with a clamorous thud. Tears blur my eyes. Shit. What the fuck did I just do? I should have just taken it off the wall and turned it around. I stumble over to it and crouch. I've all but destroyed it. The metal frame is dented, and the glass is shattered. Shards surround me. A fat tear falls through a crack and lands on the poster. And then I notice that except for the blistery mark my tear makes on Kurt's lips, the poster itself is intact. I run my quivering fingers over the splintered glass, almost caressing it, and then, one by one, I gather up the shards.

"Ow!" I yelp. One of the sharp pieces digs into my middle finger—the finger that just brought me to orgasm. I watch the blood trickle down my digit to my palm. The pain is nothing compared to the pain I feel in my heart.

I used to think a girl can dream. But now that Brandon's engaged to Katrina, it's futile. But why am I still fantasizing about him if he's not available? They say you want more of what you can't have. The truth cuts me like a piece of glass: Brandon Taylor will never be mine. My heart's bleeding too.

# Chapter 11

## Zoey

My routine with Brandon returns to normal the next day. While he swims early morning laps, I fetch him his Starbucks—an iced Grande Caffè Americano—and a hot Venti version for me. When I get back to the house, he's already at a poolside table, wearing a thick terrycloth robe and his favorite pair of Ray-Bans. His jet-black wet hair is slicked back and his face glistens in the sun.

Setting the coffees on the table, I take the empty seat opposite him and hand him a manila folder with his schedule. He likes it printed out. I act very business-like—as if my emotional and physical breakdown didn't happen last night. My minimal acting skills have come in handy. I refrain from asking him anything more about his dinner with Katrina and her mother or the rest of his night. To my relief, he offers no information. I'm glad the bitch is nowhere in sight, and I don't press him for her whereabouts. If she's not rotting in hell, I don't want to know.

I latch onto my coffee and take a sip through the plastic flap on the lid. The rich, steamy brew seeps into my veins. Brandon eyes me. My skin prickles. It's like ultra-violet rays are shooting out of the dark lenses of his shades and penetrating me.

"What happened to your finger?"

I'm in shock he's noticed the Band-Aid on my middle finger.

"Nothing," I reply, trying hard to eradicate last night's breakdown though my finger's still throbbing. "Just a paper cut."

"You should be more careful."

His voice is cold, almost reprimanding. I didn't expect him to say, "Can I kiss the boo-boo?" but yes, be a bit more compassionate. He's for sure in one of his bad moods.

His gaze stays fixed on my finger. "It's still bleeding."

I glance down. He's right. Blood is oozing through the Band-Aid. It's a bloody mess.

"Don't move," he tells me. "I'll be right back."

I sip my coffee and in five minute's he's back, holding a box of bandages and a tube of Neosporin. Setting the first aid treatments onto the table, he unwraps my nasty Band-Aid. I grimace. My jagged cut looks worst than I thought. Fiery red and inflamed.

"A paper cut?" he asks.

I splutter. "It was a thick piece of paper."

Unsure if he believes me, I hold out my quivering finger while he squirts some of the anti-bacterial ointment onto the wound and re-bandages it. One Band-Aid over my fingertip, another around it.

I wiggle my stiff finger. Not too much motion. But he's made it feel better. "You're good at first aid."

He quirks a cocky smile. "I was a lifeguard. I know how to do these things."

"Thanks."

Not acknowledging my small grateful word, he lifts his sunglasses on top of his head, and after a sip of his iced coffee, studies his schedule. His brows knit tightly.

"Why aren't we reviewing more episodes of *Kurt Kussler* together? I thought that was the plan."

"I think you've gotten the gist of it. I have many more important things to handle."

"Like what?" he challenges me, his voice as brisk as it is confrontational.

"You've got to do a gazillion press conferences. Everyone in the world wants to see you're alive and well."

"Write up some pithy lines for me. Let them know Brandon Taylor aka Kurt Kussler is ready to kick some butt."

"What should I say about your pending wedding to

K-Katrina?" It's so hard for me to say her name. In fact, I almost say Kuntrina.

Brandon's face tenses. "Just tell them we've set a date in May. To be announced shortly."

So, that's what their dinner was probably about. My heart sinks to my stomach. Suspicion confirmed. They're madly in love. I glumly mumble, "Sure."

Sipping his coffee through the straw and oblivious to my gloom, Brandon continues to review his schedule. "Who's this one o'clock lunch with?"

Sheesh. He *is* really fucked up. "Blake Burns. He's the Head of Production for Conquest Broadcasting. All shows report to him—so technically, he's *your* boss."

"Oh," he mutters. "Do I need to dress up?"

"No. You can go very casual. I'll lay out a pair of freshly laundered jeans and a tee."

"Do you want to come along?"

My stomach does a little flip. This is the first time he's ever invited me to lunch with a network executive. Probably just more of his fuckedupness.

"I can't. I have a lunch date."

"You're taking a lunch break?" he asks incredulously, cocking his brows.

I almost want to toss my coffee at him. "Seriously, Brandon. A girl's gotta eat." *Even a dieting one.*

He narrows his eyes at me. "Is it with a guy?"

I hesitate for a moment and then respond, "Yeah. A really cute one." And then a smug smile flashes across my face. "My boyfriend."

"Oh," he murmurs with a downward twist of his luscious lips.

*Got him!*

"Have I ever met him?"

"No. You've never wanted to, but you should." My smile stays on my face. Amnesia comes with its benefits.

With his brows furrowed, he takes another long sip of his iced coffee and then sets the tall cup down. "I want you to google Blake and put together a file before I leave."

"No prob."

"And be sure to be back here by two."

Frowning, he stalks off. Score one for me. He fell for my white lie. On second thought, it wasn't a lie at all.

I'm so excited about seeing Jeffrey Billings, my brother and best friend in the whole world. With our crazy schedules, it's been next to impossible to get together. I've agreed to meet him at Toast, a lively, trendy restaurant on nearby Third Street.

Wearing a hot pink crew neck sweater, he's easy to spot. I run up to him. Seated at an outdoor table, he jumps up and gives me a delicious bear hug.

"Honey, you look faa-bu-lous!" he drawls, eyeing me from head to toe. I'm wearing a tight T-shirt, a short belted skirt, and sandals. The skirt used to sit tightly on my thick waist but now it hangs loosely on my hips.

"Thanks," I say, sitting down. "I'm on my skinny side of fat."

"I'd say you're on your fat side of skinny," he counters, returning to his chair.

I laugh. Either way you look at it, I'm still not thin by Hollywood standards; in this town, an eight is a plus size. I guess I'm now what you'd call curvy. But one thing for sure, Jeffrey can always put a big smile on my face. He's done it for years, even in the darkest times. Though by birth he's my first cousin (Mama was his father's twin sister), he's always been more like a sibling. We lived nearby in Culver City and went to the same school, and when Mama died, Pete and Jo, his wonderful, big-hearted parents, took me in and made me feel like the daughter they never had. I was only five at the time so Jeffrey and I grew up together. Having a gay playmate was almost like having a big sister. We played Barbies together, and when his mom, who I've always called Auntie Jo, took us shopping, he picked out all my clothes and knew how to make an outfit from Sears look like a million bucks. And he threw me the best birthday parties ever—always with the most over the top themes—that somehow succeeded in making me not miss having my real parents (especially Mama) there to celebrate with me. It's no surprise he became an event planner—and it's even less surprising he's LA's top one.

"Did you go on a diet?" he asks, still in awe of my appearance.

"It was more like a cleanse. I was forced to go to some holistic spa for a few weeks while Brandon was in the hospital. The food sucked. If I ever see a chia seed again, it'll be too soon. And alcohol was strictly forbidden."

"Oooh!" Jeffrey sympathizes. "That's horrible."

"And on top of that, they forced me to work out. I've never sweated so much in my entire life."

"Well, at least it paid off. You look amazeballs. Wait till Chaz sees you. He's going to friggin' freak."

Chaz Clearfield is Jeffrey's significant other. A successful fashion designer. "Is he stopping by?"

Jeffrey glances down at his vintage Mickey Mouse watch. "He should be here any minute. He's been at Nordstrom's firming up an order."

"Yay!" I adore Chaz almost as much as I adore Jeffrey. They're perfect together.

"And look! There he is."

My eyes dart to Third Street where Chaz is dropping off his Jeep with the valet. He spots us immediately and joins us.

"Hi, beautiful," he gushes, giving me a double-cheek kiss. And then he does a double take. "Oh my

God. What did you do to yourself?"

He takes the chair next to mine. Jeffrey fills him in on my spa vacation after ordering iced teas for all of us from our waiter. The chilled beverages come quickly, and I take a sip of mine while Jeffrey blabbers on. Chaz is all ears.

"Zoeykins, you need a whole new wardrobe. You absolutely must come down to the showroom and pick some things out."

He's right. My clothes are all baggy on me. While I'm definitely still not the perfect Size 6 (nor will I ever be), I've definitely dropped a size from my normal Size 12.

"Wow! I'd love to—that is, if I can get away long enough from the tyrant." *Who, thanks to his amnesia, hasn't noticed my new trimmer body*, I add silently.

"How's Mr. Beautiful and Bossy doing?" asks Jeffrey, who's heard all my horror stories.

I roll my eyes. "You don't want to know. It's worse than before. I think he's bi-polar. Plus, now I have to contend with barbs from his stuck up fiancée."

"You should slap that rude bitch," quips Chaz.

My eyes widen. "You know Katrina?"

"Spare me, yes. That bitch tried to stop my friend Jennifer from marrying Blake Burns."

"The network Blake Burns?" *Who Brandon is having lunch with this very minute.*

Chaz nods. "Yup. That one."

"Holy guacamole!" I exclaim after he tells me how she stalked and drugged him and then had the audacity to show up at their wedding and object to their nuptials. Yikes! She's not just any bitch. She's a veritable psycho bitch. Devious and toxic. Does Brandon know this? Should I tell him?

Jeffrey takes a sip of his iced tea. "If you ask me, honey, your psycho boss and the bitch are a perfect match. Don't you just love that name—Bratrina?"

We all burst out in laughter. Maybe Jeffrey's right.

The waiter returns and takes our orders. Wanting to keep my weight down, I ask for a half-order Chinese Chicken salad with the dressing on the side.

"Zoester, go for the full-size," insists Jeffrey. "I promise you won't gain a pound."

He doesn't have to twist my arm. I'm starving. I go for it.

Over a sinful piece of double fudge chocolate cake, which we share (I can't resist), I mention that Brandon has amnesia. I got so caught up with all the Katrina dirt I forgot to share that.

"I know," says Jeffrey.

I gulp down my mouthful of chocolate sin. "You do?"

"Pops told me." Jeffrey's dad, Pete, who we both call Pops, is a homicide detective for the LAPD. In addition to being my loving surrogate dad, he was the one assigned to investigate my mother's brutal murder.

The senseless death of his beloved twin sister enraged him. He swore he would hunt the gunman down and personally give him his due. No matter how hard Pops worked the case or close he came, Mama's killer was never found. To this day, it haunts me that he's probably still out there. My stomach churns. I can still see his face. For a split second, I'm five again and he's pointing a gun at me. I shudder. Jeffrey's voice hurls me out of the terrifying memory.

"He's investigating Brandon's hit and run accident. Given that he's a huge star, there's a possibility some crazy stalker tried to deliberately run him over."

A shiver slithers down my spine. "You mean like a m-murder?" The word is hard for me to say.

Biting into another serving of the chocolate cake, he nods and then swallows. "He may want to talk to you."

"Ooh!" coos Chaz, a total gossip hound.

There's one last chunk of the cake remaining; Jeffrey insists it's mine. I politely decline. I've lost my appetite. The thought of someone trying to kill Brandon, my Kurt Kussler, sickens me.

*Chapter 12*

# Brandon

The Conquest Broadcasting Executive Dining Room is a formal restaurant filled with tables draped in white linen and Hollywood types, mostly men, dressed in either expensive designer jeans or suits. Blake Burns, whom I recognize thanks to Zoey, is impeccably dressed in the latter. He could be a movie star himself with his dashing good looks and athletic build. I'm shown to his table by the maître d'; along the way many people reach out their hands to shake mine and welcome me back. It's hard to believe an asshole like me is so well liked.

Blake rises as I approach his table and then rounds it to give me a man hug. "Welcome back, man. You gave us a fucking scare. How're you doing?"

Taking facing seats, I tell him I'm doing well. I decided on the way here that I wasn't going to tell him about the amnesia. What point would that serve? I found out enough about him and Conquest Broadcasting from the file Zoey put together to fake an intelligent conversation, something that shouldn't be too hard to do since I'm an actor. About my age, Blake, I learned, is the heir apparent to heading up all of Conquest Broadcasting after his father retires. He began his career as a male model, did some acting, and then decided he preferred being behind the camera. Upon joining his father's company, he started up a successful porn channel, SIN-TV, which was spun off into an even more successful women's erotica channel by his talented colleague and wife, Jennifer. The woman whose life he saved. Blake Burns, unlike Kurt Kussler, is a real life action hero.

A silver-haired waiter, in the standard white jacket and black bow tie uniform, brings us menus. "Good to see you back, Mr. Taylor," he says warmly as he hands me mine. I guess I'm a regular around this place. Blake and I peruse the menus and order, each deciding on the Conquest Club Sandwich with a side of potato salad and some Cokes. I'm hungry as a bear. The sodas, in old-fashioned Coca Cola bottles, arrive quickly.

"Everyone was freaking out we were going to lose our number one star," begins Blake.

"Nah, I'm the man of steel. Invincible," I counter with a chuckle.

"That's what I tell my wife and she actually believes me."

I laugh again. I like Blake. He's a real guy. A straight shooter.

He takes a chug of his Coke. "We honestly didn't think you'd make it to the Golden Globes. Congratulations on your nomination. We're all rooting for you."

Thank God, I googled myself. I would have had no idea that I was nominated for Best Performance by an Actor in a Dramatic Series. I humbly thank Blake.

He takes another swig of the soda. "Are you ready to get back on the set? It was quite a challenge writing you out of the show. We almost had to shut down production. Run a couple of repeats."

"Can't wait. It's a killer episode. I've got my lines down." I don't tell him that I'm still trying to figure out my character and the show. And that I haven't finished reading the most recent script, let alone rehearsed it.

"Awesome."

Our lunch arrives. Blake and I both dig into the overstuffed sandwiches.

"Hope you can come to the focus groups tonight," he comments, after swallowing a biteful.

I saw those on my schedule, but forgot to ask Zoey what they were all about.

"Definitely."

"Great. We're testing out the idea you had for the season finale. We want to make sure it works. It's quite a twist."

My stomach bunches. I have no idea what it is. I'm eager to find out.

"By the way, we want to show the season finale at MIP."

*MIP?* "Cool."

"We think it'll generate a lot excitement with our international broadcasters and licensors. You know, you've become a commodity . . . a brand."

"And what would that be?"

"Hot sexy action hero. Women love you and men want to be you. Your Q-Score is through the roof."

"What's a Q-Score?"

"Remember?"

*No.*

"Your popularity rating. You are the number one actor in the world. You're even more popular than Brad Pitt and Tom Cruise."

"Holy shit!"

"Holy shit is right. We're going to beef up our marketing and merchandising efforts. There's a *Kurt Kussler* movie in the works as well as a series of books, and Megatoys approached us about developing a line of *Kurt Kussler* action figures. Who knows, a *Kurt Kussler* animated series could be next. My wife Jennifer, who's a guru when it comes to kids' programming, thinks that's a great idea."

"Wow!" I lift my Coke bottle to my lips and take a long sip while he tells me I have a hefty profit participation in all ancillary merchandising. I make a mental note to share this information with my business manager Scott. Feeling comfortable with Blake, I change the subject. Maybe he can offer me some insight into my personal life. "Do you know my fiancée Katrina Moore?"

Blake's blue eyes darken. He pinches his lips and then responds curtly, "Yeah. What about her?"

"Do you know we're getting married live on TV? It's a ratings stunt for her reality show."

"I don't think that's a good idea, Brandon."

"Getting married live on TV?"

"No, getting married to Katrina."

I'm taken aback, but before I can ask him what he means by that, he apologizes.

"You know what, man. Forget I ever said that. It was totally out of line. I wish you and Katrina much happiness, and if we're invited, Jen and I will try to attend."

I ponder his interesting choice of the word "try." Wouldn't most people say, "love to attend" or "would be honored to attend?" Maybe, I'm reading too much into it. I mean, they're a super busy power couple and probably have tons of equally important overlapping events. I let it go. But not soon enough.

"Well, there you are!" That voice. I recognize it immediately and so does Blake. His face goes ashen. I look to the right, and there she is striding toward us in her six-inch stilettos and a thigh-high pencil skirt. Katrina! With her bouncing hair, pearly white smile, and long-legged gait, she exudes sex and confidence. Every eye is on her.

"What are you doing here?" asks Blake before I can. His raging eyes narrow and his fists ball so tightly his knuckles turn white.

"I thought I'd stop by and say hello to the two of you."

"How did you know I was here?" I ask as she slinks into the vacant chair next to mine.

"You shouldn't be so careless, darling. You left your schedule at the pool."

Before I can reply, Blake jumps in. He's still glowering at her. "How the hell did you get on the lot?"

She tuts. "Blake, darling, does Mommy have to wash your mouth out with soap?"

Blake is clearly seething. His lips flatten into a thin, angry line.

"How did you?" I repeat. Security at the gated entrance is extremely tight. It doesn't matter who you are.

"Easy peasy, as Blake would say. Money talks, people walk."

She must have bribed the security guard. I bet Blake is going to fire his sorry ass.

My eyes fix on her as she bats her cat-green eyes at him. "It's been a long time, Blakey, hasn't it?"

Blake inhales and on the loud exhale, he says icily,

"So, Kat, you're a big star now."

*Blakey? Kat?* Do they know each other intimately? Former fuck buddies? This is not the time to ask. I keep my big mouth shut.

Katrina sneers. "I would have been a bigger star if you'd picked up my show instead of that rinky-dink cable network."

"It wasn't a good fit."

"I'm sure it was a better fit than your wife's skanky little pussy."

Blake's cheeks flare and I can feel my own reddening. I can't believe what I'm hearing.

"Jesus, put a lid on it, Katrina. What's wrong with you?"

With a smirk, she slides out of the chair and saunters off. "See you later, Brandy-Poo."

I'm mortified. How could she embarrass me like that in front of my boss? The second most powerful man at Conquest Broadcasting.

"Man, I'm sorry for that. I don't know what got into her. Maybe she had too much to drink." Which I know isn't true because there was no trace of alcohol on her breath, and she sure as hell couldn't walk in those heels sloshed.

"Don't worry about it."

I can't help myself; I need to know. "Did you and she have some kind of thing?"

Blake tightens his lips once more. "My father always says: 'Sometimes the past is better left behind.' I'll leave it at that."

The irony of his words gets under my skin. If only I could remember mine. In the meantime, I'm going to find out what their story is.

# Chapter 13

## *Brandon*

I've barely stepped inside my house when Katrina comes sprinting up to me. She's dressed in a very skimpy bright red bikini that exposes her voluminous tits and her long, toned legs that seem to extend to her armpits. Her eyes are bloodshot and her face is streaked with tears. Looks like she's been crying.

She flings her arms around my shoulders, clinging to me, pressing her firm breasts against my pecs, so I can't take another step without taking her with me. In her mile-high mules, she's eye level with me.

"Let go of me, Katrina." My voice is gruff. I'm still reeling from her mortifying behavior in front of Blake Burns.

She runs one hand along the side of my jaw and bats her eyes. "Oh, Brandon, you have the right to be mad at me. The way I behaved today was so out of line.

I'm so, so, sorry. Can you ever forgive me?"

She holds me in her feline gaze imploringly. I draw in a sharp breath through my nose and exhale. "We need to talk."

She nods. And then a seductive smile slithers across her billowy lips.

"Let's take it outside." Her cloying floral cologne is smothering me. I need some fresh air.

"Can I pour myself a glass of champagne first?"

"Fine." I stab the word at her while she ambles to the kitchen with the grace of a gazelle. Her platinum mane cascades down her back and bounces along.

Five minutes later, we're seated on my terrace, my back to the guesthouse where Zoey resides. The January air is balmy. I cut to the chase.

"So, what's the story with you and Blake Burns?"

Seductively folding one bare leg over the other, Katrina takes a sip of her champagne. "I never really wanted to tell you about him, but I suppose I have no choice."

"Level with me, Katrina." My voice is authoritative. I'm all ears.

She sets the crystal flute on the small table between us. And with a lick of her upper lip, she begins.

"Blake and I have known each other almost our entire lives. Our families were best friends, and we went to the same schools right through high school. During a vacation in Capri, we fell in love. And I never stopped loving him. I thought I was destined to marry him and so did Mommy. It was a match made in heaven. Like royalty. We were practically engaged."

Her eyes narrow. "Then that repulsive peon, Jennifer McCoy, stepped into the picture, and when he chose her over me, it totally broke my heart."

My eyes bore into her. "Are you saying you're still in love with him?"

She flings her head and huffs. "Hardly. I hate his guts for what he did to me. And I hate his wife even more. The bitch did something really evil and manipulative that I can never forget. Or forgive."

"Like what?"

Her face darkens and her voice grows cold with fury. "I can't talk about it, but let's just say it'll follow me everywhere."

She brushes her long manicured nails across a faint scar below her collarbone that shimmers in the late afternoon sun. I've never noticed it before on account of the high necklines she favors. It looks like the remnants of a former tattoo. A five-letter name. I can vaguely make out the first letter—a "B." "B" like in B-L-A-K-E? While curious, I fold my arms in my lap and let her continue.

"So, darling, when I found out you were having lunch today with Blake, I couldn't resist."

Despite her explanation, another surge of anger blasts through my chest. "It was an important business lunch, Katrina. You had no right to be there. Your behavior and the things you said totally mortified me."

"I couldn't help it. I was just acting out my anger." Her pouty expression begs for sympathy. "I hope you can understand."

No, I don't understand, but the past is the past. Not dwelling on the irony of that thought, I blow out a breath. "Just don't let anything like that ever happen again."

"Is that a threat, Brandon?" Her voice is pitchy, as if she's challenging me.

"No, it's an order."

Tears cluster in her cat-green eyes. "I'm sorry. I'm working on my anger issues with my therapist."

"That's good." My voice is monotone.

"Can you forgive me?" She returns to the champagne.

"Yes." I don't tell her that I'm not going to forget about this incident. Forgetting anything is the last thing I want to do in my amnesiac state.

"Thank you, darling." A few fat tears roll down her high cheekbones, taking some of her mascara with them. My eyes stay on her as she rises and repositions herself in front of me. Squatting down, she works the button of my jeans and then yanks down my fly. My big flaccid dick sits parked between my legs.

"What are you doing?"

"I want to make it up to you," she purrs.

I don't stir. And then without warning, she dumps the remainder of her champagne on my shaft, soaking my cock, my balls, and my jeans. I jolt from the sudden cold sensation.

"Jesus, Katrina. What the fuck?"

"Do you still love me?" She rolls her tongue around the circumference of my dripping wet crown.

My breath hitches. I seriously don't know the answer to that question. And it's like my drenched cock is rolling its eyes and saying: *Don't look at me. I have no clue.*

"Show me you love me," she lilts, gripping the base. Her billowy lips descend on my length and then make their way back up. She repeats the movements, picking up speed. My soft cock doesn't respond. I just want to tuck it back into my jeans and get away from her.

"Dammit, Brandon. What's wrong with you?" she growls before going down on me again.

Squeezing my eyes, I groan loudly and almost leap up from my chair. "Christ. What the hell are you doing?"

An unexpected answer. "I'm delivering your sides—the lines you need to rehearse for this week's upcoming shoot."

My eyes pop open. Shit. Zoey.

She slaps a folder down on the table. "I'm sorry to interrupt something so important."

"Zo—"

She cuts me off. "I'm off to a meeting with my dad. I'll have my phone with me so call or text me if anything else 'important' comes up." In addition to air-quoting the word important, she puts a sarcastic emphasis on the last two words.

"No, wait." My voice takes on urgency that borders on panic. Like I'm silently saying, "Please don't leave me alone with Katrina." My cock smarts.

Too late. She stoically marches off after her eyes clash with my fiancée's.

Sliding my sore cock back into my soaked jeans, I jump up from my chair to tell her what happened, but lithe Katrina springs to her feet simultaneously and shoves me back down.

She snaps at me like a rabid beast. "We have business to finish up here."

I leap back to my feet and this time I shove her out of the way.

She gasps. I curse under my breath. Zoey's gone. I grab the file on the table.

"I'm heading back in. I've got lines to figure out." And that's not all I need to figure out. My mind's confused; my heart's confused; and my cock's confused.

"Fine." Katrina flings the word at me and then dives into the pool.

# Chapter 14

## Zoey

A trip to the precinct is just what I need to banish the image of Brandon and Katrina. Right before I caught Bratrina in that lurid sex act, I got a call from Pops, asking me if I had time to come in for some questioning. The timing was perfect.

I haven't been here in ages. The last time I was here was when I was in high school. When the kids in my civics class found out that my father worked for the LAPD, they all wanted to see what that was like. After learning this, Pops arranged a field trip to the precinct with my teacher. My classmates loved every minute. Especially the part when they got to look through a one-way mirror and watch Pops question a suspected murderer—a wealthy woman whose millionaire husband had mysteriously been poisoned. Pops was so good at squeezing information out of the suspect. My very own Columbo! All of us gasped when the suspect broke down in tears and finally confessed everything. It was just like a scene out of *CSI*—of course, the husband was having a secret affair, and the vengeful wife wanted him dead to inherit all his money.

The downtown precinct is bustling with a colorful cast of characters, and phones don't stop ringing. I walk up to the bulletproof front desk window and tell one of the busy clerks on duty that I'm here to see Detective Billings. Her name, Alma Lopez, is on her badge. I give her my name and tell her I have an appointment. She scans her computer and calls my father to let him know I'm here.

"You're Zoey Hart, Pete's daughter?" she asks, filling out a visitor's badge for me.

I smile at her. "Yes."

Her eyes brighten. "The one who works for Brandon Taylor?"

"Yeah." There's little enthusiasm in my voice.

Alma grows animated. "Oh my God! You're so lucky! I'm so jealous! What's it like to work for him?"

Taking the badge from her, I paste it on my short-sleeved tee. "Trust me, you're much better off working here."

At that moment, Pops bursts through the door, chomping on a fat sandwich. As usual, his shirt is rumpled with the sleeves rolled up, and there's a mustard stain on it. Jacketless, his holster is crossed over his torso. My adoptive dad may be a loveable schlub, but there's something so powerful about him carrying a gun. After my mother's horrific murder, I felt he could protect me. I only wish he'd found her killer. It's still an unsolved case that haunts us both.

"Pops!" I run up to him and give him a hug.

"Hi, babycakes," he says with food in his mouth. "Glad you could come by. Come on back."

Five minutes later, I'm in his office. It's rare for any LAPD detective to have his own office, but the force felt he deserved one. Pops has been on active duty for almost forty years—the longest serving member of the department. A legend. No one has cracked as many cases as he has or brought so many heinous criminals to justice. He keeps saying he's going to retire, but both Auntie Jo and I know that's never going to happen.

The office is small and windowless, lit by unflattering fluorescent lighting. Some of his awards hang on the grungy walls, but they're mostly covered with a messy array of cases in progress. His simple wooden desk is piled high with thick folders. Next to his computer is a large framed family photo—the four of us, Auntie Jo, Pops, Jeffrey, and me. And there's also a photo of him and Mama when they were kids. Despite being twins, they look as different as night and day. Mama, frail and pale with a mop of flaming red hair; Pops, big-boned and swarthy with a crown of jet-black locks. He's told me so many hilarious stories about their New Jersey childhoods. Poor elegant Mama was always trying to turn him into a proper gentleman, but she could never even get him to tuck his shirt in. I wish she were alive to see him now.

After that melancholy thought, I inwardly laugh. Things haven't changed. Pops is as disheveled as ever. The clutter on the walls and on his desk goes with his personality. Buried on his messy desk is a paper plate with the other half of the pastrami sandwich along with a bottle of root beer. He sinks into his faded pleather desk chair while I take a seat in one of the two worn out upholstered chairs facing him. His office furnishings are rather decrepit, but budget cutbacks have prohibited replacements. And truthfully, knowing Pops, he wouldn't replace them if he could.

"Late lunch," he says, taking another chomp of his sandwich. "Want the other half?"

I'm tempted. The juicy Pastrami sandwich looks and smells so good, but I force myself to pass.

"You not feeling good or something? You look like you lost weight."

My dad, the detective, is very perceptive. "I'm fine. I'm just watching it." God, I'd love a bite. But I know I won't be able to stop with just one.

Pops puts down his half-eaten sandwich. "Thanks for coming by. You know I'm investigating the Brandon Taylor hit and run."

I nod. My stomach twists at the mention of his

name. "Jeffrey told me you met with him."

"Yeah, he couldn't have been nicer."

Ha! He must have met the wrong person.

"He even autographed the box of DVDs I brought along for your mother. She's in seventh heaven."

Jeez. How embarrassing! I suddenly feel bad I never got her a signed set. She begged me for one so many times. I just never felt comfortable asking. Leave it to my outspoken, fearless father. A total charmer.

Pops takes a long swig of his soda and then sets the bottle down. "Unfortunately, he wasn't very helpful. The poor bloke's got post traumatic stress and can't remember a thing. Lucky he didn't get killed in that accident."

"Jeffrey told me you're treating it as a possible homicide."

"I have no choice. He's a major celebrity. Something in my gut tells me someone wanted him dead."

A shiver creeps up my spine. As many times as I've wanted to kill him for driving me crazy, including today, the thought of Brandon Taylor dead rattles me. Pops's gut feelings are always spot on. A troubling thought crosses my mind. My stomach knots up and my pulse accelerates.

"Pops, am I a suspect?"

Pops laughs his hearty laugh. "Of course not, baby-cakes. You're the one who found him. If you hadn't, he would have bled to death. Plus, if you recall, you were running errands at the purported time of the accident. All the shop owners have confirmed that as well as Brandon's gardener, who, by the way we questioned, and is not a suspect either.

Though I've tried to block it out, I flashback to that fateful day. Driving home from my final stop, the drycleaner, I was halfway up the private road to Brandon's house when I spotted his lifeless body sprawled on the ground. Blood was pouring from his head. Wearing his running clothes, he was already swimming in a crimson pool. My car came to a screeching halt and so did my heart. In a panic, I leapt out of my car and rushed over to him. At the time, I had no idea what had happened—I thought perhaps he'd taken a terrible tumble—but I knew he needed help. Fast! With trembling fingers, I called 911. I cradled him in my arms as I awaited the paramedics. Tears filled my eyes. Fear filled my mind. Grief filled my heart. I talked to him. Told him to hang in there. Told him it wasn't his time. And then I spilled my heart out. My tears trickled onto his soft face and I . . .

My father's husky, Jersey-accented voice catapults me back to the moment. "You okay, babycakes?"

I nod though I feel shaken. "Yeah, I was just think-ing about that day."

"It must have been hard on you."

"Yeah, it was." He has no idea.

"Do you remember anything unusual about it?"

I shake my head. "It was just like any day. Brandon went for a jog. I was doing errands."

Pops takes a deep breath. "Can you think of anyone who would want Brandon Taylor dead?"

I rack my brain and shake my head again.

"A crazy fan? An ex-assistant? An employee? Someone who works on the show?"

"No, Pops. To the best of my knowledge, everyone worships him and he's never been stalked."

"What's his manager Scott Turner like?"

"A total slime bucket."

"A murderer?"

"No, Pops, he's slimy in that icky slick Hollywood kind of way, but that's about it. He's been with Brandon since the beginning of his career. He's the last person who would want Brandon dead. He's all about Brandon. And Brandon, in return, treats him well."

"How much do you think he makes?"

"Not sure, but probably a couple hundred thousand dollars a year. Plus, he gets hefty bonuses. Last Christmas, he bought himself a brand new Corvette thanks to Brandon."

"What about Brandon's fiancée, Katrina Moore?"

The mention of her name makes my stomach churn, and once more the repulsive image of her sucking him off flashes in my mind.

"She's a piece of work, but again no murderer. I mean, she's marrying a superstar. The sexiest man in the world. Something every woman in the world dreams of. If that was me, I sure wouldn't want him dead."

*If that was me.* I inwardly sigh. I don't hold a candle to Katrina. She's Hollywood royalty. Supermodel beautiful. America's It Girl. She may be a bitch to me, but she's the perfect woman for Brandon. Second thoughts bombard me—maybe, I should implicate the bitch. Get rid of her!

My father bites into the other half of his sandwich. "Sure you don't want some?"

It looks so damn delicious. I'm mentally drooling, but I pass once again. Where there's a will, there's a way.

My father swallows, but not before getting another mustard stain on his light blue shirt. Smiling with amusement, I hand him a paper napkin.

"Thanks, babycakes." He swipes at the yellow blotch. "Your mother's gonna kill me."

I laugh while he asks me another question.

"Do you know Katrina well?"

I tell my dad just well enough to know she's a bitch. Like Pops, I'm a straight shooter. I tell it like it is. Although I can't say the same when it comes to my feelings about my boss.

He chuckles. "Was she involved with Brandon for a long time before getting engaged to him?"

"To be honest, I met her only once—shortly before

Brandon's accident—and then again at the hospital. Except for having me make restaurant and hotel room reservations for his hook-ups, he's never shared his social life with me. I've usually found out about whom he's seeing from the tabloids and online celebrity gossip sites."

"Was Katrina one of his hook-ups?"

I shrug, gazing longingly at the sandwich. "I don't know. *People Magazine* said it was love at first sight and a whirlwind romance."

Pops takes another messy bite of his thick sand-wich. "You know, you can't always believe what you read."

Pops is right, especially when it comes to the tab-loids, which survive on blowing up celebrities' lives even if it means feeding the gossip-hungry public utter bullshit. *People Magazine* is different. You can believe what you read in it, and I defend the periodical's honor to my dad, the penultimate detective.

Pops chuckles again. "Your mom swears by *People*."

I smile. That's Auntie Jo for you. Like my brother Jeffrey, she's a total celebrity hound. Brandon is number one on her list. She almost fainted when she saw that he was named *People's* "Sexiest Man Alive."

Pops wipes his mouth with the back of his hand, missing a crumb of bread on his upper lip. I reach across the desk and flick it off with a finger.

"Thanks, babycakes." He washes the sandwich down with more of the root beer. "Have you ever watched her show?"

Opening my mouth, I point my index finger at it and feign barfing. "Once was enough. Ugh! It almost made me throw up. The only talent she has is being famous for being famous. Her spoiled rich girl antics make Paris Hilton look like Goldilocks."

Pops picks up a piece of greasy pastrami that's fallen onto his desk and stuffs it into his mouth. I wish I'd gotten to it first. My stomach rumbles.

"You know she's not actually rich," he says matter-of-factly.

My salivating eyes widen. "What do you mean?"

"She's ten million dollars in debt. Maxed out on all her credit cards."

"Wow! But aren't her parents rich?"

"They used to be, but they've recently gone through tough times. Her father is serving time in prison for tax evasion and fraud. All his assets were seized by the feds. And his ex-wife Enid recently declared bankrupt-cy."

I didn't know this. "Did you learn anything more about Katrina?"

"Yes. She was sent to a mental institution right after high school."

I'm surprised and not surprised. She is after all a psycho bitch. "What for?"

The hospital wouldn't release any information to me. They gave me that damn doctor-patient privilege bullshit."

"Maybe Chaz can give you some info. He told me Katrina stalked Blake Burns, the television executive, and drugged him."

My father's burly brows shoot up. He grabs a pen and writes himself a note on a yellow pad of paper. "I didn't know that. I'll definitely talk to him."

"I'm sorry, Pops. I should have told you this earlier. I just found it out today."

He scratches his full head of ebony hair. Lucky Pops, with his Irish ancestry, has not a single gray hair among them and he hasn't lost a single strand. "So maybe she's crazy enough to murder someone?"

"Honestly, Pops, I kind of hate her, but she's definitely not a murderer. She's totally in love with Brandon Taylor."

"Do they fight?"

"I suppose they fight. All couples fight. And if you read the tabloids, celebrity couples seem to fight more than others."

"Has she ever assaulted him?"

Other than groping him with her hands or attacking his cock with her mouth? Bile rises to my throat. I swallow it down before I say no.

With a deep breath, I compose myself. I need to end this line of questioning. I don't want to think or talk about Katrina anymore. She makes me sick.

"Pops, you must know they're getting married on national TV. On a special edition of her TV show in May. The wedding is going to make her a bigger household name than she already is. Send her ratings through the roof. And probably make her a shitload of money. And even if it doesn't, why would she want to kill a man who can take care of her financially? Brandon's loaded. He can wipe out her credit card debts and enable her extravagant lifestyle. I bet she's already spending gobs of his money. Seriously, Pops, she's as much a murderer as I am." (Though truthfully, we'd both *love* to kill one another.)

Pops polishes off his sandwich and takes another glug of the root beer. "You're probably right. I'm barking up the wrong tree."

I smile. "Pops, has it ever crossed your twisted mind it was just someone driving through the neighborhood who accidentally ran Brandon over and then freaked out and took off? There are a lot of crazy drivers in the Hollywood Hills, and that's not counting the ones who drink and do drugs all day long."

Pops rakes his stubby fingers—the ones that have fired a gun—through his thick shiny hair. "You're probably right. It's just gonna be hard to find that person. Right after the accident, a city street sweeper came by and erased all tire tracks and footprints. We couldn't even find a single hair to connect us to the suspect. We only have one clue."

"Something captured on a surveillance camera?" *Or someone.*

Pops shakes his head. "I wish, but there are no surveillance cams on Brandon's private road until you get to his house."

"What about in the neighborhood?"

A look of frustration washes over his face. His shoulders slouch. "There was a power outage that morning. Some motherfucker moving van took down a power line, and everyone within three miles lost power."

That happens frequently in The Hills. The outages can sometimes last for hours . . . until the DWP fixes the problem. Brandon's house was probably affected that day as well though I wasn't aware of it. I rode with him in the ambulance to the hospital and didn't get back home till late in the night. The sound of the blaring siren resounds in my head, arousing more vivid memories. Unconscious, with his head bandaged, his face drained of all color, and his breathing labored beneath an oxygen mask, Brandon didn't look like he'd make it. A lapsed Catholic, I prayed for him and hoped God heard my words and witnessed my tears. Losing him was unfathomable.

"Babycakes, I want to show you something."

Pops's voice once again jolts me out of the excruciating memory. Just like the day Mama was murdered, it's unforgettable. I think I'll relive it forever and ever. Forcing it to the back of my mind, I focus my eyes on my father as he yanks open a creaky desk drawer. He reaches into it and retrieves a small zip lock bag. He slides it open and shakes out what's inside. I study the heart-shaped green object that's now sitting in the palm of his wide hand.

"We found this close to the crime scene."

At the words crime scene, a chill sweeps over me. Pops explains to me that even if Brandon's accident wasn't a premeditated murder, his hit and run could be tried as a felony because of the severe nature of his injury—punishable with a big fine and up to five years in prison. Personally, I think that's too lenient; whoever ran over Brandon should get a much longer term.

"Do you have any clue what this is?" he asks, glancing down at the evidence. "All we know is that it's a piece of Venetian glass from Italy."

"It looks like it could be part of an earring or some kind of pendant. Why is it so chipped and scratched?"

"Probably, it was brushed along the street by the sweeper or it got stepped on before anyone noticed. Does it look at all familiar to you?"

I shake my head. "I don't recognize it."

"Is it something Katrina would wear?"

I roll my eyes at him. "Pops, I thought we were done with her. But if you really want to know, I don't think she'd wear anything that didn't come from

Tiffany's or one of those other fancy shmancy Beverly Hills jewelry stores."

Chewing on his bottom lip, he rubs his dimpled chin with the thumb of his other hand. He always does this when he's thinking or onto something. "I have a hunch that whoever ran over Brandon Taylor was wearing this."

I play devil's advocate. "A lot of super rich women jog up and down Brandon's street. The housewives of Beverly Hills. It could have simply fallen off one of them. And with all their money, they may not have noticed or cared."

"Yup. That's a definite possibility." I sense a tinge of frustration in my father's voice, but know he's not going to give up. Even though it's now considered a cold case, he's never stopped looking for Mama's murderer.

I play detective. "Were you able to get any finger-prints off it?"

"No luck. The surface is too scratched."

"That's too bad."

Pinching his lips, Pops puts the evidence back into the plastic bag and after sealing it, returns it to the drawer. He glances down at his watch. A wedding gift from Auntie Jo, he never takes it off. They've been married thirty years. The frayed brown leather band shows its age.

He pushes himself away from his desk. "Gotta go.

Your mother's made her famous pot roast and I promised I'd be home by six."

He shrugs on his signature last century trench coat and rounds his desk as I stand up. He gives me a bear hug.

"Put some meat on those bones, babycakes. Come by one night; your mother will fatten you up."

I laugh. The last thing former size-twelve me needs is fattening up.

"Give my love to Jo." I pause. "And tell her I'll work on getting her onto the set so she can personally meet Brandon Taylor."

Pops's face lights up like a Christmas tree. "Oh boy, you're gonna make her night. She'd love that! That woman is totally in love with him."

Every woman in the world is in love with Brandon Taylor. Except he's giving his heart to only one. A sharp pang of jealousy stabs me. I hate her.

# Chapter 15

## *Brandon*

Goddamn LA traffic. What I thought would only take twenty minutes takes me almost an hour. The bumper-to-bumper rush hour traffic on La Cienega is a nightmare, and there's a fender bender that slows things down even more. I seriously want to shoot the two bickering idiots who collided. There's a reason for road rage.

When I get to the Conquest lot, I pull my Lambo into my VIP reserved parking spot and jog over to the building where the focus groups are being held. I forgot how big the lot is—practically the size of a college campus—and it takes me more time than I thought to get there. I'm late for the focus groups. Glancing down at my watch, I come to the conclusion I've already missed the first one with men. Dammit!

I fly into the observation room and apologize for

my tardiness. Despite my lateness, all the attendees are thrilled to see me and are totally understanding. Thanks to a file Zoey left me, I recognize all their faces and know their names.

Seated on an oversized leather couch with his long legs outstretched on the coffee table and a sandwich on his lap, Blake smiles.

"No problem, man. Grab a sandwich and take a seat. Libby's about to start the women's group." He chomps into his sandwich.

Before I can join him, the others in the room all jump up and successively give me man hugs.

"So good to see you, Brand-O," says Doug DeMille, the show's slick Executive Producer.

"You wouldn't believe how many emails and letters we've gotten wanting to know when you'd be coming back," chimes in Trevor Reeves, the suited-up Blake wannabe VP of Drama.

"It sucked dick having to write you out of the script," quips Mitch Steiner, the show's scruffy head writer.

I laugh at his light-hearted gripe and head over to the platter of sandwiches on the credenza. I help myself to a tuna on rye and grab a Coke. Setting the paper plate and soda can down on the coffee table, I take a seat next to Blake.

"How's it been going?" I ask him after taking a bite of the tasty sandwich.

"Great. The men's group was really receptive to your story idea."

I still don't know what the hell that is, but I don't ask him. I look through the wall-to-wall one-way mirror and focus my attention on the women's group in progress. There's a total of nine respondents, various ages and ethnicities. I'd say the youngest is in her twenties, the oldest in her fifties. From what I've learned, *Kurt Kussler* has widespread appeal, the core viewers being 18-49. At the head of the table sits a bright-eyed woman with a mop of copper curls, likely in her twenties. Addressing the group of women, she must be Libby, the group moderator.

"Remember, there are no right or wrong answers. What matters are your true and honest opinions."

Her voice is warm but authoritative. While she continues to explain focus group rules and regulations, Blake tells me the group is composed of "heavy" *Kurt Kussler* viewers.

"What does that mean?" I ask after swallowing a glug of Coke.

"They watch the show three or more times a week."

My eyes widen with shock. "But it airs only once a week."

Blake fills me in. "These women record and watch it over and over. They also download old episodes. They can't get enough of *Kurt Kussler*."

Holy shit! I guess they can't, I muse as Libby segues into the first discussion question.

"Okay, ladies, what do you think of the show *Kurt Kussler*?"

Despite being told to talk one at a time, the women break out into pandemonium. I hear a cacophonous chorus of "Oh my God! The best show ever! I love it!"

Reminding the women not to shout out all at once, Libby launches into a series of questions about what they like and dislike about the show.

The long and short of it:

Likes: Everything. Especially the lead character Kurt. They love the action-packed stories and all the flashbacks of him and his late wife Alisha. They also adore the secondary characters, especially Kurt's faithful assistant Mel.

Dislikes: Kurt's nemesis, The Locust, whom they love to hate. And the fact they have to wait a week for the next episode. A couple of women complain about my recent absence on account of my accident. They're all relieved to hear that I'm okay and will be in all the new upcoming episodes.

After a quick sip of her bottled water, Libby tells the group they're doing a great job and focuses her questions on the character I play.

"Okay, ladies. Let's talk a little bit about the character, Kurt Kussler."

Again, another outburst.

"Oh my God, sex on a stick!"

"I love him!"

An older woman fans herself. "Holy hotness Batman. He's so amazing!"

"Totally!" gush several respondents in unison.

"What about Brandon Taylor, the actor who plays the part?" asks Libby.

Yet another uncontrollable outburst. A few of the women look like they're going to swoon.

"Oh my God. I'd kill to meet him!" pants one.

A shiver skittles up my spine. I'm sure she doesn't mean that literally, but the words of Detective Billings circle in my head. Would some crazy fan actually do that?

Another woman suspiciously stares at the one-way mirror. "Is he sitting behind that mirror watching us?"

Before Libby can respond, the women start shrieking. I swear they sound orgasmic. They wave and blow kisses. One even jumps out of her seat and presses her lips against the glass. She's practically in my face. I feel myself flushing. On my next breath, they're all out of their seats and peeking through the window in search of me.

Blake laughs. "Guess they're infatuated with you."

Obsessed is more like it. They're like a pack of wild dogs in heat.

Convincingly denying my presence, Libby tells the ladies to sit back down and brings order to the unruly group. She continues to probe about my character's appeal and then moves into a discussion about the other characters. After talking about Kurt's late wife Alisha, she focuses on my assistant, Melanie, who I call Mel.

"I love her," says one respondent.

"She's so cute and funny," says another.

"And she cares so much about Kurt," adds yet another.

"I feel sorry for her," comes the voice of the youngest respondent.

"Why is that?" asks Libby, totally poker faced.

"Because she's madly in love with Kurt."

"Do the rest of you agree?" Libby throws out the question to the group.

"Totally!" the respondents shout out in unison.

"Does Kurt know Mel is in love with him?"

The women chime in one after another.

"Maybe."

"Not sure."

"Yes. But he's too in love with Alisha and feels guilty."

"That's what I think. He's suppressing his feelings."

It takes no prodding for the other respondents to agree. I listen carefully to what the insightful women are saying. The image of my own assistant Zoey unexpectedly flashes in my head, and it puts a smile on my face. The smile quickly fades. I'm sure she hates me. I treat her like crap.

Blake's voice snaps me out of my thoughts. "Here

comes the big question."

Libby: "Okay, listen up. How would you feel if Kurt and Mel got together?"

"You mean, like fell in love with each other?" asks one of the respondents.

Libby nods. "Yes."

The women once again break out into orgasmic shrieks. They talk over each other, but I understand every word.

"Oh my God! That would be amazing!"

"I would love that!"

"How 'bout like yesterday!"

"I'm dying for them to kiss!"

"That would be so hot! Mel deserves happiness. So does Kurt."

"Why can't it be me?"

After a few more similar responses, Libby wraps up the group. She thanks the helpful participants and then hands out envelopes with their compensation. While the envelopes get passed around the table, she reaches beneath it and retrieves a large box. She stands up and sets it in the middle.

"I have one more thing for you . . . *Kurt Kussler* sweatshirts."

The women shriek yet again and go at the box of sweatshirts like vultures. Thanking Libby, virtually every one of them slips their sweatshirt on before departing.

Two minutes later, a beaming Libby steps into the observation room.

"Great job, Libby," Blake commends.

The show execs second the motion.

Her smile widens. "Thanks. I think you got the answer you were looking for." Her eyes zero in on me. "Brandon, viewers love your idea."

My ears perk up as she continues.

"Of having Kurt finally realize he's in love with his assistant Mel."

So, that was my story idea. I wonder what inspired it. Before I can utter a word, Executive Producer Doug opens his mouth.

"So, Brandon, are you still up for writing the season finale? You said you wanted to."

*I did?* I gulp. "Yeah, sure. It's my idea."

Blake smiles broadly. "That's great. We're going to run it as a two-hour special and promote the shit out of it."

Christ. What have I gotten myself into? I don't think I've ever written one word of a script. How am I going to do this?

Doug picks up on my anxiety. "Brandon, don't stress out. We're all going to work with you." He turns to Mitch. "Mitch and his team will be there every step of the way."

Mitch gives me a thumbs up. Maybe I should ask him to write the script, and I'll dot a few i's and cross a few t's.

Trevor, the network executive, looks up from his cell phone. "I already texted the Publicity Department." He smiles triumphantly. "They're on it. Your writing debut will be headline news in tomorrow's trades."

"Great," says Blake.

*Not great.* I'm doomed. There's no backing out. I call on my acting skills and bullshit a couple of ideas I have for the episode.

"I'm going to end the episode with a passionate kiss between Kurt and Mel." I pause searching my mind for more. Bingo! "And one of them will have their life in jeopardy."

"The Locust?" asks Trevor.

"Fantastic! A killer cliffhanger!" exclaims Blake before I can respond. "Our viewers are going to love it! The ratings will go through the stratosphere, and they'll be salivating for more."

Kiss-up Doug pats me on the back "Brandon, I've got to hand it to you. At first when I heard your idea, I had my doubts, but now I'm totally convinced. I have to ask you—what inspired that twist?"

I stare at him blankly and stammer, "I don't re-member."

I truly don't. Damn my amnesia. Maybe I discussed my storyline idea with Zoey and she knows. Mental note: Talk to her.

Blake packs up his briefcase. "Listen, everyone, one

last thing . . . I don't want any of you to share what's going to happen on the season finale with anyone. And I mean anyone. Especially your co-workers. I want this to be top secret. It stays in this room. You'll each be receiving a non-disclosure agreement from Legal tomorrow. Trevor, take care of that."

Blake's soldier readily agrees.

Well, I guess that means I can't discuss my script with Zoey. That sucks. She could be helpful since she knows the show so well. Read over what I've written and make suggestions. Even fix lines and typos I miss. Take dictation. My stomach tenses at the daunting task that lies ahead. Will the action hero make it as an action writer?

With this ponderous question weighing on my mind, I follow Blake to the exit door. As I'm about to split, Libby corners me.

"So glad to finally meet you. Give my best to Zoey."

My brows shoot up, "You know her?"

"Yes. My brother Chaz is dating her brother."

"I didn't know that." The truth is I don't know much about Zoey at all.

"I'm surprised she never told you."

I heckle. "Maybe she mentioned it once, but I must have forgotten." That's likely the truth too.

Blake, checking his briefcase before he leaves, chimes in. "Libby and Chaz happen to be my wife's best friends."

Confused, I say, "Five degrees of separation." Part statement, part question.

Libby corrects me. "In this town, it's more like two."

I laugh lightly. She's right. Given her connections, I bet she knows my fiancée. I give it a shot.

"Do you know my fiancée, Katrina Moore?" I ask after Blake and the others take off.

She snickers. "Sure. Everyone knows your fiancée. She's America's It Girl."

"I mean, do you know her personally?"

She gathers up her belongings. "I have to go. I want to start writing up the focus group report while the findings are fresh in my mind." She extends her right hand, the one that's not holding a giant tote bag. "Really, so great to finally meet you, Brandon. And way to go on the season finale story direction. I can't wait to see the episode."

I shake her hand. My mother always said if you don't have anything nice to say, don't say it at all. Libby totally avoided my question. There's no doubt in my mind she has nothing nice to say about Katrina. Does anyone?

Five minutes later, I'm back outside. The night air is crisp and I walk briskly back to my car. Ideas for the season finale are already spinning in my head. The idea of Kurt Kussler finally acknowledging his feelings for

his assistant Mel feels right to me. With all the emotional and physical obstacles my alter-ego faces, I just
don't know how he's going to get there. I only wish *my*
assistant Zoey could help.

# Chapter 16

## Zoey

I have a terrible case of the uglies. I'm not talking a bad hair day, major zit, or bloat. I'm talking hate, jealousy, and anger. I hate Katrina. I'm jealous of her. And I'm angry with myself for feeling the way I do.

It's seven o'clock. Brandon must be back on the Conquest Broadcasting lot watching the *Kurt Kussler* focus groups. After my meeting with Pops, I came home and put together a file of the people who would be attending from the network and show. Rather than reviewing it with him face to face, I texted him and told him that I was leaving it on the coffee table. He texted back with one word: Fine. While I should have been relieved, disappointment rippled through me. I was expecting him to ask me to meet with him. Wishful thinking. I'd set myself up for a letdown. An emotional slap in the face. Reality stung. He was probably too busy fucking Katrina. Finishing what they'd started in the afternoon.

That tormenting image moves to the back of my mind as I picture the focus groups. I wish I could be there and hear what viewers think about Kurt. I did a focus group once when I was a masseuse—to test out a new line of aromatherapy oils and lotions. It was a lot of fun. I got to give my opinions and I even got paid one hundred dollars. Plus, the beauty supply company gave all the participants a bagful of their expensive products.

I imagine what it would be like to be in the *Kurt Kussler* focus group. While I change into some comfy sweats, I play a silly game in my head: Intimate Focus Group of One.

Moderator: "What do you think about the character, Kurt Kussler?"

Me: "Oh my God. He's so sexy. Every word that comes out of his mouth makes me swoon."

Moderator: "Be more specific. What exactly do you like about him?"

Me: "His sultry voice. His gorgeous body. Those piercing violet eyes. The way he moves. His fearless-ness. His passion."

Moderator: "Is there anything you don't like about him?"

Me: "I can't think of anything."

Moderator: "What about the actor playing the part?"

Me: "You mean Brandon Taylor?" (I say his name to myself dreamily.)

Moderator: "Yes. What do you think about him?"

Me: "He's perfect . . . I mean, for the part."

Moderator: "Is there anything you don't like about him?"

Me: "Just one thing. He can never be mine."

While the moderator laughs at my response in my head, hopelessness sweeps over me. I curl up on my bed with my Kindle and some erotic romance I downloaded before my spa "vacation." I can't get past the first paragraph. My mind jumps back to that unfortunate encounter. All I can think about is what I saw. Fucking Katrina turning on the tears and then sucking Brandon off. Believe me, I know fake tears and Katrina's were the premium crocodile type. But Brandon fell for them and then fell for her blowjob big time. The scene, culminating with his ecstatic groan of relief and his impassioned expression, plays again and again like it's on a loop.

*Stop it, Zoey. Stop it!* You're a chunky, lowlife assistant who gets lost in the crowd. Brandon has never looked at me as anything more than his go-to girl. His personal slave. Sure, the slave driver's been a little nicer, but that's likely because he's lost his mind. Maybe he'll remember . . .

One hour later, I'm still on the first page of the book. Make that the first sentence. I just can't focus. I need to clear my head. Maybe chill outside . . . inhale the cool evening air . . . and watch the lights of the city twinkle like stars.

Once outdoors, I pick a chaise by the deep end of the pool and stretch out. The mid-January night air is chilly, easily in the forties, and I'm glad I threw on my treasured *Kurt Kussler* sweatshirt. It was another Christmas gift from Brandon—again nothing special since he gave one to everyone in the world. But no one wears Kurt Kussler on their heart the way I do. My ventricles thrum.

I inhale an invigorating deep breath of the crisp, quiet air. On the exhale, all the tension of the day dissipates. A much needed peacefulness washes over me. Brandon's property is a little bit of heaven so high above the hustle and bustle of the City of Angels below. Lit with soft pastel lights, the heated pool shimmers, throwing off a cloud of steam, and blends in beautifully with the canvas of the twinkling LA skyline. Numerous photographers and set designers have begged to shoot up here, but Brandon always makes me turn them down. He enjoys his privacy.

Talking about privacy, it looks like I have company. A tall, lean figure in a long white robe slinks around the pool, moving like a lioness. Katrina. Unaware of my presence, she shrugs off her robe at the edge of the deep end. My eyes stay riveted on her. I'm in awe of her beauty and her grace. The full moon illuminates her flawless porcelain skin, long sinewy muscles, and broad sculpted shoulders. She's wearing a sleek white tank bathing suit that's cut to make her impossibly long legs look longer and to bring out every sensuous curve of her perfectly proportioned body. The slender five-foot nine beauty looks like a goddess. The perfect mate for a sex god like Brandon. I watch as she gathers up her golden mane into a high ponytail, lowers her goggles over her eyes, and then lifts her long, toned arms above her head into a diving position. Without hesitation, she springs off the side of the pool, headfirst into the water. Her arched form is perfect, elegant just like her, and she meets the water with only the tiniest of splashes. She immediately segues into a graceful yet powerful breaststroke, lifting her head minimally for a breath of air. Swimming lap after lap, she looks like a siren. I can't take my eyes off her.

About twenty swift laps in, she catches sight of me on a breath. She swims my way to the edge of the pool. Lifting her goggles atop her head, she rests her elbows on the ledge and meets my gaze. A wicked glint lights her cat-green eyes.

"Well, well, well, if it isn't the gopher."

I simmer. "My name *is* Zoey."

"Just hanging out?"

"Yeah, just hanging out."

"You should come in for a swim. The water is warm and delicious. And God knows, you sure could use the exercise."

The insult stings, but I bite back my tongue. "I'm not dressed for a swim." *And it's not my thing.*

"Just take off your clothes and go for a skinny dip. Or should I say fatty dip." She laughs at her own cleverness.

Rage whips through my bloodstream like an angry cobra. I want to sink my fangs into her. But I can't. She's my boss's fiancée.

"Katrina, I'm going to head in."

Her face darkens. "Please don't. We need to have a little chat."

"There's nothing to chat about."

Her eyes narrow into poisonous arrows. "I don't like you hanging around Brandon so much. I want you to stop it."

"That's my job and I don't take orders from you."

"Well, you better get used to it because soon I'm going to be the boss of this house."

I've had enough. "I'm leaving."

Katrina scowls at my defiance. "Show a little re-spect, Zo-eeeey."

"Excuse me." I push myself off the chaise to a standing position.

"Don't leave me."

I don't respond and start to walk away.

"Excuse *me*. Do you have a hearing problem? I said not to leave."

On my next step, I feel a cold clamp clutching my ankle. I look down. It's Katrina. I try to free my foot from her grip, but her hand grasps it tight like a shackle.

"Let go!" I yell, struggling to free myself.

"Bitch! You're not going anywhere."

Tightening her grip, she yanks my ankle so forcefully I lose my balance, and on my next breath, I'm flying into the deep end of the pool. I hit the water hard and open my mouth to scream, but as I go under, the warm salt water rushes in, choking me, burning my throat. Tumbling in all directions, I somehow manage to rise to the surface.

"Enjoy your little swim," snickers Katrina as she hoists herself out of the pool.

Flailing, I plead, "Don't leave me."

She looms above me and scoffs. "Funny, that's just what I said to you."

My head goes back under. Water rushes through my mouth and my nose, this time filling and searing my lungs. I frantically wave my hands and kick my legs in all directions. I rise to the surface again, only to see Katrina loping toward her robe. Terror fills me.

"Katrina," I shout out. "Come back! I can't swim."

She ignores me. Panic sets in.

Oh, God! I'm drowning! I'm going to die the same way my mother did.

The weight of my soaked sweatshirt—and pure panic—pulls me under again. I try breathing through my nose, only to have more water break in and enter my lungs. The terrifying cycle repeats itself. I manage to surface, but it's only a few seconds until I'm back under. More water gathers in my lungs, permeating and burning every crevice.

Gasping for air, I resurface, my head barely above the water. I struggle not to sink back under, but I'm literally and figuratively in over my head. I shout out another desperate plea for help. I glimpse Katrina, smirking. Tears of despair gather in my eyes.

In full-blown panic mode, my mind races. *Think, Zoey. Think!* If I could only grab on to the edge. It's my only hope. But all my thrashing is pulling me farther and farther away, closer to the middle of the pool. I feel helpless and hopeless. And I'm growing exhausted.

This time when I go under, I squeeze my eyes shut. Maybe it's just a nightmare. A bad dream. This can't be happening to me. No, it can't be! It's not my time. I try to wish it away. But as more water seeps through my lungs, my horrid reality sets back in. I don't know how to swim. The pool is my nemesis. I'm a drowning fool.

When my head slices through the water, I blink open my eyes and see Katrina hovering over me. A smug smile plays on her lips.

"Katrina, please! Help me!" I choke. Tears pour from my stinging eyes.

She sneers. "You are so pathetic."

I grow desperate. "Help! Help! Help!" Maybe God

will hear me and rescue me.

He doesn't because after my next fading cry for help I'm under again. My lungs are aching. It feels like my chest is going to burst because the air wants to come out so badly. But I don't want to let it go. It's the only air I have. For the first time, I notice swirls of colorful lights beneath the water. Suddenly, I feel like I'm suffocating, drowning in a sea of Kool-Aid. And then, a peacefulness washes over me. I'm floating. I belong to the water now. To my astonishment, I see my mother's serene face, her long Celtic-red hair fanned out all around her. She's floating toward me, her slender arms extended with those beautiful fingers beckoning me. I reach out for them. *Oh, Mama! You've come back for me. We're together again!*

"Baby girl, I'm going to take you to Papa." Her melodic voice ripples in my ears.

A vortex of white light shrouds me and then I sink into a black abyss.

# Chapter 17

## *Brandon*

After the focus group, I drive straight home. Before I dive into the season finale, I need to finish reading the script that's shooting this week and go over my lines. In just two days, I'll be on the set again, something that both excites and unnerves me.

I pull my car into my garage and head into my adjoining house. I step into the kitchen and go straight to the fridge. I swing open the door and pull out a beer. Then, I meander to the living room. The sides that Zoey printed out are still on the coffee table where I left them. Twisting open the bottle cap, I sink into the couch and take a swig.

I haven't seen my assistant since the Katrina incident. After coming back from her meeting with her father, she avoided me like the plague and figured out a way to get all my requests done without having to see me. Maybe I should have asked her to undress me, but the smart-mouth would have probably told me: "Taking your clothes off is not part of my contract." *Nah-nah-nah-nah!* The truth, disrobing me probably isn't one of her job requirements. Whoever negotiated this contract should have their ass fired.

My eyes shift to my sides. An uplifting thought crosses my mind. It's almost a light bulb moment. I can ask her to rehearse my lines with me. She told me she does that as part of her job. Setting the beer down next to the sides folder, I slip my phone out from my jeans pocket and text her.

*I need u to help me with my lines. I'm home.*

I hit send and wait for a response. *Nada.* The little tease is playing games with me again. *Tick. Tick. Tick.* My patience is wearing thin. I text her again.

*COME NOW!*

My cock twitches as I type those two shouty words. And my pulse quickens. Why does this girl affect me? Considering Katrina and the gorgeous women I've been associated with in the past, she's definitely not my type. Plus, she's got the bristly personality of a porcupine. I'm always waiting for her to shower me with quills. Yet, inexplicably, I'm attracted to her—her lush curves and her sharp wit. Her fine ass and sass trump Katrina's fine bones and class.

Once again, she doesn't respond. From where I'm sitting, I can glimpse her little house and the lights are out. Maybe she's sleeping and doesn't hear her phone. Or has it turned off. *Or* maybe she's out with her boyfriend again. The unsettling thought rattles me. Mental note: Talk to her tomorrow and make it crystal-clear she must tell me where she is and what she's doing at *all* times. Maybe throw in some restrictions. Like you can't see your boyfriend while working for me.

It's late. Taking another chug of beer, I remove my sides from the folder and begin to study my lines. Repeating them over and over. Forget it. I take a deep, frustrated breath. I've gone over this scene a dozen times today, and I'm just not feeling it. And it's shooting in just a couple days. It's a flashback—a heavy-duty love scene between Kurt and his late wife Alisha. It takes place in their shower. It's not like there are many lines. More moans and groans than words. But I can't seem to instill the few lines I have with any real emotion and make them convincing. I sound passive when I should sound passionate. Apathetic when I should sound orgasmic. Have I lost it?

Rehearsing the lines again, I have a small memory breakthrough. I hear the husky voice of my acting coach, Bella Stadler, telling me to draw from experi-ence. Bring what you've lived to every part you play. If you need to feel sad and cry, think about your pet dog or a loved one that died. Thinking about putting down my lab Buddy or my parents' fatal car crash is not going to help me. This is a love scene, a very sensuous one. From what I've read, me-the-player never did love . . . well, up until Katrina. I've loved her enough to ask her to marry me and exchange "until death do us part" vows, but still cannot remember a damn thing about our history or relationship. Thanks to my amnesia, it's a void in my life. I feel nothing toward her. Dig deep, I tell myself. I try to remember. America's It Girl doesn't do it for me. Nothing comes to mind.

Halfway into my next line, screams for help steal my attention. I listen carefully. A woman's voice; the cries grow louder. They're coming from the pool area. It must be Katrina. She told me she loves to take late night swims. My panic button sounds. Something's wrong. Very wrong. Dropping the pages of the script, I fly out of my house.

Adrenaline is pumping through my veins. I arrive at the pool in no time. Breathing hard, I need to reset my mental button. Katrina is there, but she's not the one in trouble. It's Zoey. Her body is floating across the surface of the water. I brush past my dumb-founded fiancée and, fully clothed, jump in. With a few adrenaline-powered strokes, I reach my assistant and immediately flip her onto her back and then manage to drag her through the water to safety. Cradling her in my arms, I hoist her lifeless body out of the pool onto the cement deck. In a rapid heartbeat, I'm by her side on my knees. All color is drained from her angelic face; she's as limp as rag doll.

"Zoey!" I shout out. No response. "Zoey!" Then it hits me.

Panic grips me by the balls. "She's not breathing!" I say aloud while a half-amused Katrina with her arms folded casually looks on.

"Puh-lease. It's just an attention-seeking act," she snips.

I think my fiancée is wrong. Not wasting a second, I begin to administer CPR. Having been a lifeguard before I was an actor, it's something I know and remember how to do. Parting Zoey's bowed, bluish lips, I immediately cover them with mine and breathe into her mouth. Mouth-to-mouth resuscitation. The kiss of life.

"C'mon Zoey, breathe," I plead as I take a brief reprieve to catch my own breath. Renewed with oxygen, my mouth goes back down on her hers. I resume breathing into it. "C'mon, Zoey," I silently pray. My sinking heart almost beats out of my chest.

"Jesus Christ." *Nada.*

# Chapter 18

## Zoey

"*Z*oey."

It's God. His warm lips are breathing life back into me. His strong hands pump my heart rhythmically.

*"Breathe, Zoey, breathe!"* The heavenly voice is louder, more desperate. He pumps me harder, faster, his soft lips touching down on mine once again.

*"C'mon, Zoey!"*

All life is ebbing out of me. I've gone to a higher place.

*"Jesus Christ!"*

He's called out his name. I'm with Mama. I'm His.

*"Damn it, Zoey. Breathe!"*

The words drift into my ear. Consciousness seeps into my veins. Wait a minute. God doesn't cuss. I'm not in heaven. Nowhere near. Heaven, so close to the sun, is supposed to feel light and airy. Wherever I am feels cold, hard, and wet. My eyes flutter open, and as they do, I cough up water. Reality sets in. Soaked to the bone, I'm lying flat on my back on a slab of cement. I blink again. The vision of my blurred, stinging eyes grows clearer. Kneeling next to me is another god. My boss. The sexiest man on the planet . . . Brandon Taylor. His glistening face looms over mine. His lips are dangerously close to my mouth, his breath so close I can feel it heat my cheeks. His violet eyes are wide with worry. When I cough again, his anxious expression eases up. Dripping wet in a T-shirt and jeans, he gently lifts my head into his arms.

"Hey." His voice is soft and breathy.

Still choking, I can't get a word out.

"You all right?" Genuine concern fills his eyes.

Catching my breath, I nod and give him a little smile.

He smiles back with a sigh of relief. "Jeez, Zo. You almost drowned."

The memory of my near-death experience rears up like an angry sea serpent. Brandon's fiancée, Katrina, yanked me into the pool. On purpose. I'm almost sure of it. And she just watched me flounder even though I was crying out desperate for help. My eyes dart around the circumference of the patio. Katrina is nowhere to be found. I shiver. In part, because I'm so wet and cold; in part, because of the harrowing experience, and in part, because Brandon is holding me.

Rage and revenge rising, I debate about telling him what happened, but in the end, I simply don't have the strength. Or desire. Besides, I can't prove the evil bitch's actions were deliberate. It could easily end up being a nasty my word against hers shouting match with my ass getting fired.

"I guess I'd better be going." My voice is hoarse, and my throat burns from all the salt water I've swallowed.

Slowly, I lift myself to sit up, but before I can get into an upright position, Brandon scoops me into his strong arms as if I'm a mere waif. An incredible lightness of being sweeps over me as he carries me to safety. Depleted of energy, I wrap my arms around his neck and lean my head against his wet, chiseled chest. His heart beats into my ear like a psalm. *Now,* I'm in heaven.

# Chapter 19

## *Brandon*

Zoey clings to me like I'm a lifesaver. In reality, that's what I am. If I hadn't jump into the pool as fast as I did, she might have been a goner. The thought rattles me in my steps.

She feels so light in my arms. Wet and delicious. I could carry her for miles, but arrive at her guesthouse at the end of my property in no time. I kick open the front door and transport her straight to her bathroom. I set her gently down on the tiled counter. It's impeccably neat and organized. A reflection of her personality.

The question—how did she end up in the pool?—is hot on my mind, but right now my assistant needs attention. Dripping wet, she's shivering like crazy, her teeth chattering madly. I rake my fingers through her soaked straggly hair, brushing errant strands out of her eyes. I meet her waterlogged gaze. "You need to take a hot bath."

"I prefer a shower." She smiles at me, her bluish lips quivering from the chill. "You need one too."

She reminds me that I'm as drenched as she is, and I admit I'm a little chilled too. With a shudder of my own, the thought of taking a shower with her enters my mind. While her soaked oversized sweatshirt and baggie sweats leave a lot to the imagination, in my mind's eye, I picture her luscious curves, scrumptious ass, and her bountiful tits. What would it be like to shower with her . . . wash every ounce of her . . . part her long chestnut hair and plant a kiss on the nape of her neck . . . trail my mouth down her spine to her ass . . . and spread those sweet cheeks and . . .

What's wrong with me? I keep fantasizing about my assistant. Maybe this hit and run accident messed with my head in more ways than one. Is it possible that my inexplicable attraction to her is related to my amnesia? Her soft raspy voice cuts into my mental ramblings.

"Brandon, you'd better get going. The last thing you need is to get sick before your first day back on the set."

She's right. After being out of commission from my accident for almost a month, I don't need to get sick. And I sure as hell don't need to get carried away with her, especially when she's so vulnerable. I should say goodnight, but I don't want to leave her quite yet. "Are you sure you don't need anything? I can make you some tea."

Her eyes light up with silent laughter.

"What's so funny?"

She grins. "The thought of the macho man who plays vigilante Kurt Kussler making and drinking tea. It's so . . . contradictory."

A sudden electrical current zaps my brain and I blink several times. A mixture of pain and pleasure consumes me. It's like a memory is trying to poke through my thick skull. *Tea*. There's something special about tea. I like it and drank it with someone before. But who?

"Are you okay?" asks Zoey, responding to the pinched look on my face. I can see my reflection in the mirror above the bathroom counter. There's a deep crease between my brows and an equally deep frown line that slices across my forehead.

"Yeah. I was just remembering something. Nothing important."

Her eyes search mine, and then she struggles to pull off her sopping wet sweatshirt. Her arms flailing, it's quite amusing. And sexy.

"Here, let me help you," I say, moving my hands toward her. "Keep your arms up."

She obliges. With ease, I lift the top over her head and toss it onto the nearby hamper. Beneath it, she's wearing a cotton T-shirt. She's braless. The thin, wet fabric molds to her ample tits. They're nothing like

Katrina's all too perfect man-made ones. They're supple, rounded mounds that complement her curvy body. The inviting kind you want to hold in your palms. I can see the outline of her puckered pink nipples, the bullet-like crowns straining against the sheer fabric. They're so enticing. I fight back the impulse to tweak them between my fingers and then nip them between my teeth. Instead, I grab a bath towel off the nearby rack and wrap it around her to warm her. The truth is I'd rather be wrapping my arms around her and blanketing her body with mine.

"Well, I'd better get going." My voice is unsteady. Unconvincing.

"Yeah." Her shaky voice mirrors mine.

"Sleep tight. And stay out of trouble."

Another small, smile plays on her face. "Yeah, you too."

Her voice is suggestive. Has she been reading my mind? Leaving her on the counter, I turn on my heel. One foot out the door, her voice sounds once more in my ears.

"By the way, Brandon, thanks for rescuing me."

I keep moving without looking back so she can't see the proud, triumphant smile on my lips. Move over Kurt Kussler. Brandon Taylor is a real-life action hero.

And she doesn't see it fall off like a scab when the reality of Katrina sets in.

Where the hell is she? My eyes circle the pool area. My fiancée is nowhere in sight. My rage mounting, I storm back to my house, taking angry giants steps. I need answers. Now!

"What the hell happened out there?" I yell as I tear into the living room. Katrina, freshly showered and now in a jade silk robe, is curled up on the couch, her long legs tucked beneath her and a magazine in her hands.

"Oh, darling! There's a wonderful article about us in *The Enquirer,*" she responds, not once looking up from the tabloid. "With such a great photo. Don't you love the way everyone's now calling us Bratrina?"

I don't give a rat's ass. And I hate that name Bratrina. I stomp up to her and rip the magazine out of her grip. I toss it across the room, thankful I don't break anything in its path.

Katrina straightens. Fury washes over her face. "Why the hell did you do that?" she hisses, examining one of her long crimson nails. "You almost broke one of my nails."

"Right now, I don't give a shit about your nails or some stupid ass magazine." My voice grows louder by an octave and my gaze fierce. "I asked you a question. I expect an answer."

Katrina huffs. "Doesn't someone need a chill pill."

Her response enrages me further. Trust me, nothing

can calm me down. Not even the world's best Scotch. I almost lost my trusted assistant and want to get to the bottom of this.

Katrina is totally non-plussed. She rises, taking a graceful step toward her precious magazine. Impulsively, I shove her back onto the couch. She gasps.

"Jesus, Brandon. Is this anyway to treat your fiancée?"

"Just tell me what happened out there." My voice is fiery.

She flings her head back and runs her fingers through her long wet platinum hair. "If you really want to know, I was just protecting you. That ungainly assistant of yours was insistent on seeing you at this ungodly hour, and I told her it wasn't a wise idea. I tried to hold her back, but she tripped on the slippery deck and fell into the pool. A total accident."

Leaving her insults aside and the fact that I did text Zoey to help me with my lines, I ask my fiancée why she didn't help her when she saw she was obviously drowning. Katrina's a strong swimmer.

"Darling, a combination of factors, but mostly, I thought that conniving little twit was just faking it. Just a clever maneuver to have me jump back into the pool so she could get me all wet again."

"She almost drowned." The frightening, unforgettable image of her unconscious body floating in the water flashes into my head.

"Actually, with her weight, I'm surprised she didn't sink."

I clench my fists by my sides so tightly I can feel my nails dig into my palms. It takes all my willpower not to slap her or fling her across the room. I may have a history with so-called bad girls, but Katrina keeps testing my limits. The rage I feel toward her disquiets me. Almost frightens me.

Breathing through my nose with my lips pressed tight, I try to control my temper. Silence. Tense silence. And then Katrina looks up at me. Her eyes flutter. "I'm sorry, darling. I didn't mean that. I just really don't like that girl. She's everything I'm not."

Unpretentious. Funny. Sassy. Caring. And she has an inviting body with soft, luscious curves that I find more attractive than Katrina's razor-sharp edges and plastic enhancements. After several deep breaths, I calm down enough to retrieve Katrina's tabloid. She snatches it from me and immediately goes back to scanning the pages.

"I'm going to call it a night," I say stiffly, eager to get away from her and out of my wet clothes.

She looks up from the magazine and smiles. "No problem, darling. I have an early call in the morning. I'm going to head home shortly."

Great. I need to sleep alone tonight or at least not with her. We still haven't spent a night together since my hospital release.

Still seething, I head for my bedroom. I strip off my soaked clothes and then lope to the adjacent bathroom where I turn on a hot shower. The cascading water immediately warms me. But it does nothing to undo my stress. I'm wound up as tight as a spring. I beat myself off to release the tension that's been rising in me like a fever. My rage toward my infuriating fiancée fuels my libido and my undeniable attraction to my indispensable assistant sets me off. I come powerfully and quickly. My first orgasm since my accident. It's like my cock is saying: "Now what?" I don't know. Stepping out of the shower, I gaze out the bathroom window, which offers me a perfect view of the guesthouse. The lights are out. At least I know Zoey is safely asleep.

# Chapter 20

## Zoey

The sound of my phone alarm comes as a rude awakening. I hardly slept a wink. Tossing and turning, I couldn't stop thinking about last night's events.

Brandon Taylor saved my life. My real-life Kurt Kussler rescued me from drowning. Gave me mouth-to-mouth resuscitation and carried me in his arms. I couldn't stop reliving the feeling of his soft lips on mine, breathing life into me, his heartbeat singing in my ears, and being in his strong arms, mine wrapped around his neck, clinging to him. Never wanting to let go. Never wanting him to leave me.

Peeling one eye open after the other, my exhilaration gives way to the reality that today is just another humdrum day of being his overworked assistant and back at his beck and call. What happened last night was just a fluke thing. He did what any good Samaritan would do. Except Brandon Taylor isn't any ordinary citizen. He's my boss. TV's highest paid actor. *People Magazine*'s "Sexiest Man Alive." And let's get very real. He's totally unavailable. He's engaged to Katrina Moore, America's It Girl. And they're getting married on national TV.

Still tucked under my covers, I gaze up at the ceiling like I'm looking for answers. Fucking Katrina. Did she yank me into the pool or did I slip? While she did try to stop me from leaving, I can't be sure. Pointing a finger at her is not going to pay off. The manipulative bitch will throw insults in my face and twist things so I look like some dumb-ass spaz who doesn't know how to swim. In my head, I can hear her apologizing to Brandon in her kiss-up saccharine voice for not helping me while I was drowning. In my best impersonation of her, I mouth, "I'm sorry, Brandy-Poo. I had no clue." And then, the lying bitch will make things all right by pulling down his fly . . .

My alarm rings again. Just in time to stop my imagination from going to repugnant X-rated places. It's time to get up and down to business. Groggily, I lift myself to a sitting position and reach for my phone on my night table. I routinely go to my emails to check what's on today's agenda before getting dressed and heading off to Starbucks. Sure enough, there's one from Brandon with "IMPORTANT" written in the subject line.

My pulse quickening, I click on it and read it:

*As soon as you're up, meet me at the pool and be sure to wear a bathing suit.*

Anxiety blasts through me. The pool is the last place I want to hang out with him. And I sure as hell don't want to put on a bathing suit. I only own one—a one-piece I've had for years that covers up most of my imperfections. I've actually never worn it and dread putting it on. I email him back.

*Do I really need to wear a bathing suit? I'd rather not.*

I hit send and get an instant reply.

*Yes. Get your ass to the pool now.*

Fuck. Boss's orders. He's back to being an asshole.

When I get to the pool, he's already in the water swimming laps—something he does daily while I go to Starbucks to fetch his must-have Grande iced coffee. He cuts through the water like a shark, each powerful stroke propelling him forward, the muscles of his tanned arms and back rhythmically contracting. On a breath, he catches sight of me and swims up to where I'm standing. His head rises from the water, his skin and hair glistening. Lifting his goggles atop of his head, he rests his beautiful arms along the edge, flexing those well-formed biceps. His thick-lashed violet eyes gleam into mine.

"Good morning," I say, holding it together despite a flurry of flutters. "What's on the agenda?"

"Jump in."

My stomach twists. "Excuse me?"

"You heard me. Take off your robe and jump in. I assume you're wearing a bathing suit."

I nervously tug at the belt of my worn velour robe. "If you recall, I don't swim."

"That's unacceptable. You're a liability. Now, please take off your robe."

Slowly, I shrug off my robe until it's puddled at my feet. His eyes travel from my head to my toes, lingering on some places he has no right to be. While all my lady parts are hidden, I feel like I'm totally bared to him. Divulging every imperfection. A shiver runs up my spine while I tug on the edge of my tank suit to make sure it's covering my big butt.

"You look good in a bathing suit. Now, let's get you wet."

I read more than I should into his words. A rush of hot tingles bombards me.

"I'm a little nervous." Make that scared shitless. My fear of drowning is so great I don't take baths, and when I was at that spa, I never stepped foot in the hot tub.

"Jump in," he orders again, his voice louder and gruffer.

Clenching my fists, I stand as still as a stone statue. I'm paralyzed with fear.

He scowls at me. "If you don't do it, I'm going to hoist myself out of the pool and throw you in."

I gulp. Though I suppose I could threaten him for harassment, he's not giving me much choice. I chew on my bottom lip.

He breaks into a smug smile. "Don't worry. I'll catch every little bit of you."

The thought of being held again in those magnificent arms motivates me. Okay, here goes. My heart racing, on the silent count of three, I squeeze my eyes shut and jump into the pool. The deep end, no less. *Splash!* As quickly as I sink in the tepid water so deep my toes skim the bottom, I torpedo to the surface. My head powers through the water and I find myself eye level with Brandon who's holding me tightly. His firm hands cinch my waist. Face to face, we're just a palm's width apart. Anxiously, I grasp his broad shoulders for extra support and security. Or should I say irresistibly?

He smirks. "See, that wasn't too bad."

His warm breath heats my moist cheeks. "Okay, are we done now?" Truthfully, I don't want to let go of him.

His smirk morphs into a fiendish grin. "We've only just begun. I'm giving you a swimming lesson. Something you've obviously never had."

"Um, uh, my parents never got around to it," I

stammer. Brandon knows very little about my family or past. He's never asked. Right now, the pathetic excuse will have to suffice. It's not the time to tell him about my mother's tragic death.

He cocks a brow. "Whatever. By the time we're done today, you're going to be able to swim a lap all on your own."

My breath hitches in my throat. "I don't think so."

Without responding, he transports me to the shallow end of the pool where we can both stand up. He sets me down on my feet. While the water comes to my chest, it hits his six-foot-two frame just above his waist. His shimmering pecs and six-pack are in full view. They take my breath away.

Almost ironically he says, "Okay, the first thing you need to learn how to do is breathe. It's simple."

I watch as he dips his head into the water and blows out little bubbles. After thirty seconds or so, he lifts it out and shakes off some excess water. Somehow, I find that sexy as sin and a new set of hot tingles rushes to my core.

My turn. I imitate his actions, and with pursed lips, I blow out bubbles, trying to breathe normally. The soft percolating sound echoes through my ears. Finally, when I can no longer hold my breath and my lungs feel on the verge of bursting, my head pops out of the water. I inhale a deep breath of the warm morning air to replenish my lungs. My gaze meets Brandon's.

His eyes are wide. "Wow! You have amazing breath control. How'd you learn to do that?"

One two-syllable word is on the tip of my tongue. *Blowjobs*. Sadly forgettable. I bite it back and shrug. "I suppose it's just a special skill I have."

He smirks again, his eyes narrowing seductively. "I bet you have lots of special skills I don't know about. You're lucky. I'm going to add swimming to your repertoire."

Fucking in the water would be more like it. If we weren't in a pool, he could feel how really wet I am. Here I go again! What's wrong with me?

He licks his delectable lips, a small gesture that sends more distracting flutters to my gut . . . and beyond. "Okay, now relax."

Before I can utter a word, he's repositions me so I'm lying horizontally on my belly across the water in the palms of his large hands. I can feel them pressing dangerously close to my sex. The tingly sensation intensifies between my legs as his sultry voice sounds in my ears.

"Now, stretch your arms out in front of you, keeping them as close together as possible."

I do as I'm told and await further instruction.

"Good. Now, put your head in the water, being sure to blow out bubbles like I taught you."

In goes my head. But as soon as I begin blowing bubbles, I no longer feel his grip. I panic and flounder. I lose control of my breathing. Water infiltrates my nostrils, and coursing past my throat, quickly fills my lungs. My arms and legs flail in a tangle. I gasp for air, only to swallow a burning mouthful of the salty water. My fear of drowning swarms me.

And then I'm back in his arms. This time my legs wrapped around his hips like a pretzel, my arms folded tightly around his neck. My breathing is heavy. Close to hyperventilating.

He tenderly brushes away a few wet tendrils of hair that have fallen into my face. I hope he can't tell I'm on the verge of tears. "I'm sorry," I whisper, my voice watery.

He puts a finger to my lips to silence me. "Shh. It's okay. I should have told you I was going to let you go." His tone is compassionate, not gruff or judgmental. "Let's try this again. Remember, just relax and blow bubbles. When I let go, the water will carry you. Ready?"

I nod because I know if I open my mouth a whimper will escape. The last thing I want to do is have a breakdown in front of my demanding boss. Wordlessly, I let him rearrange me back into that horizontal position. I inhale and then exhale, the deep breath composing me. With my arms extended straight out in front of me, I draw in another sharp breath and then immerse my head in the pool. His words cut through the water.

"Nice. Now steady yourself. I'm going to let go of you."

This time, I'm prepared when his hands fly off my body. Blowing bubbles, I open my eyes. It's almost surreal. I see the little popping bubbles trail ahead of me and strands of my chestnut hair fan out like tributaries. An amazing sensation overtakes me. A magnificent lightness of being. Weightlessness. Something I've never experienced before. Holy smoke! I'm floating!

In my state of otherworldliness, I lose track of time. I don't know how long I've been under the water moving like a stealth submarine, when two hands grip my hips and lever me to a standing position. On a deep breath, I tilt my head back and gaze up at Brandon. The wide-eyed expression on his face is a mixture of angst and awe. His hands cup my shoulders.

"Jeez, Zoey. You gave me a scare. I've seriously never met anyone who can hold their breath as long as you can."

I smile sheepishly. "I did okay?"

Relaxing, he returns the smile. "You did great. An A+++."

My smile widens while he tells me there's one more thing to master before I can move on to an actual lap. Treading water. Walking my hands along the rim of the pool, I follow him as he leads the way back to the deep end.

"Hold on and watch what I'm doing." While I grip the side of the pool, he moves five feet in front of me and into a vertical position, his head above the water. He explains to me it's kind of like riding a bike. To keep pedaling my legs beneath the water and to simultaneously move my hands in a small sweeping motion. Without him asking, I dunk my head under the water to get a glimpse of his legs in motion. Flexing, they're so long, gorgeous, and powerful. And his rippled stomach muscles that give way to a perfect pelvic V are so taut. And don't get me started on that monumental bulge that's straining against his Speedo. God, he's hung!

"Get it?" he asks when I lift my head out of the water.

"Got it." I play into his signature *Kurt Kussler* line.

"Good." He winks. "Now kick off the side of the pool and float toward me."

With ease and confidence, I do as bid, and in one swift, graceful move, I reach him. He grasps my hands once again. While he continues to tread the water, I shift my body so it's perpendicular to the water like his. I start to bicycle my legs and to my surprise, I stay in a vertical position with my head above the water, though barely. My legs more than once touch his, our knees knocking. And more than once his hard length grazes my center. Deliberately? Once he sees I can stay afloat, he lets go of my hands, and I begin to paddle them. To my amazement, I rise higher above the surface of the water.

"You've got it," he shouts out while I concentrate on my movements. He's right. It's a lot like riding a bike. And I'm good at that with my strong arms and legs.

We continue to tread water for another five minutes until I grow a little short of breath. He resumes a horizontal position, but this time on his back.

"Baby, hold on to my legs and just kick. I'm going to give you a ride back to the shallow end."

For a brief moment, I'm stunned and my heart skips a beat. Did he just call me baby? It probably just slipped out of his mouth and is what he calls a lot of chicks he knows. Very Hollywood, though this is a first. I let it go and grab his ankles. As I kick behind him, he hauls me across the pool with a powerful backstroke—me loving every minute—until we're both standing in the three-foot deep shallow end at the edge of the pool. He rises from the water like a god. Water drips from every part of him and his sculpted muscles glisten in the sun.

"Turn around," he commands. His voice is authoritative.

Again, I do as asked. In a heartbeat, I feel his hard body pressing against mine. He captures both my wrists in his hands and begins to circle my arms, one after the other.

"Keep your fingers together and cut the water with them."

I follow his directions, but he reprimands me. "No, Zoey. Don't slap the water. Slice it and keep the splashes small."

"Okay," I murmur, a little crestfallen that I'm not quite getting it. Finally, after about thirty muscle-exhausting rotations, I have it down. My arms are killing me.

"I'm a little tired," I plead, craning my neck. "Maybe we can pick up where we've left off tomorrow."

He looks at me sternly. "No. You're not leaving this pool until you know how to swim. End of discussion."

I hate when he says "end of discussion." There's no twisting the egomaniac's arm. He wants what he wants and always gets his way.

We move on to the next part of the lesson. He makes me hold on to the edge of the pool along side him and mimic the way he's kicking. It's all in the ankles—a small flutter kick. Again, he tells me it's not a splash party. I do well. So, we move on to the final part of the lesson. I'm going to combine breathing with stroking and kicking. Do what's known as a crawl. He demonstrates first, swimming to the other end of the pool and back. I watch in awe as his powerful body cuts through the water with the elegance and speed of a dolphin. In no time, he's back in the shallow end.

"Okay, your turn. You're going to do one lap to the

end of the pool."

My gaze travels to the deep end. Suddenly, the pool seems a mile long. Fear creeps back into my veins. "I don't think I can do it."

He tilts my chin up with his thumb and holds it there. Another rush of tingles streams through my body from my head to my toes. I meet his intense gaze and my bottom lip quivers. He's affecting me, making me all hot and bothered. I flounder for words.

"I'm scared. I've never swum before. What if I freak out and—"

Still pressing his thumb under my chin, he cuts me off and flicks his index finger across the tip of my nose. "You won't. And besides, I'll be swimming right next to you."

That's a comforting thought, but I remain frozen in fear and some other forbidden emotion I don't want to acknowledge.

"Here. Wear these." He takes the goggles on top of his head off and puts them on me. I don't move a muscle while he adjusts them to fit my face. My eyes stayed fixed on him through the plastic lenses. Oh, God! He's beautiful! So, so beautiful!

"Are you ready?"

I don't respond. I'm too fixated on his face and his body. If God created man in his image, He must be insanely divine.

Brandon grows a little irritated. "You know, we don't have all day." Ugh! That dreaded bossy voice.

"So let's get to it. Kick off and start swimming."

He moves out of my way. I shoot him one more doubtful look and I do it. It doesn't come easily and I know I look nothing like an Olympian, but for the first time in my life, I'm actually swimming. Propelling myself across the pool with my arms and legs. Slowly but surely. On my first breath, I see Brandon on his back, stroking idly beside me. He winks at me, and I manage a tepid smile back at him. But halfway down the length of the pool, he picks up his pace, and before I know it, he's way ahead of me. Panic grips me. I'm all by myself in the middle of the pool. The memory of my mother drowning fills my head. Her arms reaching out for me. Of me, watching, hopeless and helpless, until she disappears beneath the sea. I will it away. *Swim, Zoey! You can do it! Do it for her!*

On my next breath, a natural rhythm kicks in. Effort becomes effortless. Brandon's voice resounds in my ear when I come up for air. "Come on, Zo. You can do it. You're almost there." I manage to glimpse his impassioned face before my head slides back under the water. The end is in sight. Maybe a dozen strokes away.

Finally, my hand touches down on the rim of the pool. My head shoots out of the water, and looming above me is Brandon, all wet and beautiful. He grabs my hand and hoists me out of the water, something I have not an ounce of body strength to manage. After lifting the goggles on top of my head, he swiftly wraps a large fluffy towel around my dripping wet body and then draws me into his arms. Breathing heavily, I don't resist and rest my head against his damp manly chest. My thudding heart drowns out his. He holds me tightly. While my breathing calms down, my heartbeat speeds up. My nipples harden at the touch of his sculpted pecs, sending a blast of arousal to the triangle between my inner thighs. He presses me closer and I feel his hard length rub against me right through the thick towel. Finally, I break my head away from his chest and gaze up at his breathtaking face. His dark hair is slicked back, his eyes two sparkling amethyst gems. My eyes don't blink and my mouth doesn't move. My heartbeat hastens from a trot to a gallop.

Grinning smugly, he breaks the heated silence and rakes his hand through my soaked strands of hair. "You did it!"

"I had a great teacher," I say softly with a smile.

"There's a lot I could teach you, baby."

Oh my God. He called me baby again. But this time his lush lips stay parted. He bows his head, and I swear he's making a beeline for my mouth. Every feature on my face freezes in anticipation. He's getting closer. I can practically taste him. Oh so close. And then . . .

"What may I ask is going on here?"

Brandon jerks away, body and all. My towel falls to the ground.

It's her.

Hurricane Katrina.

# Chapter 21

## *Brandon*

"I'm just giving Zoey a swimming lesson. After last night, I thought she could use one."

With glacial eyes, Katrina gives Zoey the once over. "Some people should never put on a bathing suit."

Zoey is cringing; I can tell by the way she scrunches her face and clenches her fists. Before I can come to her defense, she excuses herself.

"Thank you, Brandon, for the lesson. I really appreciate it. I'm going to get changed and go to Starbucks."

Her tone is totally professional, and she avoids eye contact with Katrina.

Dressed in some designer white workout outfit, Katrina keeps her disdainful gaze on my assistant. I'm waiting for some kind of apology. A small smile slithers across her face and a glimmer of hope fills me.

"While you're there, get me a low-fat soy latte. And

don't forget the Sweet 'n Low."

My Mean 'n Low fiancée needs more than a package of fake sweetener. What was I thinking? There's no hope. Zoey's big brown eyes flare, but she maintains her cool. I want to say something, but she doesn't give me a chance.

"Sure." Zoey hurls the word at Katrina and takes off. My eyes stay on her backside as she heads toward the guesthouse. Her ample ass is shaped like a heart and I more than like it. I want to coddle and squeeze it. And that's just for starters.

Katrina's breathy voice hurls me out of my unscrupulous thoughts. "Darling, while we're waiting for our coffees, let's go over some wedding details." She's clutching an iPad.

"I'd like to take a hot shower and put on some jeans first."

She flings her head back with marked impatience. "Darling, can't that wait? I have yoga at nine and then I have a full day of shooting. This is important." She adjusts her sports bra. The remains of that tattoo on her chest shimmer in the morning sun. I still can't make out the name. B-U-T-C-H? Another old boyfriend?

"Please, darling," she purrs in my ear.

"Fine." I might as well just get it over with.

I take a seat opposite her at one of the poolside tables. I wish I had my damn sunglasses. Even with the umbrella, the morning sunlight is blinding me.

"So what's happening?"

I'm sorry I asked. Setting the iPad on the table, she goes over a crapload of wedding shit I have no interest or expertise in. Like seating and floral arrangements, wedding favors, bridesmaid gowns, the menu, and more.

My responses—when I can get a word in—are limited to the following: "Uh-huh. Good. Perfect. Nice."

The one-way conversation goes on for what seems like forever. While my interest dwindles, Katrina grows more and more excited with every over the top detail. "Darling, I'm so thrilled you love everything. Mommy's doing an incredible job. This wedding is simply going to be unforgettable!"

I twitch a half-smile as my mind wanders. All I can think about is my assistant. Why isn't she back yet? Starbucks is just a half-mile down the hill on Sunset. Five minutes away. But it's not my caffeine addiction that has me on edge. It's my growing addiction to her. I need her more than I need my coffee fix. Like I'm co-dependent on her. But isn't that what a relationship with a personal assistant should be?

Jolting me out of my disconcerting thoughts, Katrina clasps my hands. "Brandy-Poo, I'm just going to need one thing from you."

"What?"

"Your credit card so Mommy can put down deposits on everything."

I hesitate and then consent. According to my manager Scott, I did agree to pay for the wedding. The less I have to do with any of this shit, the better.

Katrina smiles brightly, revealing her perfect pearly white teeth. "Wonderful. Tomorrow, Mommy and I are going to Neiman's to pick out our registry. Can you come?"

I thank my lucky stars I have a full day of shooting *Kurt Kussler* tomorrow. I have no interest in picking out dinnerware and silverware and all those other ridiculous wedding necessities. As far as I'm concerned, I have everything I need. I break the news to Katrina and feign regret.

"Don't worry, darling. Mommy and I can handle everything. And we both have exquisite taste."

I take that to mean expensive.

"You're just going to love everything we pick out."

"I'm sure I will." At that moment, I see Zoey heading toward us, carrying a small Starbucks bag.

Katrina doesn't notice her and starts spewing all the registry items she has in mind. From hand painted china sets to sterling silver tea sets. I half-listen. My mind is more focused on my iced coffee, and the girl who's bringing it our way. She doesn't have movie star looks, but she's fucking adorable with her curvy-little body and that kissable, upturned mouth.

"And Brandy-Poo, one more thing we really need to think about is our honey—"

"Your coffees." Zoey sets the bag down on the table and serves us both, Katrina first.

Katrina immediately grabs her coffee without acknowledging Zoey.

"You're welcome," singsongs my assistant, her voice dripping with sarcasm.

I have to love her. She hands me mine.

"Thanks, Zo." Our eyes connect and she smiles.

"No, prob."

"Why don't you join us?"

Katrina's eyes narrow. "Zoey, why don't you go to the kitchen first and get me a cup and saucer. I don't care for drinking coffee out of a paper cup. It's so uncouth."

"You have two legs. Get them yourself." She stalks off with an air of confidence.

Score one for Zoey. Katrina's jaw drops to the ground.

"Brandon, how could you let that rude girl talk to me like that? You should fire her sorry ass."

There are a lot better things I want to do to her ass. Shit. I'm engaged. A pang of guilt assaults me.

After coffee, Katrina splits, and I take a hot shower and get dressed—jeans and a T-shirt. I spend the rest of the morning going over my *Kurt Kussler* script and rehearsing. I'm at once excited and anxious about being back on the set tomorrow. It'll be my first time since the accident. I've decided once again not to let anyone know I have amnesia. It's pointless and will put everyone on edge. I've watched enough episodes to know who's who, and Zoey put together a file of the cast and crew. I don't quite have all the crew members down—between cameramen, ADs, grips, wardrobe, hair and makeup, catering, and PA's, there's well over a hundred. It takes a village to produce a TV series. But yours truly has a plan. I'll just avoid calling people by their first names, and if I screw up, I'll just cover it up with a lighthearted excuse à la: "It's been a long time, man. It's easy to forget." *You have no clue!*

The first scene up tomorrow is the love scene between Kurt and his late wife Alisha. A flashback. No matter how many times I've rehearsed it, I'm still not getting it. Or should I say, making it work. I'm growing frustrated and anxious. The last thing I want is to suck tomorrow. I'm an Emmy and Golden Globe nominated actor. My cast and crew expect me to be good. Make that great.

At half past one, I've had it. Cussing, I crumple up my script pages in my fist, toss them across the living room, and then pour myself a Scotch. It's way to early for me to be drinking, but I've got a throbbing headache and need to de-stress.

Nursing the Scotch, an idea comes to me. The same

one I had last night before all the drama.

Zoey. Rehearsing my lines with me is on her list of job responsibilities.

Slamming my tumbler down on the coffee table, I reach for my iPhone and text her.

*Print out two more copies of my sides and get ur ass over here.*

Before I hit send, I modify my message.

*Print out two more copies of my sides and* get *ur **sweet** ass over here.*

One word can make a difference. As Jackie Gleason used to say on the *Honeymooners,* an old show from the fifties my mother loved to watch . . . *How sweet it is.*

I impatiently wait for her reply. Zippo. My feisty assistant is back to playing games with me. I text her again.

*If ur not here soon, I'm going to drag u by ur hair like a caveman.*

My cock flexes as I type the words. And I silently chuckle. The savage Neanderthal image gives me more than a rise and a laugh. The thought of dominating her like that sends a ripple of recollection through my head. I blink several times, searching for a memory I'm obviously suppressing.

Before I hit send, she responds: *Coming.*

My rigid cock strains against my jeans in anticipation.

Damn my amnesia!

Damn that girl!

# Chapter 22

## Zoey

The asshole hasn't changed one bit. He's still texting me obnoxious messages and I'm still at his beck and call. I take that back. He's gotten worse. That head injury has given him more than amnesia. I think he's gone bi-polar. One minute, he's super nice to me, the next a total jerk. I don't know what to expect.

I re-read his text and read more into it than I should. If he wants my *sweet* ass, I'm going to give him what he wants. I hastily change from my baggy sweats into a sexy tight black mini-skirt and sleeveless tank top, both courtesy of Chaz. Before heading over, I examine myself in the full-length mirror on my closet door. Before my sojourn at the spa, I made a decision to take it down once and for all—waking up to my chunky body was not the best way to start a day—but now that I've shed some pounds, I don't mind it. I study my reflection. Okay, though far from thin by Hollywood standards, I look good. Wearing all black is slenderizing. I shove my hands under my skirt to fix my top. With a couple of tugs, it hugs my solid curves perfectly. I'm wearing my best Gloria's Secret push up bra—and in this clingy top, I must say my cleavage is outstanding. Thanks to the spa, my legs are thinner and more toned, and the platforms I have on make them look longer. Retrieving the sides from my printer, Go-to-Zo is ready to go.

"Hel-lo-O. I'm here"

I catch Brandon off guard on the couch reading the trades. While most now read *The Hollywood Reporter* or *Variety* online, he still likes to read the daily paper versions. I wonder if it's because his late father owned a newsstand. He doesn't know I found that out online. I've googled just about everything about him. With my uncanny memory, I'm a walking encyclopedia when it comes to Brandon Taylor.

He looks up and stares at me. Let me rephrase. He eyes me from head to toe. "You look nice."

Surprised at the compliment, I adjust my skirt. "Thanks."

"Are you going some place special later?"

"I have a date tonight." I have no clue what made

me say that.

"Oh," he mutters under his breath. "That guy you went out to lunch with?"

I flash a smile. "Yes." *Well, it's true.*

He knits his brows. "Your boyfriend, right?"

"Yeah." That's true, too, depending on how you interpret the word "boyfriend."

He frowns and I change the subject. "I brought your sides. Two copies like you asked." I slide them out of the folder I'm holding and hand them to him.

He hands one stapled set back to me. "I need you to rehearse the first scene with me."

My breath hitches. To be honest, I didn't pay much attention to his sides. I just hit print and threw them into a folder.

"Sure, no problem."

"You should study the lines and then we'll work on them."

With the sides in hand, I plop down on the leather chair closest to him. I can feel his eyes on me as I read over the scene. I cross my legs to quell the sudden tingly sensation between them.

With every word, my pulse quickens and chest tightens. And I grow heated. It's one of those flash-backs with Kurt Kussler and his late wife. A love scene. An explicit one that takes place shortly before Alisha is brutally executed by Kurt's nemesis, The Locust.

"Okay. I know the lines." My voice falters. The

scene is so sensual and moving. I'm fraught with emotion.

Brandon lifts a brow. "So quickly?"

"Yes," I stutter. "I have an eidetic memory."

"What's that?"

"The extraordinary ability to look at anything or anyone and remember everything about them after only a few moments of exposure."

"Wow. So like a super-memory?"

"You can call it that." It's weird that I can remember everything and he can't remember a thing.

My photographic memory is the reason I've never forgotten what Mama's killer looks like. Even as a five-year old, I was able to explain to the police sketch artist every detail of his face though I only laid eyes on him for a brief moment. And it's the reason I keep reliving the day of Brandon's accident. You'd think by now it would be a blur, but every vivid detail fills my mind while every unforgettable emotion sweeps through my veins. The heart has a memory too. His pool of blood . . . my ocean of tears. The fear and despair. The pain. My beating heart is an emotional watershed, the back of my eyes a veritable damn.

Brandon's voice breaks into my inner turmoil and brings me back to the moment. "You okay?"

I take a deep breath to calm myself. "Yeah. It's a very powerful scene. Let's do it."

"I want to rehearse it in the shower."

My jaw drops and my stomach knots. "What?"

"That's where it takes place. It'll help me really feel it."

"B-but the scene calls for you and Alisha to be bared to each other." I know they use body part cover-ups, but still it requires undressing. I'm bristling all over.

"You can keep your clothes on. I'll do the same. We'll just pretend we're undressed."

My heart pounding, I process his words. His eyes stay riveted on me as if he's mentally undressing me. Fully clothed, I already feel so exposed. So vulnerable. So aroused.

"And we'll pretend the shower is running, right?"

"Wrong. We've got to go all the way."

I gulp, reading much more into his words than I should. I struggle for a comeback. "What about my outfit? It'll get all wet."

"Make that the least of your worries. I'll get it dry cleaned or buy you something new in time for your hot date."

"Fine," I splutter. My panties already need to be rung out. He's right. I'm worried about a lot more.

Brandon's bathroom is a spacious, state-of-the-art retreat, and like the rest of the house, it offers dazzling views of the city. Today, I can even see as far as the Pacific Ocean. There's an oversized whirlpool tub and a separate glass enclosed shower that's virtually the size of a room. A dozen people could easily fit inside it.

"Are you ready?" asks Brandon as he turns on the shower. It's one of those luxury hi-tech showers with a multitude of knobs. To my wide-eyed amazement, the water gushes from the ceiling like a waterfall. I've never seen anything quite like it. The room steams up instantly.

"Take your shoes off."

Kicking off my platforms, I'm having second thoughts. Anxiety is pulsing through my bloodstream and my stomach is twisting. But before I can change my mind, he takes me by my hand and leads me into the stall. The water pounds on us, soaking us quickly. In a couple breaths, we're as wet as two drowned rats.

"This is kind of fun," he laughs, shaking his dripping wet mop of ebony hair out of his eyes.

"Yeah," I laugh back, drinking in the contours of his rippled muscles that strain against his drenched tee. I gleefully tilt back my head and rake my fingers through my hair. Droplets of water catch on my tongue. I'm reminded of being a little kid and running through the sprinklers with my clothes on. It was something naughty and fun.

"Okay, now let's get serious. Do you remember your lines?"

I meet his glistening eyes. "Of course."

"Good," he says with a sexy lopsided smile. Without fair warning, he flips me around. His powerful arms circle my waist and draw me close to him. His hard body presses tight against mine. I can feel the rise and fall of his chest. My heart pitter-patters, and I'm glad for the forceful spray that washes out the sound.

"Now, remember. I'm Kurt Kussler and you're my beloved wife Alisha. We're insanely in love. Two kindred souls united by body and mind."

I nod like a bobble-head doll. Words are stuck behind a big lump in my throat. I just hope I can say my lines.

"Ready? Here goes."

I nod again. I'm wired up. Every nerve in my body is buzzing.

"Baby, did I ever tell you how sexy you are?" Brandon, I mean Kurt, breathes into my ear.

"No." Butterflies flutter in my stomach, and I try to remember this is just make-believe.

"Well, I'm telling it to you now, Mrs. Kussler." He parts my wet hair and, then wrapping his arms around me again, he nuzzles my neck. I flinch in his brawny arms at the feeling of his soft lips touching down on my flesh. Tingles swarm me.

And then he gropes my big tits, circling my nipples with his thumbs. My buds instantly harden under my clingy wet tank and another rush of tingly sparks descends to my sex. It's as if my tits and my pussy are connected by a power cord. Holy shit! He's turned up the steam.

As called for by the script, I moan. But to be honest, I can't help it. As he continues to nibble my neck and tweak my tits, my knees go weak. To my relief, an arm curls around my waist and holds me up. A trail of kisses travels down my spine, sending a shiver up it despite the heat. He lifts his other hand off my tit and cups the ample cheeks of my ass in his palm. He squeezes and caresses them.

"I love every part of you," he breathes against my neck.

I'm so caught up in the scene I almost forget my line. "You're everything to me, Kurt."

He draws me closer to him, and to my shock, he slips the hand holding me up under the waistband of my skirt. His fingers slide down my abdomen until they're cupped over the crotch of my drenched cotton undies, covering my pulsing pussy like a glove. Hissing, he leaves his hand there for a few heated breaths, and then begins to rub my clit until the sensitive bundle of nerves is a bubbling nub.

"Do you like this?"

Oh my God. Was this in the script? Am I supposed to say something? I'll just ad lib. "Oh yes. Please don't stop." My voice is a breathy, desperate plea.

"Don't worry, that's not happening." For real? He

continues to rub my clit vigorously. "You're so hot for me, baby."

I'm on fire. And if he only knew how r*eally* wet I am. Soaked with lust and desire. My breathing grows harsh. I may either jump out of my skin or faint. My burning need to come is consuming me. Taking over every ounce of my being. To make matters worse, the hardness between his legs grazes my backside. Holy cow! He's as aroused as I am! Are we acting or is this for real? The line is blurred in the haze of steam.

"I love you, Bra . . . um, uh Kurt." Fuck. I almost flubbed my line.

"The same, baby. I can't get enough of you."

He flips me around so I'm facing him. His biceps flex as his deft hands grip my bare upper arms. I soak in his impassioned face, dripping with lust, his thick-lashed eyes smoldering with desire. I brush away a wisp of his slick hair that's fallen into his eye. I think the script called for that.

Moving his hands to my face, he tilts it up, his eyes never losing contact with mine. His head moves forward. Holy smoke! He's going to kiss me! Maybe I missed that part in the script. My whole body quivers as his lips touch down on mine. Oh my God! It's a veritable movie star kiss—deep, passionate, all-consuming. A kiss like none other. Thinking I may swoon, I moan again into his mouth and dig my fingernails into his hard biceps. He bites down on my lower lip, and then his tongue darts inside my parted mouth. It finds mine and we tango like we've danced this way forever. Whirling and swirling, my tongue follows his lead. I moan again—I'm not sure if that's scripted—but I just can't help it. Every muscle in my body is trembling with anticipation and desire. Without breaking the kiss, he draws me closer to him and starts grinding against me.

"Alisha, my love, let's make a baby."

The baby they will never see. Alisha, of course, doesn't know this yet, and the thought of the tragedy that awaits her brings tears to my eyes. They mingle with the stinging needles of water, cascading over us while my character's cherished husband and lover grinds harder and faster with urgency and zeal, rubbing against my aching clit. It's all pretend, yet it feels so real. I can feel his swelling erection, straining against his soaked jeans and pulsating against me. It's so hard, so hot, so ready to come. Clutching his shoulders, I fight the urge to slide a hand down to his fly and touch his extraordinary length. A bizarre thought crosses my mind—dry humping someone has never been this wet. I'm soaked through and through, so close to the edge. There's a hot ball of fire between my legs the water can't quench, and on his next thrust, I combust with a deafening scream of his name. I'm so enraptured, I don't know if I've shouted out Kurt or Brandon, but who cares when his face contorts with pure ecstasy and he roars out, "Oh, baby."

Fade to black. I free myself from him and lean against the all-glass shower. Barely able to stand on my trembling legs, I collapse into a squat. My pussy's throbbing, my mind's murky, and my heart's working hard. Brandon joins me and wraps his arm around my shoulders. Like mine, his breathing is shallow. He looks as shell-shocked as I feel. In a cloud of steam, we sit silently side by side, our bent legs touching, until our breaths and heartbeats calm down. The shower's still on, the forceful spray still grazing us. The sound of the pounding water replaces the drum of my pulse in my ears. Brandon finally breaks our long, stunned silence.

"Wow. You're a really good actress."

"Thanks." I don't tell him I've had to be.

"Did you ever consider becoming one?"

I tell him I did and even took a few acting lessons. "But the truth is, there aren't enough parts around for a girl like me so I decided to become a full-time masseuse." I also don't tell him that I took his assistant position with the remote hope of breaking into the biz.

Twisting, he sweeps away a tangle of hair that's dangling in my eyes. "Well, I think you missed your calling."

"Thanks." My voice is a soft whisper.

"No, thank *you*. You really helped me. I've got the scene down now."

"No prob. That's part of my job." I pause. "You

were amazing." *Oh was he!* My head is already set on instant replay.

He smiles. "I may need your help again. It's been rough getting back into the swing of things."

"Sure. Anytime." I'm in love with Kurt Kussler, but I'm not supposed to fall for Brandon Taylor. That wasn't in my job description. And besides, he can never be mine. He was just acting. Nothing was real. My heart grows heavy, soaked with reality.

# Chapter 23

## *Brandon*

"Take that, you asshole!"

*POW!*

"I'm not done with you!" I grunt.

*POW! POW! POW! POW!*

Sweat pours from every crevice of my bare-chested body. Breathing heavily, I give the punching bag another hard punch, and then I prepare to give it a roundhouse kick. Distracted, I miss and I end up on my ass.

Cursing under my breath, I punch the gleaming hardwood floor of my fully equipped, spacious home gym. So hard, it hurts. Damn that girl! And this isn't the first time I've messed up. On account of my debilitating coma, I'm physically not in as good shape as I should be and mentally, I'm even worse off. I can't focus.

All afternoon, I've been working on the other scene

I'm shooting tomorrow. An action-packed one in which I've got to battle one of The Locust's henchmen. Hand to hand combat. I read online that I choreograph and do all my own stunts so I thought putting on some sweats and working out with a punching bag in my gym would be the most effective way to go. And to be honest, I thought a hard workout would get my mind off Zoey and release some of my pent-up energy. But I haven't been able to stop thinking about that shower. I've been reliving it in my head like I'm the one with an eidetic memory, my throbbing cock a relentless reminder. I let myself get carried away, and I'm not sure if I was acting or not. That inexplicable attraction I have to my curvy assistant drove the emotion of every line and took me way beyond my scripted physical moves. I kissed her like I meant it, and for the first time since my accident, I had a mind-blowing orgasm. I swear she knocked me into outer space. Sent my head spinning, no pun intended. My cock gave me a standing ovation for my performance and it still hasn't calmed down. It's like it's begging for an encore, but all it's getting is a replay. Brain to cock: *Listen, buddy, I'm engaged.* In fact, Katrina and I have a dinner date to finish the discussion we started this morning about our wedding. I'm meeting her in an hour.

Daylight morphs into dusk. Evening still comes early in mid-January. Picking myself up from the floor, I grab a towel and my cell phone that I left close by on a barbell bench. Throwing the towel around my neck, I slog over to the floor-to-ceiling window. My muscles ache almost as much as my cock. With a groan, I gaze out the glass pane, taking in the gray-pink sky and the glimmering lights of Los Angeles that dance in its midst. In the near distance, I glimpse Zoey's guest cottage. The lights are burning bright. I haven't seen her for hours. Mostly, she was out and about running errands for me. I did call her a couple times to check on her whereabouts and gave her a few dumb things to do like having my freshly laundered jeans pressed just so I could hear her voice. I acted like her boss when I wanted to act like her lover. And she fell for it.

Then, she took me up on my offer and gave me a rude reminder. Texting me from the dry cleaner, she told me he couldn't get her outfit done in time for her "hot" date. The skirt might even be ruined for good. My father was a man of honor and always told me never to break my word. So, I told her to go shopping and buy something new. Stupid me! I should have gone with her to monitor her selection to make sure it had a turtleneck and was two sizes too big.

My skin prickles with sweat. Clenching my cell phone, I text her.

*I want to see what u bought.*

That's right. My money. My eyes first. I swear if her new outfit's too sexy, I'm going to make her take it off. Even if I'm the one who has to do it.

Awaiting her reply, the rumble of a sports car in my driveway resounds in my ears.

*Ping*. Her response.

*Too late. I'm out the gate. Off on my date.* :)

The nerve of her to add a happy face! *Get your ass back here* is what I want to write back. The words are burning on my fingertips. Instead, I squeeze my phone like I want to strangle it. My blood is curdling with helpless rage. And it's turning green with uncontrollable jealousy. An emotion I know I've never experienced even with my amnesia. Seething, I pivot toward the punching bag. I need to punch it again. This time pretending it's that fucking boyfriend. And giving it to him until he cries.

Halfway there, my cell phone vibrates in my hand. Loosening my grip, I glance down at the caller ID screen. The face of a beautiful blonde meets my eyes. Dammit. Katrina.

Reluctantly, I answer.

"Darling, I just wanted to make sure you're getting ready. Our reservation is at seven."

It's been almost two weeks since I came out of my coma. I still feel nothing toward her except growing dislike.

*My* reservation has nothing to do with time.

# Chapter 24

## Zoey

I pick at my spicy tuna roll with my chopsticks. Popular Sushi Roku is one of my favorite restaurants and usually I binge out on their outrageous rolls. But tonight I have no appetite. Since that shower with Brandon, I've felt sick to my stomach. I almost canceled my date with Jeffrey. But when he told me he was feeling down because Chaz was away for a few days doing trunk shows in the Midwest, I didn't have the heart to let him down. Jeffrey's always been there for me just as I have for him.

"What's wrong, Zoester?" asks my perceptive brother. "You don't seem yourself. Are you sick or something?"

I am sick. Lovesick. I'm crushing on my boss. *People Magazine's* "Sexiest Man Alive." A man I can never have. Should I tell him? All my life, I've told

Jeffrey everything. Even my weight when it was at its highest. After a quick mental debate, I decide not to. I make up an excuse that's partially true.

"I had a hard day with Brandon." *Oh was it hard!*

Jeffrey pours some sake into our petite stoneware cups. I take a sip and the soothing hot liquid immediately seeps into my bloodstream.

"Is that slave driver asking too much of you again?"

You could say that. I sigh. "Yeah. He's wearing me down." *Emotionally and physically.*

My boyishly handsome confidant scowls. "You can't let him take advantage of you."

I take another sip of my sake and practically choke on it. Oh my God. Heading straight toward me is Mr. Slave Driver himself with a dazzling Katrina on his arms. All eyes are on the gorgeous Hollywood glamour couple. My heart beats into a frenzy. Oh, please God, don't let him see me. I may vomit if he gets within ten steps of me. Frantically, I search for a menu. Something . . . anything to cover my face. Wait! My napkin. I'll use that. I yank it off my lap, but it's too late. He's already made eye contact with me. Without a blink, he holds me fierce in his gaze.

Jeffrey eyes me strangely. "Zoester, you're acting all weird."

Bratrina is getting closer. My inner panic button sounds. "Quick, Jeffrey. Kiss me!"

"Huh?"

"Just do it! And make it look like you love me."

"I do love you."

"No, I mean like you're my boyfriend."

Jeffrey's eyes pop. "What?"

Brandon is so close I can taste him. "Hurry, just do it!"

"Zoester, you're going gross on me."

"I know. Just no tongues. Hurry!"

"You owe me."

"Fine."

Thank God, we're sitting next to each other in a circular booth. On my next breath, Jeffrey slides in closer to me and his lips touch down on mine. They're warm and silky, and taste sweet and a little salty from the sushi. While he's nothing like Brandon, I always knew he must be a good kisser and he is. Banishing the thought of how inappropriate this is, I fist his spiky hair and deepen the kiss, prolonging it as much as I can. A sultry voice breaks it. Brandon's!

"Well, Ms. Hart, fancy meeting you here."

His manly gorgeousness is looming above me. Katrina gives me an icy look as if I'm nothing more than a slice of raw fish.

I flutter my eyelids and smile at Brandon. "Well, hello."

He doesn't smile back at me. His frosty eyes stay fixed on Jeffrey. "Do you mind introducing me to your companion?"

"Oh, this is my boyfriend, Jeffrey." I give Jeffrey a kick under the table. I hope he gets the message to play along.

He does! He flashes his dazzling smile and, standing up, extends his hand. Brandon reluctantly shakes it as Jeffrey gushes.

"So nice to finally meet you. Zoey has told me so many wonderful things about you."

Brandon's eyes shift back to me. A brow lifts. "She has?"

I keep smiling smugly while Katrina gives me another dirty look. Disdain flickers in her catty eyes.

"Brandon, darling, let's not waste our time with these pe . . . people."

Bitch! I just know she was going to say "peons." I'd like to shove her superiority complex up her ass.

Without losing eye contact with me, Brandon excuses himself.

"Well, enjoy your dinner." His jaw tightens. "And, Zoey, don't forget to print out the rest of this week's sides when you get home."

*Newsflash.* "I may not be going home tonight." I shoot Jeffrey a seductive smile. He winks at me. My gay "boyfriend" deserves an Emmy. Matter of fact, give one to me too.

Brandon's violet eyes darken. Before he can say a word, the bitch wrenches him away. "Come on, darling. Our table is waiting." As she turns on her heel, she hurls a snide comment at me.

"Oh, and by the way, congratulations, Zoey. I honestly didn't think someone like you would have any luck in the boyfriend department."

Jeffrey's mouth parts, but I kick him again before he can throw an insult back at her. I'm going to play it cool.

"Thanks, Katrina. Enjoy your dinner."

She snarls at me before leading Brandon to a nearby table. Brandon is seated facing me, his eyes glued to me. Grinning, I give him a little wave. With a frown, he buries his head in a menu.

"What was that all about?" Jeffrey asks loudly.

"Shh! They may hear you."

"Well?" His voice is urgent but softer.

My chest tightens. Brandon's eyes are back on me. I give Jeffrey an affectionate kiss on the cheek. "Just keep acting like we're madly in love."

"Are you trying to make Brandon Taylor jealous?"

"Snuggle with me and wrap an arm around me. Then, smack another kiss on my lips. By the way, you're an excellent kisser."

"Thanks, but after that, no more mouth kisses."

"Deal."

Jeffrey does as bid. I keep onc eye on Brandon. Ooh! He's jealous alright. His brows furrow deep enough to make a crease while Katrina, oblivious, drinks champagne. I'm loving every minute of this charade.

Jeffrey digs into a piece of the sushi as do I. My appetite's suddenly come back with a vengeance.

"He's staring at you," Jeffrey says after swallowing a mouthful of the tender fish.

I make eyes at Brandon. My actions only taunt him more. His nostrils flare.

"Feed me a piece of sushi. Then I'll do the same. Keep smiling."

With his chopsticks, Jeffrey picks up another bite-sized sushi roll. I do the same. We exchange rolls. Nothing says love like a couple feeding each other.

Jeffrey puts his chopsticks down. "Is there something going on between the two of you? I think he likes you."

My heart skips a beat and I swallow hard. "What do you mean?"

"He's attracted to you. I can tell by the way he looked at you. He's still staring at you."

I meet Brandon's smoldering gaze and my heart races. The memory of our shower rushes back into my head. My skin prickles. I can hardly breathe. Any hope that Jeffrey might be right comes to an abrupt halt when Brandon lets Katrina take a hand to her mouth. My stomach churns watching her suck on his fingers.

Jeffrey's voice cuts into my misery. "Are you attracted to him?"

"Every woman in the world is attracted to Brandon

Taylor," I answer defensively and then inwardly sigh. Part with relief that I've come up with a good line and part with remorse that Brandon can never be mine. Even if Katrina didn't exist, I don't belong in his world of glamour and glitz.

My intuitive brother, who's inherited Pops's sixth sense for bullshit detection, rolls his long-lashed eyes. The no-nonsense straight shooter goes right for the zing. "Zoey Hart. You better level with me. You're in love with him."

It's more of a statement than a question. He's right. Is it *that* obvious?

"No," I counter, my voice thin and unconvincing. "Honestly, it's just a stupid schoolgirl crush."

"Come on, Zoester. You can't fool me for a second. I'm going to tell Chaz."

"No, please don't!" My panic only underscores the truth. I shrug in defeat. "Jeffrey, sweetie, I don't want to talk about Brandon anymore."

My beloved brother looks at me with warmth in his caramel eyes. "Just know, Zoester, I'm always here for you."

"Thanks," I say, clasping his hands. "I know that."

My voice trails off. Trying to stave off a wave of sadness, I absently play with my chopsticks. My eyes stay riveted on Brandon. I watch as he stands up and rounds his table to help Katrina out of her seat. With her heels on, they're almost the same height. He tilts her head back with a thumb and plants a kiss on her lips.

Jealousy spreads through me like a raging wildfire. Every organ inside me is burning to a crisp. Katrina saunters away—she must be going to the restroom. I wish she was going to burn in hell.

Brandon buries his face back in his menu and completely ignores me. My heart sinks like the Titanic. Game over.

Jeffrey, who's witnessed the kiss, reads me like a magazine. "You're too good for him."

I twitch a small, woeful smile. No, he's too good for me. He's way out of my league.

Jeffrey reads my mind. "C'mon. Let's get the check and get out of here."

Despondently, I ask him if I can sleep at his place.

"Sure, honey." He squeezes my hand and right now, that's just what I need.

# Chapter 25

## *Brandon*

I have a restless night's sleep. No matter how much I try, I can't get Zoey's boyfriend out of my mind. The prick is movie star handsome and a damn good dresser. That slick suit he was wearing was no off-the-rack rag. It easily cost a couple thousand bucks. And he was really into her. I had to mentally chain myself to my chair when he kissed her. I wanted to take him by his collar and throw him out the front door. And make it loud and clear to him to never touch my property again. That's right, dickwad. I own Zoey Hart. She's *my* paid assistant. Hands off!

And as if having to put up with their lovey-dovey shenanigans wasn't bad enough, Katrina and I had a huge fight. Over dinner, I told her that she and her mother were spending way too much money on the wedding. Seriously . . . five hundred thousand dollars—

and that's just in deposits. And that doesn't include Katrina's hundred thousand dollar gown. I asked her—is it studded in diamonds?

Some kind of exorbitant crystals with a name I can't remember. But that's not what made me almost spit up my meal. The real clinker was she told me she bought a dog. Using my credit card! And not just any dog. Some designer mutt—a Maltipoo—that cost ten thousand dollars. A bargain next to the twenty-five grand Paris Hilton plunked down on two teacup Pomeranians. She's already told the press the pup is a pre-nuptial present from me. By the time I dropped her off at her condo, it was all over the Internet, Instagram, and Twitter. The dog's name is Gucci. Gucci the poochie. America's "It Dog." I need a fucking dog like I need another hole in the head.

And it gets worse. When I got home, I had a splitting headache. Just my luck, I was out of Advil. So I texted Zoey to run out to the all-night Rite Aid and pick me up a bottle of the painkillers. She immediately texted me back.

*Can't. At my boyfriend's. Downtown. Plus don't have my car.*

Simmering mad, I texted her back.

*Borrow his car.*

And she replied.

*Can't. We're busy right now.*

*Doing what?*

*Use ur imagination.*

Ending the conversation, I almost threw my phone across my bedroom. And then I wanked off . . . well, tried. Zoey's damn boyfriend got in the way of my imagination. I couldn't stop thinking of him ravaging her. The asshole stole my fantasy!

So given my night, it's not surprising I feel like shit this morning. It's the butt crack of dawn. My head still hurts. My cock aches. And I'm full of piss. Stark naked, I roll out of bed and, after my bathroom routine, stagger into my walk-in closet. I yank one of my dozens of swim briefs off the built-in shelves, trying to push the events of last night out of my mind. Today's my first day back on the set. I need to get it together. Maybe a couple of extra laps in the pool will help.

The swim is just what I need. It clears my head and releases my stress. Revitalized, I hoist myself out of the pool and as I get to my feet, a beaming Zoey appears. Barefoot, she's wearing the same outfit she wore last night—a clingy little black mini dress—and her wild chestnut hair has that bedhead look going on. My stomach muscles tighten. I can feel it in my gut. Oh, yeah. She got laid. Big time.

"Hi," she says brightly, heading my way with a Starbucks bag in her hand. "I had my boyfriend stop at Starbucks and picked up your coffee." She sets it on a table while I towel dry myself.

"You're welcome," she chirps.

I hate when she does that. She never gives me a chance to say thank you. It's not like those two words don't exist in my vocabulary.

She takes my coffee out of the bag. Surprisingly, there isn't one for her. Hmm. Maybe she already had one with Jeffrey. Though he looks like the British tea-drinker type.

Wrapping the towel around my waist, I grab my iced Americano and take a sip. While my lips suck up the drink through the straw, my eyes soak in my assistant.

"Is that the dress I bought you?" The body-hugger is so short she should be arrested for indecent exposure.

"Actually, no. It's something Jeffrey bought me."

I cringe at the sound of his name on her lips. And at the thought that he buys her expensive, sexy presents. My eyes travel downward.

"Where are your shoes?"

She laughs. "I left them at his house."

An unsettling thought smacks me. Is she going to move in with him? I falter trying to make more conversation.

"How was the rest of your evening?"

She sighs dreamily. "Fabulous."

Seething inside, I fake a half-smile. "That's good."

No need for details. "What does your boyfriend do?"

"He's in finance. He does really well."

She's seriously pissing me off. I take another sip of the coffee.

"Where does he work?"

"He's a consultant. Self-employed."

"What kind of car does he drive?"

"A Mercedes 560 SL convertible. Oh, and he also has a Range Rover."

So, he's very good looking *and* rich. And he dresses really well. Kill me now. Me, the sexiest man in the world, feels threatened by some no one.

"How long have you been together?"

"We met just before your accident."

I do the math in my head. They've been together for only a few weeks. And she's already sleeping with him.

She chimes into my thoughts like a mind reader. "It was love at first sight. You know what that's like." A hand flies to her mouth. "Whoops! I forgot you don't remember meeting Katrina."

I detect sarcasm in her voice. Anger rising, I press my lips tight together.

"What's his last name?" I'm going to google the bastard. Find out everything there is to know about him.

"None of your damn business."

Well, scrap that plan.

Without warning, she changes the subject. "Are you excited about your first day back on the set?"

Her question takes my mind off Jeffrey. "Yes. Very."

"Are you cool with your lines?"

Once again, that memory of showering with her flashes into my head. I have the burning urge to shower with her again. But this time, clothes off. I want to caress her velvet flesh and savor all her sexy curves. I want to feel her skin against mine. All of it. Everywhere. My cock's telling me to rip off her dress. Brain to Brandon: *Get a grip!* I tell her I'm good.

She quirks a smile. "Great. You'd better get going. Your call time is at eight. You don't want to be late on your first day back."

"Right." My gaze stays fixed on her as she sashays toward the guesthouse. It's like my eyes have X-ray vision. I can see that big, adorable heart-shaped ass right through the fabric of her skimpy frock. My cock twitches. It's shouting out to me again. I silently give it a piece of my mind. *Hey, buddy, lay off; taking off her clothes is someone else's good fortune.* Besides, I'm committed to Katrina. But I can't silence my cock. My insatiable need for her pulses through my body. What the hell is wrong with me?

"Zoey, get undressed," I shout out, my cock egging me on.

She stops dead in her tracks and spins around.

"Excuse me?" Her eyes burn into mine.

"You heard me. Get undressed . . . and put on something comfortable. You're coming to the set with me."

"But—"

"There are no buts when you work for me. I believe that's in your contract."

She screws up her face. Damn, she's so cute.

"Asshole! I should have poisoned your coffee!"

Things are back to normal. And I'm back in control. There's no way I'm letting her out of my sight. I'm going to tie up my feisty assistant if I have to.

My first day back on the set couldn't start off better. The cast and crew are overjoyed to see me. In fact, before we start shooting, there's a little welcome back party. Nothing big or fancy—just coffee and Krispy Kreme donuts for everyone. Boxes of them. Everyone's in a great mood, including me.

"Have a donut," I tell Zoey. "They're killer good."

Dressed in jeans, sneakers, and a *Kurt Kussler* sweatshirt, my adorable assistant, who's been taking everything in, eyes me as I devour a chocolate one.

"I'm trying not to eat fattening things."

"C'mon, you're missing out." I help myself to an-other—this time, glazed. Her big brown eyes are drooling. I'm mildly amused. "Zoey, it's an order. Have one."

"All right. Just one." She chooses a cream-filled one. I watch as her full lips descend on it. She takes a whopping bite and the cream spurts out. It's like the sugarcoated donut has had an epic orgasm. She moans and swallows. It's so damn erotic. My cock flexes while she licks her upper lip.

"Hey, you missed a spot." I flick my index finger along her lip and then lick off the little bit of cream on my fingertip. The sweetness mixes with berry flavor of her lip-gloss. I savor the taste of her. And want a second helping.

"Thanks," she says softly and then polishes off the donut. "That was yummy."

*You're yummy.* "C'mon, I'll introduce you to the producer."

To my surprise, this is Zoey's first time ever on the set. She's like a little kid in a candy store—wanting to experience everything. Within minutes, she meets not only Executive Producer Doug DeMille but also my co-stars, Jewel Starr, who plays my late wife Alisha, and Kellie Fox, who plays my infatuated, devoted assistant, Mel. I haven't told her the direction the show's going—the way the season's going to end with Kurt falling hard for Mel. Under strict orders from network production chief, Blake Burns, everyone who attended the focus groups agreed to keep it under wraps, even from the cast and crew, so the twist I came up with wouldn't get leaked. In this world of social media, secrets are hard to keep.

Wide-eyed Zoey cannot contain her enthusiasm. She's especially in awe of Jewel. "Wow! You're even prettier in person!"

Clad in a bathrobe, her blond hair in curlers, Jewel's blue eyes twinkle with laughter. "Not for long. I'm going to look like a drowned rat after shooting my scene with Brandon."

"Oh my God. That shower scene was—I mean, is—so amazing. I can't wait to see it for real."

Before the gorgeous, slightly perplexed actress can respond, she's whisked off to hair and makeup. The rest of the crew is scuttling about, prepping for the shoot. I'm more than glad I've brought Zoey along. Thanks to her insane memory, she's able to put names and positions to almost everyone. I told her during our drive here that I wasn't going to tell anyone about my amnesia. She thought that was a good idea and assured me she could help me identify most of the crew. She studied the file she put together and went over it again with me in the car. Thank goodness, I was able to retain the names of several key crew members, including the Director, the first AD, a couple of camera guys, hair and makeup, and some helpful PAs so I wouldn't look like a total idiot.

Just after I finish my second donut, a young freckled-face woman, wearing a headset and carrying a clipboard, jogs up to me. She must be one of the PAs. Shit. I don't remember her name. I shoot Zoey a desperate look. She mouths the PA's name: Janine. She's the no-nonsense type.

"Brandon, let's get you into hair and makeup."

"Zo, just hang out for a while," I say, letting the PA lead the way.

Another female voice stops me in my tracks.

"Darling!"

I pivot. My body goes rigid. Katrina! Every muscle clenches. I'm still mad as hell at her. And in fact, I'm even madder. She's brought the fucking mutt to the set.

Holding the yapping ball of fur in her arms, she prances up to me. All eyes are on the statuesque beauty. She looks stunning, dressed in a tight hot pink sweater dress with matching thigh-high suede boots, her platinum hair cascading over her shoulders in perfect, soft waves. The little white dog is wearing a matching outfit—a same shade pink sweater along with a bow in his hair and a pink rhinestone-studded collar. An unsettling thought crosses my mind—shit, maybe they're diamonds. I wouldn't put that past my extravagant fiancée or to put the astronomical charge on my credit card.

"What are you doing here?" I snap, avoiding eye contact with the beast.

Katrina holds Zoey in her rabid gaze. "What's *she* doing here?"

Smiling, Zoey holds her own. "Brandon invited me."

Another PA lopes up to us with a last call for donuts. He's holding a box with the remaining few. Zoey surveys them.

"Katrina, you should help yourself to one before they run out."

"Puh-lease. Donuts are for peasants." She directs her snide comment at Zoey and then smacks her mouth on mine. Coated in a bright pink lipstick, her billowy lips taste nothing like Zoey's. I pull away. Zoey stares at her icily.

Clutching the ravenous looking dog in the crook of one arm, Katrina runs a long manicured finger around my lips. "I'm sorry, darling. I got lipstick on you."

I grit my teeth and don't move as she continues.

"Since I wasn't shooting today, I thought I should come by and wish you the best of luck on your first day back on the set. Plus, I really wanted you to meet Gucci. I just know you're going to fall in love with him."

*Him?* By now, all the crew members have taken notice of Katrina and her new pretty in pink cross-dresser dog. Or should I say, *our* new dog? Many have gathered around to congratulate her on our engagement (and glimpse the rock I gave her) and to admire the fluffy designer mutt. Everyone's a sucker for a cute dog. Being the center of attention, America's It Girl is in her glory—with "It Dog."

"Darling, why don't you pet him?" she purrs.

I want to bark at my fiancée. Tell her to get the hell out of the studio and take the damn dog with her. But with all these people around us, it sure won't look good to have a fight. Or for it to get out that I don't like dogs. That's just not the kind of publicity I need right now. Besides, I love dogs. I had a Chocolate Lab growing up. I just don't like little yappy ones.

Hesitantly, I lower my hand to the dog's head, but as I'm about to touch down, the mongrel growls and bares his tiny razor-sharp teeth. With a vicious snap, he almost takes off my fingers. I yank them away just in time.

"Jesus," I mutter under my breath, happy to have my digits intact.

"Brandon, are you okay?" asks Zoey.

Katrina shoots Zoey another predatory look and then shifts her attention to me.

"Darling, he just has to get to know you better." She makes goo-goo eyes at the monster. "You're a very sweet little dog, right baby boy?" She kisses the still growling beast on his head, leaving an outline of her pink lips on his white fur.

The PA named Janine impatiently butts in. "Brandon, we've got to go. It's getting late."

"Katrina, I have to get ready," I say, happy to have an excuse to get away from her. The hostile dog growls at me again. I've had it. This time I growl back. It whimpers. Ha! I'll show the furry little beast who's the alpha male around this joint.

Katrina fires me a dirty look and comforts the shaking pup. "Poor baby, don't let him scare you."

Zoey cups her mouth to stifle her laughter. We exchange an eye roll. Score one for me.

Five minutes later, I'm back on the set. I'm wearing a bathrobe, monogrammed with my name, but beneath it I'm stark naked except for a flesh-colored cock sock. Jewel, in a similar bathrobe, joins me. Her hair coiffed, she looks ready to get started.

I spot Zoey. I've had a PA set her up in my folding chair by the director's camera. I've told her the best way to watch the filming is on his monitor. Numerous cameras will be in play to capture different angles, including an overhead one on a crane and a handheld one for close-ups, but the director's monitor captures the first cameraman's master shot. In editing, they'll splice together the various angles to make the scene dynamic and then later in post add sound effects and music.

Niall Davies, the episode's wiry director, strides up to us. In addition to being the show's Emmy-winning primary director, he's married to Jewel, my co-star. They met on the set.

"Ready to rehearse the scene, my man?" he asks in his charming British accent.

"I don't need to rehearse it. I've got it nailed." I shoot Zoey a look. Our eyes connect. Smiling, she gives me a good luck thumbs up. Smiling back, I suddenly realize Katrina's nowhere in sight. Maybe she took the damn dog for a walk. Just as well. The last thing I need is for the mutt to start yapping in the middle of my scene.

Niall turns to his wife. "Are you all right with that, gorgeous?"

Jewel smiles. "Let's go for it, baby."

Stripping off our bathrobes, we step into the already steamed up shower. Water sprays from the many overhead jets. In seconds, we're soaked and in position.

"Quiet on the set," shouts out the first AD.

The next three words are music to my ears. It's as if I've heard them my entire life. Is my memory coming back?

"Lights. Camera. Action!"

# Chapter 26

## *Zoey*

"Lights! Camera! Action!"

The words echo in my ears. I'm so wet I may stain Brandon's canvas chair. When I first saw Brandon in the raw—just seconds ago—my jaw crashed to the floor and my heart almost rocketed out of my chest.

I've seen him in Speedos and tight jeans and I've given him massages in his boxers, but nothing's prepared me for the sight of his manliness full on. Sure, he's wearing some kind of flesh-colored sheath that wraps around his genitals like a bag of leprechaun's gold, but it doesn't camouflage his size. Holy mother of God! I mean, I knew he was endowed when I felt his hardness against me in the shower. But not this big. And his enormity is sans an erection.

Still in a state of shock, I soak in the rest of his body. It's as if he's been sculpted by an Italian master.

A seamless combination of lean muscle and bronze with washboard abs, a perfect pelvic-V, long worked-out legs, and a chiseled ass that belongs in a museum. As the cameras start rolling, my temperature rises and hot tingles storm my body. I'm throbbing so hard between my legs I can hear it.

I can't keep my eyes off him. My pupils dart back and forth between the director's monitor and the set, a near replica of Brandon's home bathroom. It's bathed in a cloud of steam and sensually lit in a way that makes Brandon and Jewel glow like two ethereal lovers. Like the stars they are.

Under the powerful spray, Brandon and Jewel magically transform into the characters they play—CIA agent Kurt Kussler and his beloved wife Alisha. Alit with love and lust, Brandon holds his co-star in his arms just as he held me. After he tells her how sexy she is, he fondles her perfect, nipple-covered tits and nuzzles her long, slender neck. I relive every moment, every word. New sensations overtake me, both emotionally and physically. An unexpected bolt of envy shoots through me. Brandon and Jewel look so beautiful together. So comfortable in their skin; so comfortable with their nudity. So oblivious to the cameramen surrounding them. Passion dances in their eyes as the water pounds them. Their flesh glistens. The steam intensifies. I know they're only acting, but every word, every action seems so real. I wonder—did

Brandon ever fuck Jewel? With her blond goddess looks, she's just his type. Are they possibly drawing from experience?

The thought fades as I watch the scene unfold on the monitor. I hardly blink my eyes as I glom on to every word. I know them so well they're forming on my lips, and I hear myself saying them in my head. As Brandon sensuously touches Jewel in all the places he touched me, my breathing grows shallow. His moans and groans sing in my ears, causing a fresh rush of hot tingles to swarm me. I can't stop reliving every minute of my shower with Brandon.

Every touch of his deft fingers.

Every brush of his hard body.

Every sound of his sultry voice.

Every pulse of his wondrous cock.

Any jealousy I harbor gives way to feverish lust and desire. *You're everything to me, Kurt.* My breathing grows harsher, and my heart beats like a hammer. Every nerve in my body is sparking as a fire rages between my legs. I have the burning urge to touch myself. To quell the white-hot flame that's searing every inch of my being. I squirm in the chair and cross my legs. My upper thighs stick together, slicked with wetness. I'm positive now I've stained Brandon's chair. I feel faint like I may pass out any minute. Thank God, I'm sitting.

A thoughtful PA notices my condition.

"Can I bring you some water, Ms. Hart?"

"Yes, please," I breathe out. "That would be great."

Waiting for the water, I keep my eyes on the monitor and watch Brandon and Jewel heatedly play out the rest of the scene, making me believe the passion between Kurt and Alisha is so real. And then that kiss. That unforgettable kiss with his lips on mine, our tongues entwined in an erotic dance. Our bodies melded like one. Unable to erase the taste of him, I can't watch anymore. I'm either going to melt or detonate. I jump off the tall chair and rush to the restroom. I dash into a stall and shove down my jeans. And finger myself until my lips silently cry out his name.

# Chapter 27

## *Brandon*

"Oh, baby!" The final words of the scene tumble out of my mouth. I'm so close to coming, but one little word stops an orgasm of epic proportions.

"Cut!"

Emotionally drained and physically aroused, my head falls onto Alisha's. Breathing hard, we hold each other, our soaking wet bodies slick against the other's. It takes a long moment for the word to register. It's not until some PA hops into the stall and turns off the pounding water. I slowly lift up my head and meet my co-star's gaze. She's no longer Alisha but Jewel.

Her wide-set blue eyes penetrate mine. "Brandon, that was amazing. *You* were amazing."

My breathing calms. "So were you."

"Thanks." My technique worked. To get into the scene, I drew from experience. The most erotic shower experience I ever had. Or at least can remember.

Freeing herself, Jewel casts her eyes downward. My enormous erection stares her in the face.

She smiles playfully. "Brandon Taylor, did I give you a boner?"

I ponder her question for a few quick seconds. "No."

Jewel laughs. But that's the truth. Someone else did. While I acted out the scene, she was in my bloodstream, filling my mind and my heart. I tasted *her* sweetness and felt *her* soft curves against my body. Dripping wet, I step out of the shower and look for her. My eyes dart around the studio.

Zoey Hart is nowhere to be found. My cock sinks as a PA hands me a towel and helps me shrug on my robe. Jewel joins me. There's raucous applause and cheers amongst the crew. I just shot my first scene since my accident, and I've blown them away.

Jewel's director husband runs up to us. He hugs his beautiful wife. I wish there was someone to hug me.

Envy grabs me by the balls. To watch and film the woman you love kiss another man must be so challenging. Let alone *People Magazine's* "Sexiest Man Alive." But he doesn't seem threatened. Though likely twenty years older, he and Jewel must have a very strong marriage. Something beyond sex. Soul mates? Like my parents?

Breaking from the embrace, Niall pats me on the

back. "Brandon, my man, you were absolutely brilliant. You nailed it."

Before I can thank him, a familiar breathy voice calls out my name. My eyes find her quickly. Katrina. With the dog on a leash, she breezes my way.

"Where have you been?" I ask her while the little monster sniffs around my bare feet. I curl my toes, fearful he'll bite.

"Oh darling, I'm so sorry I missed the scene, but I had to take Gucci for a walk. He needed to make a wee-wee."

I mentally roll my eyes. She turns her attention to Jewel and Niall. Niall's arm is wrapped around his wife.

"Darling, introduce us," Katrina insists.

Reluctantly, I introduce my co-star and director to my fiancée.

Katrina plays up to them. "So wonderful to meet you! I do hope the two of you will be coming to our wedding."

At the word wedding, I feel a tightening in my chest. It's something I don't want to think about. Make that the last thing I want to think about.

"Wouldn't miss it for the world," says Jewel. "In fact, we just received the invitation. So clever to have it attached to a miniature horse-driven pumpkin carriage. I assume you're going to be a Cinderella bride?"

Katrina's face brightens. "Yes!"

Niall chimes in. "We'll be there for sure."

Jewel excuses herself to get changed while Niall tells us he's going to review the shot list for the upcoming action scene. Alone with my fiancée, I change the subject to the only one on my mind. "Katrina, did you by chance see Zoey while you were outside?"

She contorts her face with disgust. "Yes. I wish you hadn't reminded me. That pathetic girl was throwing up by your car."

My pulse speeds up. "Is she okay?"

Katrina huffs. "How the hell would I know? I don't associate with her. And besides, how could you even think I'd get close to a pool of vomit!?"

Before I can respond, something that feels like molten liquid trickles down my ankle. I look down and rage whips through me. The goddamn dog has peed on me! Its leg is still lifted.

Katrina gushes. "Finally! That is so cute! Gucci thought you were a fire hydrant."

Fuming, I clench my fists by my sides. As if enduring this humiliation isn't enough, on my next exasperated breath, the fucking dog bites me. I yelp and then shout some expletives. Blood is pouring. An observant PA runs to get me a Band-Aid. She returns quickly and wraps it around my big toe. I thank her, wishing I were thanking Zoey.

"Bad boy," scolds Katrina, lifting the dog into her

arms. "You're getting a time out!"

The little dog cowers at the sound of her harsh voice. For a minute, I almost feel sorry for him, especially when his big brown woeful eyes meet mine. Katrina marches off with the dog. The pup's gaze stays on me as if he's expecting me to rescue him from whatever inevitable punishment he faces.

While the crew prepares for the next set up, I hobble to my dressing room. Collecting my cell phone, I sink into the couch and immediately speed dial Zoey. It rings and rings. No answer. Next, I text her. No answer. Finally, I email her. No answer.

Worry washes over me. It's not like her not to respond. If I didn't have to dive right into the next scene and spend the afternoon shooting an action sequence, I'd go home and check on her. Suddenly, I wish this day could be over.

I take a deep breath. It doesn't calm me. I don't remember the last time I cared so much about a girl. Or if I ever really did.

# Chapter 28

## Zoey

I'm surveying the contents of Brandon's refrigerator so I know what to order tomorrow when I hear a car pull into the adjacent garage. It must be Brandon. It's after seven. He must be done with his shoot.

"Are you okay?" he asks, stepping into the kitchen. His voice sounds urgent.

Closing the refrigerator door, I spin around to face him. "What do you mean?"

"Katrina told me she saw you puking in the parking lot."

"I must have eaten something funky from craft services. Or maybe that donut did me in. I Ubered home. I'm much better now."

At least, part of my white lie is true. I do feel better. My sudden bout of nausea, however, had nothing to do with what I ate. The panty-melting, passionate shower scene Brandon filmed with Jewel made me more than hot and bothered; it made me sick to my stomach. I had to leave. And then outside, at the sight of Katrina, nausea rocketed to my chest. After puking my guts out, I managed to call for an Uber car and went home. Totally wiped out, I crawled into bed and spent the rest of the day sleeping it off. I still don't feel one hundred percent and his presence doesn't help.

Brandon's violet eyes darken. "Why the hell didn't you answer my texts or calls?

His angry voice intimidates me. "I turned my phone off and fell asleep."

"Don't *ever* do that again." His curt tone is reprimanding. "I need to know where you are every minute of the day."

*Control freak.* "Maybe you should put me on a leash or insert a tracking device under my skin."

"Maybe I should. A collar and leash would suit you."

From the tone of his voice, I think he's serious. The image of me in Gucci's rhinestone accessories pops into my head with an amusing yet arousing mental montage. Master and Slave Girl. *Sit. Beg. Come.* Flushing, I quickly change the subject.

"How'd the rest of the shoot go?"

With a deep breath, he rakes his perfectly mussed up ebony hair with his right hand. My eyes grow wide. It looks like Frankenstein's. Every finger except his thumb is bandaged in splints.

"Jeez. What happened to your fingers?"

"Fucking jammed them," he mutters, heading toward me.

"How'd you do that?"

"I did my own stunt. I was supposed to punch my assailant. But just as I was about to make contact with him, Katrina's damn dog got loose and bit the guy's ankle. He flinched and I ended up bashing a wall."

"Ouch! That must have hurt."

"Hurt like hell," he says, swinging open the fridge door with his left hand.

"Are you sure they're not broken?"

"Pretty sure. The set doctor said they'd be more misshapen. It's just a sprain." He grabs a beer with the good hand and with his thumb, struggles to pop off the bottle cap. I'm mildly amused he can't get it off and let him struggle. He's obviously not ambidextrous—well, at least when it comes to little things.

"Fuck," he grumbles, frustrated.

"Let me do it," I finally say, taking the bottle from him. I twist the top off easily. "Piece of cake. Here." With a smug smile, I hand him back the bottle. He takes it from me with his good hand.

"Thanks." His voice is small, surprisingly humble. Leaning seductively against the counter, he takes a chug of the beer, arching his head back and squeezing his eyes shut. He looks sexy as sin. Almost orgasmic.

"Aah! Just what I needed," he says after the long swig. "Do you want some?"

"I don't think there are any more beers left."

"No, I mean a sip of mine."

My heart does a little jump. He's never shared anything with me, unless you count the nasty flu he gave me last year. Oh, yeah . . . and those fries the other night.

"Sure, thanks," I say hesitantly. I take the bottle from him and wrap my mouth around the throat. Tilting my head back and squeezing my eyes the way he did, I take a lengthy sip. The frothy beverage fills my mouth and then I swallow. The cold, refreshing liquid courses down past the back of my throat. I open my eyes and let out a satisfied sigh before licking my upper lip. His violet gaze is on me.

A saucy smile lights up his face. "I like a girl who can drink beer like a man."

"Doesn't K-Katrina drink beer?" Shit. I almost said Kuntrina again. A Freudian slip?

"Nah. She's strictly a champagne girl." To my utter shock, he dusts my lips with one of his fingertips. Goosebumps pop along my arms.

"Have some more."

Eagerly, I take another gulp. But this time, the frothy liquid goes down the wrong pipe and I choke. In the throes of a fit of coughing, I feel my face reddening, my eyes watering.

"Jeez, are you okay?" Brandon pats my back vigorously with his good hand while I continue to wheeze.

I nod my head like one of those stupid bobble-head dolls. *Not really*. I can't catch my breath. Harsh, suffocating coughs still clog my throat. After almost vomiting up the beer, I finally calm. My cheeks are heated with embarrassment, and my eyes are tearing.

Brandon's eyes soak me in playfully. "Stop showing off."

"I wasn't showing off," I croak back.

"You were." He snatches the bottle from me and sets it down on the granite counter.

"I'll be right back. Would you whip me up a sandwich?"

"Sure."

"And promise you won't drink any more beer, at least while I'm not here. I don't want you to choke to death. A repeat of last night is the last thing I need. I can't live without you."

Of course, he can't live without me, I think as he disappears. No other assistant could put up with all his shit. So far, I'm the only one who's made it past three months. All the others quit or were fired by his majesty. The one before me had a nervous breakdown. Brandon doesn't remember any of them. I guess that's some kind of blessing in disguise. They were all gorgeous. Blond and willowy—I checked out a few on Facebook. Just his type. He probably fucked them into submission and broke their hearts. Or worked them to the bone.

I swing open the fridge door and survey the shelves for what I can use to make a sandwich. Slim pickings. I make a mental note to call Bristol Farms first thing in the morning to stock up; our high-end neighborhood supermarket delivers. In addition to Brandon's must-haves, I suppose I should also order a few bottles of expensive champagne to appease Katrina. The last thing I need is a hissy fit from the bitch.

Despite his fame and fortune, Brandon's taste in food leans toward all-American basics—the hearty, down-to-earth brands I grew up on with Auntie Jo and Uncle Pete. Like Oscar Meyer bacon . . . Skippy Peanut Butter . . . Kraft Mac and Cheese . . . and Campbell's Soup. He's somewhat of a junk food junkie and prefers a good steak and potatoes to a frou-frou gourmet entrée. Not having much to work with, I settle on an open can of Bumble Bee tuna. With the can in hand along with a jar of mayo, I pad over to the island and start fixing my demanding boss a sandwich. While I search for some bread, Brandon's voice bellows in my ears.

"ZO-EEEY!!!!"

"WHA-AAAT?"

"I NEED YOU!"

"WHERE ARE YOU?"

"IN THE BATHROOM. HURRY!"

I drop what I'm doing and head over to the pantry adjacent to the kitchen. It must be one of his toilet paper emergencies. I grab a roll and scurry to his bathroom.

I knock on the door. "I'm throwing in a roll of toilet paper." As my fingers curl around the knob, he yells at me again.

"Get your ripe ass in here NOW."

Huh? Hesitantly, I turn the knob and open the door. Brandon's pacing his large, state-of-the-art bathroom. His left hand without the splints is fiddling with his fly.

"What's the matter?"

"I can't take a dump."

"You're constipated?" Oh, fuck. I hope I don't have to stick an enema up his ass. I read on Facebook somewhere that one of his former assistants had to do that. Surprisingly, she didn't get slammed with a lawsuit for violating her non-disclosure agreement.

"Hardly. I'm practically shitting my pants. I can't unbutton my fly!"

I can't help it. I burst out in laughter. Loud snorty laughter that makes me double over in hysterics. I'm laughing so hard I'm crying. Falling out of my hand, the roll of toilet paper tumbles to the floor and unravels.

"Why the hell are you laughing?" he barks.

"That's the funniest thing I've ever heard!" I can barely get the words out. So much for gazillion dollar designer jeans.

"This is serious. I'm going to shit any minute."

I swipe at my tears. "Okay. Stand still."

He does as bid. A breath away from him, I work the

button of his low-slung jeans. My hand grazes his cock. A bulge rises between his legs. Correct me if I'm wrong, but I think he's getting a hard-on. Holy shit! My fingers fumble. This is much harder than I thought. *It's much harder.* I can't concentrate. My fingers keep skimming his hard as rock length. It's all I can think about.

"Zoey! How are you doing?" His voice sounds panicked.

"Not good. I can't get this fucking button through the hole. It's so tight." To my horror, my words are loaded with sexual innuendo. An electrical current zaps my body and travels straight to my core.

"Figure it out!"

"I'm trying! I'm trying!" I reply, fiddling madly with the impossible button, my hand grazing his swelling organ. I need a new approach. So, I sink to my knees. His bulge is in my face. I work feverishly at the button.

"Hurry, Zoey. It's coming!"

"Hold on!" In my mind, I wish he were saying, "I'm coming."

With one more push through the buttonhole, I manage to unbutton his tight-ass jeans. "Did it!"

"Phew!" His good hand immediately pulls at the zipper tab. Panic fills his voice.

"Fuck! The zipper's stuck!"

Oh, God. No!

"Do something, Zoey!"

In a dither, I try shoving down the fly, jiggling and joggling it. It won't fucking budge. My knuckles brush his rigid length beneath the denim with each successive tug.

He hisses. "Shit!"

At the sound of that word, I grow more heated and frantic. Breaking into a sweat, I work at the zipper harder, faster. His cock grows bigger, harder. I can feel it pulsating!

"Jesus, Zoey! I'm so close!"

Close to what? Pooping? Or coming? Either way, his voice sounds so desperate. Without stopping my movements, I pray to the fly gods. Please! Please! Help me! On my next forceful tug, a miracle! The zipper slides down with ease.

My jaw drops to the floor and my eyes grow as wide as saucers. He's commando. At full attention. All rock-hard ten-inches are in my face. So close I can smell his manliness, feel his heat on my cheeks, and practically taste him in my mouth. Speechless, I behold his erection like a magnificent piece of abstract art. Seeing it shrouded today at a distance and on a monitor was one thing. But seeing it in its full glory, up close and personal, is another.

I can't take my eyes off it. His cock is spectacular— a monstrous pink sculpture with a violet vein that matches the color of his hypnotic eyes. Its unexpected beauty takes my breath away as it arouses every one of my senses. It takes all I have to fight my burning desire to touch it . . . wrap my hand around his girth and feel the hot pulsing velvet in my palm. And then wrap my mouth around the crown, suck it, and then slide my lips and tongue down his length, tasting and inhaling the essence of him. And that's just for starters.

Brandon doesn't give me much time to stretch my imagination. Hastily, he shoves his jeans below his knees with his good hand and plunks down on the toilet. His enormous package parks to the right. My eyes don't stray.

"I'd better be going," I manage.

His intense gaze meets mine. Our eyes connect.

"No, Zoey. Don't leave; stay with me. I may need you."

Oh, God. Is he going to ask me to wipe his ass? Millions of women would kill to do that. But seriously?

He grimaces. "Don't worry. I just want to look at you." And then he grunts.

Watching Brandon Taylor take a shit with his violet eyes on me becomes the most perversely sensuous experience of my life. Personal assistant has a whole new meaning.

The bathroom incident is just the beginning of my week

from hell. In addition to enduring the wrath of Hurricane Katrina for ordering the wrong brand of champagne (Dom Pérignon instead of Cristal), physically challenged Brandon is totally co-dependent on me. While he's taken to wearing easy to pull on and off sweats, there are so many things he can't manage. I only hope fingering Katrina is one of them.

On top of everything, the Golden Globes are coming up. They're being held on Sunday at the Beverly Hilton. Brandon's nominated for one in the Best Actor in a Television Series, Drama category. Half my days I spend dealing with his stylist and publicity team; the other half schlepping him to the set and various pre-awards events. Since both of Brandon's sports cars are shifts, he can't drive them with his splinted fingers. The spoiled brat refuses to ride in my cute little Mini. He says it's too small for him—there's not enough legroom and his head almost hits the roof. The truth is there's barely enough room for his cock in the front seat. So, I'm stuck taking him around in his Hummer, which he also refuses to drive. His excuse: he'd rather sit back and use the time to study the file of nominees and presenters I put together for him. With his amnesia, he doesn't know who's who.

The bright red Hummer isn't a car. It's a veritable monster that takes up two lanes. I can barely navigate it let alone see above the steering wheel. It's made for someone built like Brandon, not diminutive five-foot three me. Every time I get in it, sweat pours from behind my knees, and I think my heart is going to ricochet out the windshield. Today's no exception.

"Can't you drive any faster?" Brandon yells at me. "We're going to be late."

Tightening my grip on the steering wheel, I gulp. Driving at a snail's pace is the best I can muster. Mr. Impatient will get to his pre-awards luncheon whenever. And that may be never. As the Hummer slowly winds down the narrow twisting Hollywood Hills streets, a speeding Jag comes at us at full force. Oh, no! We're going to collide! With an ear-piercing screech, I swerve off the road.

"Jesus! What the fuck are you doing, Zoey?" screams Brandon as I jam down on the breaks. "You're going to get us killed!"

I narrowly miss crashing into the hillside. Catching my breath, I'm near tears. "I don't know how to drive this car. It's too big for me."

"Well, you better learn because you're going to be driving it for a while."

Hasn't he heard of the words "Uber" or "taxi"? And there's a new service called Lip Service. My entire body shaking, I get back on course and silently pray that we'll both still be alive for the awards. Five minutes later, I sideswipe a delivery truck.

By Friday, as if all this Golden Globes stuff isn't enough, I'm dealing with one insurance claim after another. I've hit so many cars parking the fucking monster I've lost count. While there's hardly a dent on the invincible Hummer, the damage I've caused is substantial. I even knocked someone's fender off. Brandon's insurance premium is going to skyrocket.

I do some online research. It could take several weeks for a finger jam to heal. I'm not sure I'll last that long with him. I'm exhausted from everything I've had to do for the invalid. From driving to spoon-feeding him. You'd think he'd be appreciative, but he's not. He's been in a bad mood all week. And with each passing day, he's grown testier—a combination of frustration and pre-awards show jitters. He no longer talks; he growls.

Saturday rolls along with the force of an avalanche. The Golden Globes are only a day away, and he still hasn't written his acceptance speech should he win. We're engaged in a working lunch. Awaiting our delivery order from Brandon's favorite Chinese restaurant, Chin Chin on Sunset, we're sitting side by side on the couch. He's so close to me I can feel his warm breath on my face. His long, muscular legs are stretched out onto the coffee table. I'm sitting cross-legged with my laptop on my thighs.

"Let's try this . . . " He's dictating his latest version of the speech to me. "This has been the greatest year of my life."

I hastily type the words. I'm a super-fast typist . . .

another one of my outstanding personal assistant skills.

"Scratch that. That's so untrue. Someone ran me over. I've got fucking amnesia. I can't remember a goddamn thing. For all I know, this year sucked."

I hit delete. "Why don't you just keep it simple? You only have a minute or so. Just thank the Hollywood Foreign Press and the most important people in your professional and personal life."

His face brightens. "That's a good idea. Why didn't you think of that before?"

I mentally roll my eyes. "Thinking for you isn't part of my job description."

"It is now. I'm giving you a raise." He tugs on my messy ponytail. A jolt of electricity bolts through me.

"Okay, go for it." My fingertips are on the keyboard, ready to go.

"Got it." He pauses briefly. "Thank you, members of the Hollywood Foreign Press for this incredible honor. There are so many individuals I want to thank, but tonight I'm just going to thank the most important people in my life. A big shout-out to Conquest Broadcasting and Blake Burns for believing in *Kurt Kussler* . . . my producer Doug DeMille and our wonderful production team . . . my amazing co-stars, the beautiful Jewel Starr and the funny and talented Kellie Fox . . . my faithful, long time manager, Scott Turner . . . my late parents for believing in me . . . um . . . uh . . . "

He tugs at his bottom lip with his thumb while I chime in. "You should thank your mentor."

"My mentor, Stella Adler . . . "

"Bella Stadler." I quickly correct him.

"Right." He quirks a grateful little smile. "And last but not least . . . "

Feverishly typing away, my heartbeat speeds up as I await the final mention.

" . . . My beautiful fiancée, Katrina Moore, for never leaving my side when I needed her most."

My heart sinks to my stomach. My fingers quiver. I force myself to type her name. "Is that it?"

"Yeah. I think that does it."

I fight back hot tears. And forget to hit save.

# Chapter 29

## *Zoey*

"You've got to be kidding." Brandon is pacing the living room, his cell phone pressed to his ear. His brows knit. "I can't fucking believe it."

He ends the call. "Shit!"

"What's the matter?" I've been running over his schedule. His stylist along with the hair and makeup team should be here any minute to get him ready for the Golden Globes. While the actual awards ceremony doesn't start until five o'clock, he needs to be at the Beverly Hilton by three to walk the red carpet and get settled.

"That was Scott. The van with my entourage got into an accident on the 101."

"Oh my God. Are they okay?"

"Minor injuries, but they've all been taken to the hospital." He looks at me beseechingly. "Zoey, I need your help."

I knew that was coming. Go-to-Zo. That's me. "Why can't your 'beautiful fiancée Katrina' help you get ready?" I make air quotes with my fingers. My tone is snippy.

"Because she's at her condo getting ready herself. She's been at it all day. Make that all week. She wants everyone to look at her on the red carpet."

I cringe at the thought of them doing the walk of fame, arm in arm, all smiles and waves, the paparazzi having a field day. Technically, I shouldn't even be working. Sunday is my one day off. But because of the Golden Globes, Brandon demanded my presence. I have no choice.

Brandon tosses his cell phone on the coffee table. "I'm going to shower. Meet me in my bathroom in ten minutes."

The still steamy bathroom smells intoxicating, a mix of Brandon's expensive hair products, body lotion, and cologne. Clad in a thick white towel that hangs low on his hips, he's perched at the vanity counter, studying himself in the lit-up, wall-to-wall mirror. I stare at his reflection, mesmerized by his sculpted pecs, muscled arms, and gorgeous face. A few strands of his unruly damp hair dangle just above his dark brows. His violet eyes sparkle. He's everything a movie star should be.

With his good hand, he scratches his beard. With his sprained fingers, he hasn't been able to shave all weekend. Usually he has a faint trace of stubble along his sharp jaw line, but it's grown in thick like thistle. It's a new form of sexy that I rather like. I long to run my fingers through it and try to imagine what it feels like. Wet velvet? Raw silk? Sweet blades of grass?

Catching my reflection in the mirror, he narrows his eyes. "I need to shave."

"You look good with a beard."

He cocks a brow. "You think so?"

"Totally."

He quirks a sexy smile and strokes his jaw again. "My fans won't like it. It's got to go."

He's right-handed. His right hand is useless. It takes me a second to decode his words. Gah! He wants me to give him a shave. Take a razor to his face.

"You trust me to shave you?" I ask nervously.

"I have no choice. Have you ever shaved some-one?"

"Yeah. I shave my armpits and legs all the time."

He rolls his eyes. "No, I mean a man."

I used to pretend-shave my Ken doll when I was little, but that doesn't count. I shake my head no.

He hoists himself on the marble counter and faces me. We're almost eye-level.

"What if I cut you?"

"You won't. Just follow my instructions and you'll do fine."

He has more confidence in me than I do.

A few minutes later, I'm gripping a badger brush and lathering his face in circular motions with his shaving cream. It smells clean and rich, intoxicating like him. His warm, minty breath tickles my neck. My skin is prickling.

He brushes the fingertips of his left hand along his foamy beard. "Perfection."

I beam. A tingly sensation sweeps through my body. Mr. Put Down just gave me a compliment. My confidence surges.

I set the brush back down on a silver tray and take hold of the shaver. It's an old-fashion safety razor, not a disposable one. With a hint of melancholy, Brandon tells me that it and the brush belonged to his late father. I have the burning urge to ask more about his deceased parents, but we're short on time and I don't want to arouse any more memories that may dampen his spirits on this big night. Maybe some other time. What I've learned, however, is that behind his macho, controlling façade is some tenderness and vulnerability.

My heart leaps back into my throat as I put the razor to his face. What if I screw up? Mutilate him? Make him bleed to death? Even the tiniest nick can spell disaster. All these worries bombard me as I glide the sharp blade downward toward his jaw with my unsteady hand. He holds himself perfectly still as I clear his bristle. Bingo! I repeat my actions, and before long, I've cleared the entire right side of his face. I can't help running my fingers along his jaw. It feels smooth, but I've managed to leave just a fine layer of stubble. He mimics my action.

That dazzling smile flashes on his face. "You're good at playing barber."

I smile back at him while I rinse the blade and then shave the other side of his face. My confidence is soaring. And so is the bubble of sexual energy rising inside me. This sensuous experience is turning me on. And then when I set the blade down, my eyes pop at the sight of a tent between his legs. Holy shit! It's turned him on too! Beneath the towel, he's got a raging hard-on! I swallow hard. My heart pounds. So close to him, I'm sure he can hear it.

A smug smile curves up his delicious lips. Oh yeah, he knows. "Are you okay?"

"I'm fine," I stammer. Who am I kidding? I'm so sexually charged I may combust.

"Good. You're almost there. You just need to douse my face with some of my aftershave." He points to the bottle on the counter. I grab it and pour a little of the lavender-scented French cologne onto my palm. And then I splash it on his smooth skin, cupping his breathtaking face in my hands, his lips dangerously close to mine. My hands linger and my mind wanders back to that shower with him. I replay his kiss. And feel those luscious lips back on my own. My mouth parts involuntarily as if ready for his deft tongue.

"Zoey, we don't have all day. I need you to help me blow dry my hair."

His gruff voice puts an end to my reverie. My hands fly off his jaw. "Right."

Fifteen minutes later, I've styled his hair perfectly and know all his secret products. At the last minute, I rake my fingers through his thick onyx locks to give him that groomed tousled look he's famous for.

He jumps off the counter and faces the mirror. "Wow! You're good with hair too."

I meet his breathtaking reflection. "I was raised by a hairdresser. She taught me a few tricks." It's a shame I don't use them on my own hair. Like Mama's, it's long, thick, and lustrous. Usually, I just throw it into a utilitarian ponytail and never make a fuss. It drives Auntie Jo nuts.

While my gaze stays riveted on him, Brandon glances down at his watch. "C'mon. We don't have much time. Help me get into my tux."

Before I can say a word, he grabs my hand with his good one and leads me to his bedroom. Just like the rest of the house, it's furnished with hi-end Italian furniture. A giant king-sized bed with a mountain of fluffy pillows dominates the room and faces a mirrored wall. A shudder runs through me. Is this where he fucks

Katrina? I haven't thought about her until now. Jealousy rears its ugly head.

"Where's your tux?" I ask glumly.

"It's in that garment bag hanging on the closet. Everything you need is inside it, including my shoes." He points to it, and with my back toward him, I retrieve it.

When I swivel around, my jaw crashes to the floor and my eyes pop. He's standing stark naked before me. The towel is pooled by his feet.

"What's the matter, Zoey?"

I can't get my mouth to move. Or my feet.

"Are your legs stuck in cement?"

A croak escapes my throat.

"Sheesh, Zoey. You've seen my cock before. And my body. And seriously, how did you expect to get me dressed if I didn't undress?"

He makes some valid points. But right now, there's no room in my head for any form of rationality when the epitome of manly perfection is standing before me.

Holy mother of Jesus! His body is a total work of art. All lean, polished bronze muscle, his chiseled torso and limbs fitting together to make the whole greater than the sum of its parts. It belongs in a museum or something. Except there's no fig leaf big enough in the world to cover up his package. His cock is the size of Texas and below it, a big sac of balls hangs low. He moves to the bed and I get a glimpse of his gorgeous ass before he sits down. Holy cow! Sculpted buns of steel! They're practically surreal!

"Zoey, come on, now." He's beginning to sound irritated. "I'm not the big bad wolf. I'm not going to bite."

That's *just* the problem. I *want* him to bite. I want him to tear off every stitch of my clothing with his teeth, mark my body, and bite down on my lips. And then ravage me. Lick me with his tongue. Suck me with his lips. And then fuck me every which way he can.

We remain at a gridlock. I still haven't taken a step or said a word. His violet eyes burn into me.

"Zoey, please don't make me stand up and fetch you. If you do, I'm going to throw you over my knees and spank you."

I gulp. My first words: "You would?"

"Of course not, that would be sexual harassment, *n'est-ce pas?* Maybe even assault and battery."

*Assault me! Take me now!*

"Zo-eeey. Please. You're beginning to stress me out. A limo will be here to pick me up in fifteen minutes. Now, come over here, and give me a quick shoulder massage and then help me get dressed." He crooks his left index finger and signals for me.

"Okay," I squeak. With the garment bag draped over my arm, I take one baby step after another. I'm walking like I'm on tightrope about to fall off, except there's no safety net to catch me.

"Good girl, Zoey," he says as I near his bed. "Now, lay the garment bag down, and hop on the bed so you can massage my shoulders."

I'm teetering between fainting and jumping him. Somehow, I will myself to do as asked. I lay the garment bag flat on the giant bed and then crawl on to it so I'm kneeling behind him. I soak in his beautiful muscled back and his broad sculpted shoulders. The body of a swimmer. An Olympian. A God!

Wordlessly, I cup my hands over his shoulders and dig my fingers deep into his bronzed skin, pressing and kneading. He *is* tensed up; I can feel his knots, especially in his neck, and press deeper to loosen them.

He moans. "Ah, Zoey. So, so, so good. Your hands really are magic." He moans melodically again, and I wonder: Is this what he sounds like after he has a satisfying orgasm? My own body heats up, and wetness gathers between my legs.

"How do you feel?" I stammer.

"Better." His voice is sultry and soft. "I'm nervous about tonight."

"Don't be. You're going to win."

"I doubt it. I have some pretty stiff competition."

I don't think he has any competition in the stiffness department. I glance over his shoulder. His monstrous cock is still as hard as a rock. Every nerve in my body is sparking, and another surge of wet heat drips down my thighs. I'm so turned on I could cry.

Rolling his shoulders and head, he lets me know he's loosened up. "Enough. Help get me dressed now."

My legs Jell-O, I stumble off the bed and unzip the garment bag. I behold a magnificent black suit draped over a crisp white tux shirt with a plaque of "invisible" buttons and extra long cuffs. A purple bow tie that matches the color of his eyes is wrapped around the hook of the padded hanger, and a pair of black velvet slippers peak out of a shoe bag.

"Start with my shirt," he orders.

I remove the jacket, laying it gently on the bed, and slide the dress shirt off the hanger, the cool, starched cotton a sharp contrast to my heated hands. He takes it from me and slips it on. "I need you to button it."

"Okay." Starting from the bottom button, I do as asked. My eyes stay fixed on his six-pack, and I feel the ripple of each finely honed muscle against my fiery fingertips. I get to the top button and adjust the wing-tipped collar.

He glances down at his hands. "After I put the jacket on, I'm going to need you to do the cuffs."

My stomach scrunches. I have no experience with cuffs or cufflinks. But next, I have to help him with the slacks. I rummage through the bag for some underwear. Nada.

"Um, uh, aren't you going to put on some underwear first?"

"Zoey, I don't wear underwear. I thought you knew

that."

"Oh," I mutter. So, that fine cock is going to strain against the fine fabric of his trousers. I hope he gives himself plenty of crotch room. I take the satin-piped pants out from the bag.

Squatting down, I slip his two feet into the leg openings and inch the formal pants up to his knees. I'm salivating. His gorgeous cock is only a mouthful way. I can practically taste it. "Stand up."

At my command, he rises, and I'm once again awed by his imposing size. He looms over me. Gripping the pants by the waistband, I rise, sliding them up his long, muscular legs as I do. I try not to gaze at his erection or get too close to it. Impossible. He smirks at me. Asshole! Tucking in his shirt, I zip up the fly and hook the clasp. Thank goodness, I don't have to deal with a repeat of the jeans incident.

We're getting there. I hand him his single-button jacket and he slips it on. I do the button and flatten the satin lapels. It fits him so perfectly, accentuating his wide shoulders and his tapered, athletic physique. The wide cuffs of his shirt, however, hang out from the sleeves. Okay, now I'm in trouble.

"Zoey, the cufflinks are in the bag with my shoes. I reach for the bag and set the black velvet slippers on the floor, arranged so he can easily step into them. I then dip my hand back in the shoe bag and easily find a small silk pouch containing the cufflinks. I shake them out of the delicate see-through bag onto my palm. I study them. They're simple but elegant gold disks engraved with the letters ET.

"You're an *ET* fan? That's one of my favorite movies too."

He laughs. "Not at all." And then his expression turns a bit somber. "These cufflinks belonged to my father. His name was Edward."

"Oh," I mumble, covering up my embarrassment. I catch sight of a family photo on his nightstand and can see the powerful resemblance.

"They're my lucky cufflinks. My most treasured possession. I may win tonight if I wear them."

A wave of anxiety sweeps over me. What if I break them or can't fasten them? It'll jinx his chance of winning the Best Actor award. Oh, God! What should I do?

Brandon's impatient voice cuts into my despair. "Zoey, what are you waiting for?" Using his splint-free fingers, he plucks one of the cufflinks out of my hand. "I'll hold this one while you insert the other."

After a short internal debate, I decide not to tell him that I don't know the first thing about cufflinks. I don't even know where to start. Logic tells me I'm supposed fold up the cuff that drapes over the back of his hand, lining up the two sets of button holes, and then insert the cufflink into each slit to hold the cuff together. Fumbling, I manage to fold up the stiff, starched fabric and line up the holes. A fine layer of soft dark hair dusts the edge of his large, manly hand.

Pinching the edges of the cuff together with one hand, I attempt to slip the bottom half of the cufflink through the top slit with the other. Makes sense. Except I can't get the disk through no matter how hard I try. My hands are shaking and the damn buttonhole won't give an inch.

"Zoey, what's taking so long? The limo will be here any minute."

At the sound of Brandon's miffed voice, I panic, and the cufflink slips through the cracks of my fingers.

"Oh shit!"

"What's the matter?"

"I just dropped your cufflink."

"Jesus," he says, following my eyes to the carpeted floor.

*Crap. Where is it?*

"I don't see it!" he exclaims.

"Me neither!" My voice is thick with despair. I drop down on all fours and frantically search the carpet. Brandon follows suit, getting down on his hands and knees in his tux, the unfolded cuff trailing along the floor. We circle each other in our desperate scavenger hunt. Why can't we find it? It couldn't have gone far. And it shouldn't be that hard to spot.

Guilt stabs me in the gut and shoots through my blood. These are his lucky cufflinks—a family heirloom. If he doesn't wear them, he may not win tonight and it'll be all my fault. My eyes start to water. Several rebel tears escape and fall to the carpet.

"Why are you crying?" To my surprise, Brandon's voice is soft and sweet.

"I feel terrible. If we don't find it, I'll jinx your chances of winning. I'm so, so sorry."

I've never failed him like this. But to my even greater surprise, Brandon grabs the edge of the loose cuff and dabs at my tears. "Stop it. We're going to find it. It has to be here. Maybe it's on the bed." He stands up, slipping his bare feet into his tux slippers.

"Ow!" he shouts out.

Plunking back down on the fluffy bed, he removes one of the slippers and gives it a little shake. His face brightens with an ear-to-ear grin.

"Look what I just found!" He holds up the cufflink.

"Phew! Thank, God," I say with a loud sigh of relief. I leap to my feet.

He winks at me. "Here. Try again."

Before he can hand it to me, I draw in another sharp breath and, on the exhale, tell him the truth. "Brandon, I have a confession. I don't know a damn thing about cufflinks." With my help or without it, he may not be wearing his lucky charms. A resurgence of guilt mixes with despair.

"Don't worry about it. I'll do them myself."

*What!?*

My eyes almost pop out of their sockets as I watch him yank the splints off his fingers and fling them across the room.

"B-but—"

"My fingers are just fine now," he says as he fastens the cufflinks with ease.

For the second time tonight, my mouth crashes to the floor and I can't get a word to form. Finally, while he adjusts his bow tie around his collar, my mouth moves.

"Why the hell—"

He cuts me off. "Because I was having too much fun with you. I liked having you feed me and dress me."

I want to kill him! The asshole—make that, the sadistic bastard—tricked me. Played me for a patsy. He's done a lot of things to piss me off, but nothing comes close to this. I'm humiliated and furious. My blood is curdling. Did I tell you how much I really, really want to kill him?? His voice hurls me out of my treacherous thoughts.

"How do I look?" Smiling, he makes a final adjustment to his bow tie. The rich purple color turns his eyes an even deeper shade of violet. Two sparkling amethysts.

Holy hotness! My heart flutters and my pussy pulses. I'm melting like a popsicle. He looks breathtaking. Devastating. Sexy as sin. Every bit the big star he is.

"Y-you look . . . beautiful." *So, so, beautiful.* I think I'm going to die.

He flicks my chin, and the very touch of him brings me closer to my inevitable demise. A glint in his eyes and a small grateful smile light up his face. "Thanks, Zoey."

Before I can reply, I hear a car pull into the driveway. He hears it too.

"That must be my limo."

With a sinking heart, I follow him into the living room. It takes another nosedive at the sight of Katrina. Clad in a body-hugging sparkly gown in an eye-catching shade of coral, she looks like a goddess. Her golden hair cascades over her shoulders like a shimmering cape and an array of glittering diamonds light her up like the glimmering North Star. She completely ignores me. It's as if I don't exist.

She grabs Brandon's hand. "Come on, darling, let's go. I don't want to miss one red carpet opportunity."

"Good luck tonight, Brandon," I say, meaning it from the bottom of my heart. Yet, every word's an effort.

He looks over his shoulder as Katrina hurls him toward the door. Our eyes connect. I swear there are sparks flying between us. The ache in my core is palpable.

His eyes never leave mine as he quirks a small melancholic smile. "Thanks, Zoey. Look for me on TV."

Fighting back tears, I simply nod. They disappear, and after a forlorn sigh, I hear the limo pull away.

I slump down onto the couch and bury my head between my hands. I feel like poor Cinderella, left behind for the ball. Except Cinderella was way better off. At least she had a couple of cute mice to hang out with to cheer her up along with a trusty fairy godmother to make her dreams come true. Bippity-boppity-boo.

# Chapter 30

## Brandon

Flash! My eyes flutter madly. My head hurts. I'm having a memory breakthrough. I remember something and silently curse. I hate this shit. It's a goddamn circus. A media frenzy. The part of being a megastar that I despise. Our limo pulls up to the entrance of the Beverly Hilton, and even before we step out of the car, paparazzi storm us. *Click! Click! Click!* The never-ending flashes blind my eyes and clog my eardrums. I fake a megawatt Hollywood smile when really what I want to do is smash each and every one of these assholes' cameras. Wearing Katrina on my arm like a clunky piece of jewelry, the walk of fame down the red carpet feels like an eternity. That's because my fiancée insists on talking to every E! Entertainment reporter who accosts her and mugging for the paparazzi and glamcams. While zealous fans gathered outside the hotel are roaring "We love you, Bratrina!" and hoping to get a shot of us with their phones, I seriously feel like Mr. Katrina Moore.

A fashion blogger runs up to Katrina. "I love your dress. Who are you wearing?"

"Monique Hervé. She's also designing my wedding gown."

"When are the two of you getting married?"

Looking straight into a camera, she spews the date. "Saturday, May twenty-third, six p.m. Pacific Standard Time. Check your local listings and be sure to tune into Celebrity-TV for the special edition of *America's It Girl*."

Flashing a big smile and her ring, she sounds like a walking commercial for our wedding. I want to vomit.

Another female reporter runs up to us. "Bratrina, so glad to have you here. Tell me, Brandon, with your recent accident, did you ever think you'd *not* see this night?"

"Well—"

Katrina cuts me off. "We always knew this moment would come. I prayed for it every minute while I sat by his bedside in the hospital."

The reporter's face turns to mush. "That's so beautiful I could cry. Oh, and congratulations on your engagement. The best of luck to the both of you."

We're stopped yet another time. The bubbly Asian reporter shoves a mike into my face. "Congratulations on your nomination, Brandon. Do you think you're going to win tonight?"

I shrug my shoulders. "I'm wearing my father's lucky cufflinks. So there's a chance."

Katrina: "Darling, of course you're going to win."

"Is there anyone at home you want to say hello to?" the reporter asks.

Katrina grabs the mike. "Hi, Mommy." She waves. "And Daddy, if you're watching this from prison, just know I love you."

I have to say I'm a little touched. The reporter takes the mike and angles it back at me. "And what about you, Brandon?"

Just one person. "Yo, Zoey." I blow her a kiss. I hope she's watching and catches it wherever she is.

Katrina shoots me a dirty look. Make that a look that can kill.

Is everyone and their mother nominated for an award? The Emmy's, now that I remember, are bad enough, but the Golden Globes go on ad nauseam because they cover both motion pictures and television. Oh, and now they even give awards to online shows produced by Amazon and Netflix among others.

The only thing that makes these awards bearable is that you get to eat and drink during the show. Unlike the Emmy's where you're trapped for hours in a stadium-sized auditorium downtown, at the Globes, you're served a full-course gourmet dinner in the expansive but more intimate Beverly Hilton ballroom. The place looks spectacular with dazzling arrangements of flowers on every table and is overflowing with Hollywood glitterati dressed to the hilt. If I had to guess, there must be over two thousand attendees and that's not counting the press.

Everyone looks like they're having a blast. A chumminess saturates the room—reminiscent of a camp reunion. Hugs and kisses abound. As we make our way to our table, I'm both astounded and humbled by the number of people who stop to congratulate me and express their relief that I'm okay. Wow! Even De Niro and Scorsese give me man hugs and Glenn Close gives me a big kiss on the cheek. But most I don't recognize on account of my amnesia. Especially those nominated for all these cable series and movies I can't recall. Zoey's briefing only went so far. Sometimes I feel like I'll never catch up.

Our table consists of the Conquest Broadcasting nominees. In addition to me, there are several other stars, directors, and producers nominated, including *Kurt Kussler* director, Niall Davies. Also at our table is CBC production chief, Blake Burns and his lovely wife Jennifer, the head of MY-SIN TV, the women's erotica channel that's part of Conquest Broadcasting. We chat and I learn that several of her series are up for awards.

"When you have the time, you really must do one of our telenovelas," she tells me over the salad course. "We're putting *Shards of Glass*, another one of Arianne Richmonde's erotic romances into development, and you'd be perfect to play the lead, Daniel Glass. Women love you. Oh, and by the way, I love *Kurt Kussler*. I so hope you win tonight."

"Thanks," I reply. "I'd love to be considered for the role if my production schedule allows." So far, except for a short hiatus over the summer, the chances aren't good.

She takes a sip of her champagne. "Oh, and I suppose I should congratulate you on your engagement. I'm glad it's working out between you and Kat. More than you'll ever know."

Just like Blake, she calls my fiancée Kat. She's a little bit more supportive of our nuptials though hardly what I'd call enthusiastic. There's something unspoken. Do I really know the whole story? Maybe there's more to learn, but tonight's not the night.

Katrina is seated on the other side of me. After a very cold but cordial hello to both Jennifer and Blake, she's been on good behavior. Thank God. Most of the time, to be honest, she's been working the room, hobnobbing with every A-list celebrity, talking to reporters, and posing for photographers. And when she's not up and about, she's been tweeting non-stop, snapping photos, and taking selfies with her iPhone.

Comediennes Tina Fey and Amy Poehler are co-hosting this year's awards, and they've had the audience roaring with laughter. Though they're not on my memory radar, they're two funny chicks. While their opening jibe about Bratrina becoming a popular baby name and their ensuing *Kurt Kussler* "Get it. Got it? Good." spoof had me flushing with embarrassment, the audience was in stitches as was Katrina. The presenters, however, haven't been as entertaining, and now they're going through a phase of documentary film awards that I could care less about. Naturally, they leave all the big awards like mine to the end so viewers will stay tuned. I'm getting restless, plus Katrina is bugging me to take selfies with her that she can post on Instagram. No thank you. During a commercial break, I take a run to the little boys' room.

There are a couple of men taking leaks in the bathroom, none of whom I recognize. I find an empty stall and sit down on the toilet seat. I don't really need to take a dump. I just need a quiet place where no one will fawn all over me. I mean, it's nice to feel the love, but it can get to be too much. And besides, there's only one person I want to talk to. I pull out my phone from my trouser pocket and text Zoey.

*Are u watching?*

I hit send and wait impatiently for a reply. Finally.

*Yes. I saw u on the red carpet.*

:) *Are u alone?*

For some reason, I'm sorry I asked that question after I hit send. My pulse accelerates waiting for her reply.

*No.*

My stomach twists.

*Who are u with?*

It'd better be a girlfriend. Or her mother.

*Someone really cute.*

My blood runs cold. It's her fucking boyfriend.

*We're cuddling in bed.*

My blood sizzles.

*WHO?*

*Teddy.*

Jesus. A new boyfriend?

*Teddy who?*

*Bear. LOL! We're sharing a quart of Häagen-Dazs.*

Relieved, I smile.

*What flavor?*

*Coffee chip.*

*My fave.* :)

*I know. I stole it from your freezer.*

I laugh.

*U better replace it.*

*I will.*

*What do u think of the show?*

*Boooring! But Tina and Amy are funny.*

*Agree. What's going on now?*

*They're giving* the *Best Actress in a TV Drama award.*

*Who won?*

*Julianna Margulies for The Good Wife.*

*Oh.*

*BTW, where are u?*

*Men's room.*

*Taking a dump?*

*No. Just texting u.*

*No shit! LOL!*

*:-D*

*Shit!*

*What's wrong?*

*They're about to announce the Best Actor in a Tele-vision Series . . . Drama!!!! They mentioned ur name!*

*Fuck!*

I leap up from the toilet seat and dash out of the bathroom.

Jet-propelling myself back to the ballroom, I dig my hand into my breast pocket to retrieve my acceptance speech should I win. Except it isn't there. I fucking forgot it!

My heart beats into a frenzy as I speed dial Zoey. Panicked, I shout into the phone. "Email me my speech!"

Silence.

"Zoey, what's going on?"

"Hmm . . . can't find it."

"What?"

"It must not have saved. Just wing it."

"Balls!"

"Oh my God! You just won. They're looking for you! Hurry!"

"I'm almost there!" I end the call and slip the phone back into the pocket.

My heart is practically beating out of my chest as I race into the ballroom and sprint up to the stage. Applause and cheers boom in my ears. I can't believe it. I won the Golden Globe!

Breathless, I accept the award from my presenter, Kevin Spacey. All eyes are on me. I take a deep, calming breath, but my heart's still beating a hundred miles a minute. Clutching my award, I manage to get my brain to communicate with my mouth.

"WOW! This is amazing and so unexpected. Thank you members of the Hollywood Foreign Press. Um . . . uh, I also want to thank Conquest Broadcasting and Blake Burns for believing in *Kurt Kussler* . . . my incredible producer, Doug DeMille and his stellar production team . . . my talented, wonderful co-stars, Kellie Fox and Jewel Starr . . . my outstanding fellow nominees . . . my dear parents, Phyllis and Edward, and my mentor, Bella Stadler . . . and last but not least, I want to thank my beautiful assistant, Zoey Hart, for all you do for me. Love you!"

I triumphantly hold up the award and soak in the

audience. Holy shit! A standing ovation! Everyone is applauding and cheering wildly except one person. Katrina. She's in her seat, seething.

What the hell?

# Chapter 31

## Zoey

Jumping up and down on my bed, I'm literally doing a happy dance. I don't even care if I break a spring and the mattress crashes to the floor. I can't believe it! Brandon just won the Golden Globe and thanked *me* on national television! In front of a gazillion people! Called me beautiful! And then said, "Love you."

My cell phone rings. The strings of my heart go zing. It must be him. I hop off the bed and make a beeline for my phone. A tinge of disappointment. It's Jeffrey. We're on FaceTime.

"Girl, that was so exciting!"

"You're watching the awards?" My TV's still on, but I'm not paying attention.

"Of course. You're practically a household name. You're already trending on Twitter."

I laugh and then laugh harder when he tells me

about Katrina.

"Did you see the expression on Katrina's face when Brandon thanked you?"

I tell him I missed that.

"Don't worry. I recorded everything. There was a camera on her. Everyone in the audience stood up and gave Brandon a standing ovation except her. She was fuming. I thought she was going to throw a plate at the lens."

My laughter dies down, but a question burns on my tongue. "Jeffrey, I have to ask you something." I can tell him anything. And you can always count on a gay guy to tell it like it is. Brutal honesty.

"Shoot, Zoester."

"You know, when he said 'love you'? What do you think he meant by that?"

"Honey, this man's going to sweep you off your feet."

The breath in my throat hitches. In the corner of my eye, I glimpse the *Kurt Kussler* poster I shattered in a fit of madness. It's leaning against a wall. I still haven't fixed it, and now I regret my actions. Before I can get down on myself, Jeffrey's boyfriend Chaz gets on FaceTime and makes me laugh again. He berates Katrina's red carpet performance.

"Oh my friggin' God! I wanted to barf. That bitch was in everyone's face. I wanted to slap her! And can you believe that dress? It was so *vomiticious!* Oh and when Brandon blew you a kiss, she practically blew a fuse."

I'm laughing my head off. I so love Jeffrey and Chaz. They're my equivalent of Cinderella's chattering, adorable, supportive mice. We watch the rest of the Golden Globes together, and we all squeal when *Kurt Kussler* wins for "Best Drama Series" near the very end. The cast and crew rush to the stage and swarm a blown-away Brandon. Executive Producer Doug DeMille speaks for them all. What a night for the show! What a night for Brandon! What a night for me! I only wish I could be there with Brandon to celebrate.

After Tina and Amy congratulate all the winners and thank everyone for watching, I bid Jeffrey and Chaz goodnight. In no time, I'm hugging Teddy, dreaming of my Prince Charming.

The subconscious is a strange place. When I doze off, all of tonight's events come together in a fantastical dream that plays out in my head like a surreal fairy tale.

It's the night of the most anticipated event in Lala-land. The Golden Globe Ball. Everyone who's anyone will be there. A glittering gathering of Hollywood royalty. It's being given by Prince Brandon, the most eligible and handsome bachelor in the land. Rumor has it he's seeking the woman of his dreams—his princess bride. He's my idol. My sigh master. The love of my life. I long to attend, but my chances are nil.

"I'd like to go too," I plead to my evil stepmother, Enid, already dressed to the nines and hopeful that my stepsister will be the one to marry Prince Brandon.

She rolls her eyes. "Puh-lease. Peasants don't attend balls."

Her equally evil and done up daughter Katrina snorts with wicked laughter. "Mommy, she probably couldn't even find a ball gown to fit her."

Their words sting me like a hornet. She's right. I can't even fit into my beloved late mama's beautiful vintage dresses. In her haughty voice, Katrina demands that I zip up her coral ball gown. Reluctantly, I do as bid when what I really want to do is rip the dress off her back.

Not even a thank you.

"Now, Zoella, while we're gone, I want you to mop the floor and polish the furniture," pouts Enid as she heads toward the front door, arm in arm with her stunning daughter.

I sigh silently. I'm more of servant than a step-daughter. I'm thanklessly worked to the bone. Expected to tend to their every whim and need. Dear Papa had no clue when he married Enid and left her his two cents.

Their imposing black limo awaits them outside, leaving me behind with Katrina's sweet little white mutt, Gucci. Weighted with gloom, I sink into the couch. Life's so not fair. The fluffy pup dances around my feet, licking my ankles in an attempt to cheer me up. With tears in my eyes, I gather him up in my lap.

"Oh, Gooch, it's futile. They're right. I'm just a no one." My tears give way to uncontrollable sobs. I squeeze my eyes shut while my body heaves. I don't know how long I've been crying when Gucci barks madly, hurtling me out of my misery. My eyes blink open and my jaw drops to the floor. Standing before me are two boyishly handsome men dressed alike in flamboyant sequined jumpsuits. Each holds a sparkling wand.

"Who are you?" I gasp.

"We're your fairy godmothers," says the slightly taller of the two. "I'm Jeffrey and this is my life partner, Chaz."

"Wow! I have two fairy godmothers?"

"Double the pleasure. Double the fun," they reply in unison.

"Now, darling, dry your tears," says Chaz. "It's bad for your complexion."

"And you can't go to the ball with red eyes," chimes in Jeffrey.

My eyes grow wide. "I'm going to the ball?"

"That's the goal here." Chaz surveys me.

I look down at my sweats and then back at Chaz. "But I have nothing to wear."

"No worries. I'm a fashion designer by day, a fairy

godmother by night."

Jeffrey glances at his Mickey Mouse watch. "Oh dear, we're going to have to work fast. Are you ready?"

With a nod, I squeal out an eager "yes."

"Chaz, do you remember the incantation?" Jeffrey asks his partner.

"Abracadabra?"

Jeffrey rolls his eyes dismissively "No, honey, that's so last year. It's bippity-boppity-boo."

Chaz blushes. "Right."

I stand as still as a statue while the twosome recite the magic words and wave their glittery wands. On my next breath, I find myself shrouded in a cloud of sparkling fairy dust. And when the dust settles, I'm dressed in the most beautiful ball gown I've ever set eyes on. A sexy tulle and lace pouf in a color that's reminiscent of Prince Brandon's famous violet eyes. I gasp. "Oh my God, it's beautiful!" Tears of joy spring to my eyes.

Proud of their handiwork, my two fairy godmothers give me the once over.

"We need to accessorize," comments Jeffrey.

"Totally." Reciting another incantation, Chaz waves his magic wand. With a whoosh, he transforms my worn slippers into shimmering glass stilettos and my tears into a breathtaking pair of diamond teardrop earrings.

"Come look at yourself, honey," says Jeffrey. Taking me by the hand, he leads me to a floor-to-ceiling gold-leaf mirror. I gasp at my reflection. I hardly recognize myself. My hair is done up in a crown of dark curls, and I'm wearing a stunning spaghetti-strap dress that hugs all my curves and compliments my cleavage. I look like a princess! And then my heart sinks.

"Fairy Godmothers, how am I going to get to the ball?" The thought of driving my little Mini-Cooper in this voluminous gown doesn't sit well. Plus, I'm so anxious I'll probably get into an accident. Or pee.

"No worries. Where's your car?" asks Jeffrey. "I'm an event planner by day. I'm a whiz at these things."

I tell him it's in the driveway, and on my next in-hale, the duo escorts me outside. Wagging his tail, Gooch trails behind us. Jeffrey waves his magic wand over the miniscule white car, and before my stunned eyes, it magically transforms into a majestic Rolls Royce. It's fit for Hollywood royalty.

"Oh my God," I mutter under my breath. "It's out-rageous, but there's no way I can drive that to the ball. I'll crash it for sure."

"No worries." Grinning, Jeffrey recites another incantation over panting Gooch, shrouding him in a pouf of fairy dust. My eyes grow wide again as the little dog magically transforms into an adorable shaggy, white-haired livery.

"Meet your new driver." Jeffrey beams.

"Shall we, Madame?" says Gooch, gallantly opening the passenger door for me with a sweep of his arm.

Pinch me. This can't be real. I slip into the car as gracefully as I can while Gooch gets into the driver's seat.

"Get ready to par-tay," chants Chaz.

"Enjoy the ball," chimes in Jeffrey. "But there's one caveat. At the last stroke of midnight, our spell will be broken. The Rolls will turn back into a Mini, the driver back into a mutt, and you back to a simple servant girl."

A shiver skitters up my spine, but I'm still grateful for the incredible opportunity they've given me. "Fairy Godmothers! How can I ever thank you?"

"Give us hugs and be off. Have fun!" replies Jeffrey with a smile.

"Oh, and give the Prince a kiss from us," adds in Chaz.

In twenty short magical minutes, we pull up to the entrance of the Prince's majestic palace. It looks just like the castle at Disneyland. The valets take the car and escort me to the ballroom. For the third time tonight, my eyes grow as wide as spinning saucers. It's a veritable spectacle filled with the glitterati of Hollywood. All eyes are on me, but my eyes are on only one person. Heart-stoppingly beautiful Prince Brandon. Our eyes connect instantly. He meets me halfway on my walk down the red carpet until we're a mere breath apart. His violet eyes sparkle while a dazzling smile curls on his lips.

My heart flutters, my body trembles, and my legs go weak.

"You're beautiful," he breathes against my neck. "What is your name?"

"Zoella. But you can call me Zoey." I'm tingling all over. Every fiber of my being is sparkling like fairy dust. For the first time in my life, I *feel* beautiful.

"Zoey, may I please have this dance," he asks me. It's more of a command than a question.

Before I can respond, a perturbed Katrina clamors up to us. "Brandon, you promised you'd dance with *me*!" She shoots me a what-the-fuck-are-you-doing-here look.

Prince Brandon shoves her away. She lands hard on her bony ass at the feet of her nearby mother and shrieks.

"Mommy, do something!"

Her shrieks fade in the distance as Brandon sweeps me into his arms and waltzes me away.

I'm his. Melting into him, I lose sight of everyone around me. My body follows his as if we're sewn together. As if we've danced this way forever. He draws me in closer to him. His hard body brushes against my chest and his hard length against my center. My heartbeat accelerates and wetness beads between my legs.

"C'mon, let's blow this pop stand," he whispers in my ear and then whisks me away.

A few breaths later, we're in his royal highness's private chamber. Lit by candlelight, the cavernous room is dominated by a massive four-poster bed draped in violet satin and fit for a king. A tall grandfather clock sits in the corner. I can't make out the time. I'm too distracted. Too caught up in the moment.

Bathed in the glow of the amber light, Brandon holds me tightly in his arms. His soft lips kiss my neck, shoulders, arms, and face, touching every ounce of flesh they can latch onto.

"Oh, Zoey," he breathes against my neck. "From the minute I laid eyes on you, I knew you were the one."

My heart beating a mile a minute, my skin heating with fever, I lift my head and meet his smoldering gaze. Those violet eyes that dance with a glint of lust and love.

"Oh, Brandon. I've dreamt about you forever."

Before I can say another word, his luscious mouth captures mine and he continues our erotic dance with his warm waltzing tongue. Each sensuous sweep takes me further to the edge until we're entwined on a precipice. Fisting his silky hair, I deepen the kiss. I can't get enough of him.

Without losing contact with my mouth, he tugs at the back zipper of my gown, and glides the dress down my body until it puddles at my feet. To my shock, I'm totally bare and wonder if my fairy godmothers deliberately left out underwear. Pulling away from me, Brandon beholds me. I feel terribly naked and ashamed under his gaze, but his sincere words ease my discomfort.

"Zoey, you're even more beautiful than I imagined. A vision of womanly perfection."

While I tremble with rapture, his mouth repossesses mine with a fierce kiss and his hands coast from my ass to my tits, lingering on all my curves. Moaning into my mouth, he gropes my bare breasts. His thumbs rub my sensitive nipples and send a tingly rush of wetness to my sex. My hands move back to his head, but this time I cradle his gorgeous face between my fingers. Capturing one of my wrists, he places a hand between his thighs. His hot rigid length sears my palm. He's as aroused as I am. I feel the fiery desire that's consuming us both.

"Oh, Zoey, you make me feel so good," he breathes into my mouth, breaking the delicious kiss. His lips return to mine yet again before he rips off his clothes in a fit of passion. My fingernails dig deep into his heated flesh as he scoops me into his arms and lays me down on his regal bed. The sea of satin sheets feels cool against my flaming skin.

He climbs onto the bed. Every inch of his virile magnificence makes my skin prickle. I've never set eyes on a man as beautiful as he is. And have never wanted anyone more. Straddling me, his muscled legs pressed against my hips, he trails hot kisses from the ticklish crook of my neck, all over my breasts, and then past my abdomen until his head is buried between my thighs. After an inhale, he kisses my delicate folds with urgency and reverence.

"Oh, my sweet Zoey. You smell and taste divine. And you're so hot and wet."

"Oh, Your Highness, My Lord! What you do to me!"

"My beauty, I love that you call me Your Lord." His hand caresses my fluttering sex, a thumb running over my quivering clit. I moan from the ecstasy he's giving me.

"I want to own you. Possess you. Treasure you. Rule you."

"My body is your kingdom," I whisper.

"Your wish is my command," he hisses back. "What do you want, Zoey?"

"I want you to ravage me."

"You want to be my princess?"

"Oh yes, please."

"Please, what?"

"My Lord! Oh My Lord!" My voice is a breathless, desperate plea.

"Good girl."

On my next rapid heartbeat, he spreads my legs with his powerful knees.

"Show me what you want, Zoey."

My hand trembling, I wrap my fingers around his pulsing girth and guide it to my ever-ready entrance. The very touch of him at my door to pleasure sends a ripple of white-hot desire to my core. I let out an audible gasp as he drives his magnificent cock inside me, one glorious inch after another. I groan at the size of him, stretching me apart, filling me beyond measure. I want him all.

"Take me, My Lord," I cry out with equal pain and pleasure.

"You're mine," he growls. "I'm going to fuck you royally." With a loud grunt, he pushes all the way into me until his shaft hits a spot that makes me wince from the impact.

"Jesus, my love. You're so fucking tight and wet. You're pussy fits my cock better than a glove. Like a rare glass slipper . . . the perfect fit."

At his words, my muscles clench around his erection like a carnal hug.

"Christ, you're amazing," he sighs before pulling away. A heartbeat later, he lunges right back into me, and I groan when he hits my womb.

"Oh, Brandon, My Lord. Fuck me hard."

"How hard?" he taunts as he withdraws again. "This hard?" He rams into me with savage force.

"Oh yes!"

On my next heated breath, he pummels me with reckless abandon, rubbing along my clit and hitting my magic spot over and over. My body arches into him, and with each thrust, my moans grow louder.

"I've never had anyone like you," he mumbles breathlessly. "You feel so fucking good."

I'm speechless. I'm too consumed with the most indescribable feeling I've ever experienced, his body joined with mine, his cock filling me and taking me to a place where I've never been.

He puts his hands under my ass, his firm grasp making me gasp again from the intensity and pure ecstasy of his thrusts. My legs wrap around his hips, wanting to hold on, wanting this to never end as an orgasm begins to crescendo inside me. I rock my hips to meet his thrusts, each breath, each thrust harsher than the one before. A symphony of our breaths, flesh against flesh, fills my ears.

"You're so damn sexy," he pants out, picking up his pace and jamming me harder, as if harder is possible. "I can't fucking get enough of you."

The pressure inside me is so intense I think I'm going to die. Fisting the satin sheets so tightly, my hands begin to ache. My desperation for a release overtakes me.

"I need to come!" I scream out, ecstasy pulsating inside me.

"Not yet, my love."

"Please, My Lord, I beg you!" I can no longer hang on.

"No, Zoey. You will come when I say you can. I own you. Your orgasm is under my command."

I'm so close to coming. I bite down on my lip to keep from screaming. And squeeze my eyes shut.

"Don't hold back, Zoey. Open your eyes and let me hear you."

I do as I'm told. But as my eyes open and meet his impassioned gaze, the sound of a gong coming from the clock chimes in my ears. Gah! I've lost track of time. It must be going on midnight!

"My Lord, I must go!" I panic as the gong sounds again and again.

"No, Zoey, you can't leave." He grips my hips tightly, holding me prisoner. "You're mine."

"I must!" I cry out, so close to combusting. I'm silently counting the gongs. Oh no, the clock's on seven. I have only five seconds to escape. I can't let him see me for who I really am.

On the next powerful thrust and a pinch of my clit, I come with a cry of his name and a release so thunder-ous my whole body convulses. *Gong!* His cock shudders inside me with his own explosive release.

"Fuck!" he roars before he slowly withdraws.

The gong goes on ten. I only have two seconds.

Frantically, I bolt up and shimmy into my gown. Still in my stilettos, I dash out of his chamber. I can hear rapid footsteps behind me. I look over my shoulder. Wrapped in a satin sheet, he's coming after me. I run like there's no tomorrow through the ballroom of shocked onlookers until I'm out the palace doors.

"Come back, Zoey!" Prince Brandon's voice trails behind me.

Thank God, the valets have left my Rolls Royce parked in the driveway in front of the palace. Gooch is in the driver's seat waiting diligently for me. But as I approach the car, I trip. A glass slipper falls off. In a panic, I pick myself up, leaving it behind.

*Gong!*

It's too late! I'm too late! Before my eyes, the Rolls transforms back to my Mini, and Gooch is once again a little fluffy white dog who's looking out the window and wagging his tail at the sight of me. Back in my baggy sweats, I clamber into the car. I turn on the ignition, but the sedan won't start up.

Prince Brandon, with my glass slipper in one hand, runs up to me and tugs at the locked door. "Open up, Zoey. Let me in!"

I can't face him. Touch him. Bear the pain of my desire. Finally, the ignition catches. But Brandon is still clutching the handle of the door and banging on the window.

"Brandon, please let go! Please! My Lord, I beg you!"

"Zoey, if you leave me now, I will fuck every woman in the kingdom until I find my princess. My cock belongs in only one pussy. I'll find you again. I will know when I slip it inside you. The girl who's the perfect fit."

My core on fire and tears scorching my cheeks, I jam down on the gas and peel off the curb.

Another loud bang brings my dream to a screeching halt. Tossing and turning, I'm drenched in a cold sweat. But between my thighs, I feel a hot bed of moisture and relentless throbbing. The banging persists.

"Open the door, Zoey!"

Is he still clinging to the car door? I'm dazed and disoriented. Lost in a gray space between dreamland and the real world.

"Fucking open up!" The pounding grows louder.

My Prince . . . he's come for me.

"Zoey, if you don't open up, I'm going to knock down the door."

I blink several times while my heartbeat slows down. I glance at my cell phone. It's midnight. I made it home in time! I'm still treading the fine line between reality and fantasy.

The line fades and reality seeps into my veins. Fully awake, I realize I'm in my house—in the real Lalaland. I roll out of my bed, and after grabbing my robe, I stagger to the front door and unbolt it.

It's him! Brandon! A disheveled version of the gorgeous man I dressed earlier. His hair is unkempt, his eyes bloodshot, and his bowtie undone. I can smell alcohol on his breath. He may be more than a little drunk.

"What do you want?" I ask, my voice shaky from my dream. Embarrassment mixes with anticipation. There's a part of me that thinks he's come here to sweep me off my feet and devour me. My wet dream is as vivid in my head as when I dreamt it.

"You ate *all* my ice cream?" With each word, his voice rises with rage.

"Yes," I squeak. "There was only a little bit to begin with."

"But now, there's none. And I'm starving. We're going out to buy some."

"Now?"

"Now. End of discussion."

My ego deflates like a balloon that's been stuck by a pin. Who am I kidding? I'm no princess. I'm his personal assistant. His workhorse and slave.

Ten minutes later, we're at all-night "Rock 'n Roll" Ralph's on Sunset, pushing a shopping cart through the packed supermarket's freezer section. Though I'm dressed in my pajamas and he's in his tux, no one so much as gives us a glance or a damn who he is. Everyone's stoned or on some kind of high. Silence prevails. Still shaken from my dream, all I can think about is what would it be like to really fuck Brandon Fucking Taylor.

I'm more and more convinced this man's gone bi-polar. I mean, how can someone who's just had the biggest and best moment of his life be in such a bad mood? He hasn't said a word to me since rudely knocking at my door and waking me up. Seriously, if he doesn't stop frowning, he's going to get a permanent frown mark that won't add anything to his character.

"Are you happy now that you've got your ice cream?" I ask him, my voice thick with attitude.

Wordlessly, he sits at the island in the kitchen and rips off the lid.

"I'll get you a bowl and spoon," I say, heading toward the cabinets, "and then I'm going back to bed."

"Forget the bowl," he growls. "Just get two spoons. We'll eat the ice cream straight from the carton."

*We'll?* I don't think so.

I fetch him a spoon and say goodnight as I pad toward the back door.

"Where do you think you're going?"

"To sleep."

"No, you're not. Get your ass over here."

It's one o'clock in the fucking morning. It's now Monday. So contractually, I'm on duty, back to officially being his majesty's lowly personal assistant at his beck and call. With resignation, I join him at the island and hop onto a stool cattycorner to his. Glimpsing the shiny Golden Globe statuette on one of the kitchen counters, I falter trying to make conversation.

"Congratulations on winning. I guess your lucky cufflinks really worked."

No response. Silently, he picks up the spoon and digs into the ice cream. One heaping teaspoon after another. My elbows are anchored on the counter, my head sunk between my palms. I glumly watch him devour the container of Häagen-Dazs, my eyes riveted on his sensuous hands and mouth. You'd think I'd be drooling over the caloric ice cream, but I'm too consumed by my erotic dream. And the way he licks the melting dessert off his spoon.

"Why aren't you having some?"

"I'm not hungry." I squirm on my stool to quell the throbbing between my legs.

"Eat." He scoops up a heaping teaspoon of the ice cream and puts it to my mouth. "Open."

I part my lips and clamp my mouth over the cold spoon. His eyes stay on me while I gulp down the creamy dessert and lick off the remains.

"Have some more."

"Why aren't you at one of those awards parties?" I ask, ignoring his order.

He looks up from the ice cream. "I had a big fight with Katrina."

My ears perk up. And so does my mood. "Oh. What did you fight about?"

"I fucking forgot to thank her in my speech. The press is already all over it. Tomorrow's going to be a living nightmare."

"How could you forget to thank her?" *Easy!*

"I don't know. I was nervous. Plus, I had to wing it. To be honest, I can't remember what the hell I said."

*Should I remind him? Forget it.*

His words meant nothing. My heart sinks to my stomach. Prince Charming could never forget Cinderella. But I hold no candle in Brandon Taylor's heart. Svelte Cinderella was blond and beautiful like Katrina. I'm fat and mousy. I've got to stop dreaming. A fairy tale ending is not going to be mine.

# Chapter 32

## *Brandon*

I begin my morning after the Golden Globes the same way I always do—with a swim. Except instead of my normal twenty laps, I only do ten. Booze and a quart of Häagen-Dazs don't mix well. Hoisting myself out of the pool, I spot my manager Scott. He's heading my way at breakneck speed. Already smoking, he looks agitated. I throw a towel over my shoulders and meet him halfway.

"Brandon, the shit's hit the fan. Your speech last night is the talk of the Internet. It's worse than I anticipated. Every fucking gossip columnist online is wondering why you didn't thank Katrina. He hands me his phone. He's googled me. While Scott puffs on his cigarette, I read one headline after another:

Perez Hilton: "Brandon Taylor Wins Big at the Golden Globes. But Will He Lose Katrina?"

TMZ: "After the Golden Globes, Is It Splitsville for Bratrina?"

Celebuzz: "Katrina Cusses Kussler at Awards Party!"

E! Online: "Thanks but No Thanks. Is That It for Brandon and His It Girl?"

I scroll down until I've had enough. Scott follows me as I stride to a table. He takes the chair opposite mine. I hand him back his phone.

"I fucked up."

Scott blows out a cloud of smoke. "Big time. Katrina is fuming. She hasn't spoken to the press, but she's demanding a public apology."

"Shit."

I haven't seen or spoken to Katrina since last night. The scene she created at the Conquest Broadcasting after-party was beyond embarrassing. The shrieking and expletives were just the tip of the iceberg. She went ballistic and yanked my award out of my hand. She seriously would have either struck me with it or hurled it across the room had not security reined her in. Mobbed by reporters, I was lucky Blake Burns used his clout and got me out the back door and arranged for one of his company limos to take me back home. But nonetheless, the damage was done. And I'm sure today I'm going to pay the price. I have people who deal with these kinds of things, but Katrina's a loose cannon.

Contemplating what I'm going to say to the press

and how I'm going to handle Katrina, I catch sight of Zoey coming toward us. She's carrying a folder and a Starbucks bag. At the sight of her, my mood brightens. And my cock flexes. She always has that effect on me. I'm glad she was around when I came home last night even if she seemed a little down. Eating ice cream with her more than cheered me up. It aroused me. There was something about the way she wrapped her lips around my spoon that made them so kissable. I, of course, refrained, but it wasn't easy with my raging boner. If she only knew.

Meeting my gaze, my assistant shows no emotion. If anything, an expression that borders on coldness is etched on her face. Once at our table, she silently sets down the bag. With not as much as a good morning, she hands me my regular iced Caffè Americano. Scott eyes it.

"Whatcha got for me, sweetheart?" he asks my assistant before I can thank her.

"Nothing. Not even a smile. And by the way, my name is Zoey."

Do I detect some animosity? I wonder if she's still pissed at him for sending her away while I was in the hospital.

Her voice stays icy cold. "Brandon, here's your schedule." She places the folder in front of me. I flip it open and peruse the printout. It's a fairly light day. I just need to go to the recording studio at noon to do some pickup lines.

Avoiding eye contact, she continues. "I'm outta here. I've got a lot of things to take care of."

As she whirls around, Scott grabs her by the elbow. She tries to shake herself free. "Let go of me, Scott."

"Sweetheart, you've got your work cut out for you today. I need you to draft an apology statement for Brandon. You know, something along the lines of him being so excited last night, he totally forgot to mention Katrina in his acceptance speech."

Zoey's face grows seething mad. "Since when do I take orders from you?"

Scott sneers at her. "And don't forget to mention how much he loves her and is looking forward to their wedding."

With dark, questioning eyes, Zoey looks at me for a go-ahead. I nod.

"Zoey, that would be very helpful."

"Fine. Now, let go of me, Scott."

"Scott, let her go." My voice is firm and authoritative.

Ignoring my order, my manager leers at her "That's not all. You need to respond to all the tweets and Facebook posts that are questioning the future of Bratrina. And I want you to work with their publicists and try to get the two of them booked on one of those talk shows. Jimmy Kimmel or Letterman would be perfect."

"Okay, now let me get to work." She tries again to jerk her arm free of my salacious manager.

"Scott, did you hear me? Let go of her. Now!"

A smirk crosses Scott's lips. Rage crescendos inside me. My hands ball into fists. I'm so close to punching him I can feel the pain of the impact on my knuckles. Just in time, he releases her and blows a cloud of smoke in her face.

Zoey's eye narrow and her bowed lips press thin. "You know, you shouldn't be smoking. It's actually not allowed in the Hollywood Hills. It causes fires."

"Aren't we a Miss Know-It-All?" Scott deliberately blows another puff of smoke at her.

This time she waves it away and glowers at him. "Maybe you'd feel differently if *your* father died putting out a wildfire."

My brows lift. That's news to me. I swear the other day after she witnessed Katrina sucking me off, she told me she was going to see her father. Maybe in my mortified state, I heard her wrong. Or my fucked-up mind was playing tricks on me.

"Brandon, text me if you need anything." She stalks off before I can say another word.

Scott takes yet another drag of the cigarette. The repulsive smell of the smoke and tobacco is getting to me. I'm done with being Mr. Nice Guy. I'm going to tell him to put the damn thing out. Before I have a chance, he blows out another puff, flicks the ashes on the deck, and throws me another curve ball.

"You know, today's Katrina's birthday."

"It is?" *Shit!* I had no clue. My mind's so screwed up I'm lucky I remember my name or what day of the week it is.

"I'm taking her out for lunch at The Ivy. You should join us. It might help smooth things over and being seen in public with her might help quell rumors of your breakup."

"Can't. I have some pickup lines to take care of."

"Too bad. Hope you're getting her something expensive and taking her out for a nice, romantic dinner. That would definitely help calm her down. The Polo Lounge would be a great place for the two of you to be seen."

"Done." Crap. I haven't bought a thing for her or made a reservation. Mental note: Email Zoey and tell her to go to Tiffany's and pick up a bauble. Plus, make a dinner reservation at the Polo Lounge.

Scott flashes his pearly white teeth. They glow against his fake tan. They're perfect. In fact, too perfect. They've got to be caps.

"Good. You know, Katrina's mentioned you're still having a little problem in the equipment department."

I cringe. She's been sharing our sex life—or lack of one—with Scott? Okay, he might manage both of us, but it's none of his fucking business. Fucking Katrina.

Scott takes another puff and winks at me. "Brand-man, you should treat yourself to a little bauble too. A ring."

I glance at Scott's flashy pinky ring. So not my style. "I don't do a lot of jewelry."

He snorts. "I was thinking jewelry for your weiner. Trust me, those cock rings work wonders. You'll be as hard as nails and going at it for hours. Take my word, Katrina will love it."

Who is Scott to know what Katrina will or will not like when it comes to sex? Just how much does she confide in him? Or is there something more? Or maybe I'm just reading into things and Scott's just trying to be helpful.

He gives me the name of a nearby sex shop—a name that rings a bell—and I hesitantly thank him for the tip. Another errand for Zoey. She'll need to be discreet.

"Brand-man, you'll be thanking me again after you use it. Katrina will be way over the Globes screw-up."

I inwardly cringe and tell him I'll have Zoey handle it.

Scott's beady eyes darken. "You know, Brandon, I'm a straight shooter. I don't like that girl."

*And she doesn't seem to like you.* "What's your problem with her?"

"She's a little smartass. She thinks she owns you."

*She does. In more ways than one.*

"On top of that, she's been very rude to Katrina. If I

were you, I'd fire her fat ass. It's something I told you to do before your accident. You probably don't remember."

I don't. And I don't like the way my chain-smoking manager talks about Zoey. His cigarette is down to the butt. At this point, it's moot to ask him to put it out, and I'll wait till he lights up another. My mind right now is burning with more questions.

"Why did you force Zoey to go away while I was in the hospital?"

"For your own good. You don't remember shit, but that little twit's a thorn in your side."

"You had no right to do that."

"I made a big mistake."

"You did."

His lips snarl. "You're not kidding. *I* should have fired her sorry ass while you were in a coma and saved you the time and effort."

My blood is sizzling. It takes all I have to hold it together. "Scott, you may be my manager, but you have no authority to *ever* act on my behalf. I control all of my decisions at *all* times. Do you understand that? Don't *ever* cross that line again."

Scott's eye twitches. My gaze stays on him. With silent rage, I watch as he tosses his cigarette butt onto the deck and stamps it out with one of his shiny leather loafers.

"You'll be sorry you didn't listen to me. Trust me,

you could do a lot better."

Zoey is perfect for me. Maybe what I need is a new manager.

# Chapter 33

## Zoey

*Breakfast at Tiffany's* was one of Mama's favorite movies. She made me watch it with her a few months before she died. I didn't understand it. I thought the cat was cute and begged for a kitty afterward. I was allergic to cats so we never got one. But many years later, I watched it again with Jeffrey, and it brought tears to my eyes. It made me think of Mama. Unlike me, she was waifish like Audrey Hepburn, and I could hear her singing "Moon River," her angelic voice better than any movie star's. While Jeffrey gushed about Audrey's Givenchy wardrobe, I, the romantic, wished I could find true love like Holly Golightly. And could be ballerina-thin.

The melody and lyrics of "Moon River" play in my head as I float through the high-end jewelry store in Beverly Hills in a trance-like state. I hear Mama's voice. Memories of last night flicker in my head. After dressing my boss and hearing him thank me on the Golden Globes, I had high hopes. Now, I know my erotic dream was sending me a message. I'm delusional. I can never have him. Brandon Taylor is my heart breaker, not my dream maker.

The reality is he's in love with Katrina or I wouldn't be here. Believe me, the last thing I want to be doing is shopping for a glitzy birthday present for the stuck-up, evil bitch. The morning was bad enough, having to perfect a statement from Brandon about his undying love for her and assuring all his fans that their relationship was intact. Long live Bratrina! It took me hours. By the time I was done, I hated myself as much as I hated the bullshit words I finally locked down. Unshed tears brimmed in my eyes.

With a heavy heart, I roam through the main floor of the store. The Rodeo Drive outpost is not exactly the Fifth Avenue Tiffany's featured in the movie, but still it's Tiffany's. Dazzling diamond jewelry fills the display cases. Happy couples in love and wealthy matrons surround me. I don't really belong here.

"Can I help you?" asks an impeccably groomed, Audrey-thin sales associate. She tells me her name is Beatrice.

"Um . . . uh . . . yes," I stammer. "My boyfriend's looking for something special to give me for my birthday. He wants it to be right." I have no clue why

I've launched into this fantasy. Maybe I'm so mental I need to see a shrink.

The saleswoman beams. "You've come to the right place. Your boyfriend must be someone really special."

"Y-yes," I stutter. *She has no idea.*

"I suggest this diamond necklace. It's one of our signature pieces. Classic Elsa Peretti." She takes out a necklace from the display case and lays it on a black velvet pad on the counter. Under the overhead halogen lights, the bling blinds me.

"It's platinum and the diamonds are all D-colored stones . . . VVS1 quality."

Having no idea what all that code language means, I admire the stunning necklace with its abstract pavé diamond heart pendant. So sleek. So elegant. So Katrina.

"Yes. This is perfect," I splutter. *Too perfect!* "My boyfriend has an account here and told me to put it on his credit card. I hand her the "dummy" credit card Brandon gave me. To protect his identity, he has many with false names.

I stare at the exquisite necklace while Beatrice swipes Brandon's card. It'll look beautiful around Katrina's long, slender neck. I'm sure he'll give it to her at their romantic dinner tonight. The reservation at the Polo Lounge is all set. I almost didn't make it, but I was driven by my unquenchable desire to please him.

The saleswoman's breathy voice brings me back to

the moment. "Wonderful. The charge went through." Handing me the receipt, she smiles brightly. I eye it and gasp silently. Twenty-five thousand dollars. A bolt of jealousy tears through me. Score one for Katrina.

"Is your boyfriend coming by to pick it up or does he want it sent?"

"Actually, he's out of town right now and wants me to take it with me."

"Would you like it gift-wrapped?"

"Yes," I mutter, still drowning in jealousy. "He'd like that."

"Wonderful. I'll call someone." Moments later another Tiffany's staffer comes by to take the necklace to gift-wrapping.

"Thank you," I mumble as he skirts off.

Beatrice clears her throat. "In the meantime, can I show you some engagement rings? With that extravagant gift, I'm sure he's going to pop the question sometime soon. Perhaps Valentine's Day?"

Valentine's Day is just a few weeks away. The only question that pops inside my mind is—what will Brandon get Katrina for the occasion? I'm sure I'll be back here.

"So may I?" asks Beatrice, her voice pitchy.

"Sure," I say with hesitation. My stomach knots. Why am I playing this cruel game with myself?

Beaming, she leads me to the engagement ring section. I immediately spot Katrina's ring. It's hard to miss. The sparkling elliptical-shaped diamond outshines and outsizes the others by miles.

"How much is the ring in the front row center?"

Beatrice's smile widens. "Just a little over a million dollars. It's a flawless ten-carat D-colored marquise."

GAH! A million dollars? He spent *that* much on her? I feign composure.

"Would you like to try it on?"

Just the thought of this mega-expensive ring on my finger gives me butterflies. I shake my head. "It's lovely but not my style."

I sidestep to the next display case. Beatrice tracks with me.

Scanning it, my eyes take in the various beautifully displayed rings. And then I see it. A magnificent rectangular amethyst flanked by two glittering triangular diamonds. The stone is the color of Brandon's eyes. My favorite color. It's calling my name.

"May I please see the ring with the amethyst?"

"Of course." With a somewhat haughty attitude, Beatrice sizes me up. "I'm not sure if it'll fit your finger. It's a sample that's made for a very slender hand."

Inside, I'm simmering. She just called me a fattie. Well, I'll show her. In a calm, collected voice, I assure her it will.

Doubt is written all over her face. "Very well. Let's give it a try."

While she removes the ring from the case, I plant my hands on the glass countertop.

Beatrice's eyes widen with surprise. "Why, I think it'll fit you just fine. You have the most elegant fingers I've ever seen."

"Thank you," I say proudly. *Thank you, Mama.*

She sets the ring on another velvet pad. My eyes stay fixed on it. It's so, so beautiful.

"This is one of our newest settings. Many young brides prefer a colored stone to a traditional diamond. This one consists of a five-carat amethyst of the highest quality. The Trillian baguettes weigh over a carat. I think it will look lovely on you."

My heart and hands tremble in unison as I slip the exquisite ring onto my long, slender ring finger. It fits perfectly. Holding up my left hand, I admire it. My heart hammers against my chest.

Beatrice flashes a smile. "It fits you perfectly, and it looks absolutely stunning on your hand."

"It does." My voice is small and dreamy.

My eyes stay riveted on it. My pulse speeds up. Yes, this is the ring *I'd* want Brandon to give *me.*

Beatrice cuts my fantasy short. "Should I put a hold on it, dear?"

"Yes," I mutter. *A permanent hold.*

"Wonderful. Why don't you and your boyfriend come back over the weekend? You can show it to him. When he sees it on your hand, I'm sure he won't be able to resist."

I twitch a faint smile. "We'll try to do that." The tone of my voice is far from chipper. While Beatrice assures me the ring will be waiting for me, the assistant returns with a gift-wrapped blue box containing Katrina's birthday present.

"Enjoy your lovely necklace," Beatrice says as she places it inside a small Tiffany-blue shopping bag. Just like the one Audrey carried in the movie.

I take one long last look at the amethyst ring before I remove it from my finger. Reality stares back at me. Who am I kidding? Even if Brandon wasn't engaged, he'd *never* marry an overweight nobody like me. My aching heart tanks. There's no rainbow's end for me.

# Chapter 34

## *Zoey*

With now the heaviest of hearts, I run a few more errands for Brandon in Beverly Hills. I drop off a pair of his expensive Italian loafers at the "shoemaker to the stars" for re-soling, go to the beauty supply store to pick up more of his favorite grooming products, and then run into an exclusive wine store to pick up a bottle of Cristal—which I'm sure is for Katrina. Of course . . . he'll propose a toast before he showers her with that gorgeous necklace.

I have one last chore before I head back: a stop at a store in West Hollywood called The Pleasure Chest. A package is waiting there to be picked up under the name "John Steele." Another birthday present for Katrina?

When I step into the store, my eyes grow wide with shock. It sure as hell isn't Tiffany's. It's an emporium filled to the gills with all kinds of sex toys and accessories for both men and women. To my amazement, it's packed with customers, including many who look like they're close to sixty. I guess with the huge success of *Fifty Shades*, everyone's into kinky sex. An unsettling thought hits me: Is this the kind of sex Brandon and Katrina have? Or maybe tonight they're going to experiment, and he's going to surprise her with some birthday toys?

With a mixture of curiosity and apprehension—and an undeniable twinge of jealousy—I wander up and down the aisles. In the toy aisle, there are dildos and vibrators in every shape, size, and color, ranging from monstrous latex cocks to tiny vibrating bullets. I gravitate to one of the vibrators. "Sparky." It's molded like a huge pink penis and has an amusing rabbit ear attachment.

"*Bubala*, get that one," says a petite silver-haired lady standing next to me. She's got to be in her eighties and looks familiar—like maybe she's on TV or something. I'm sure I've seen her photo in one of those gossip magazines. She blabbers on in what sounds to be a Yiddish accent.

"Trust me, the other ones are *feh*. My Luigi loves using this *vun. OY! Vee* have so much fun. He loves to *vatch* me come! He says it's so sexy *shmexy.*"

Her adorable bluntness cheers me up a bit. I have to bite down on my tongue to stifle laughter. "Thanks for the recommendation," I say while she throws a couple of vibrating eggs into her shopping basket and sprightly heads down the aisle.

I follow "Grandma" down the next aisle, where she loads up on blindfolds, paddles, handcuffs, and whips. Everything you need for the total BDSM experience. "Have you ever tried these?" she asks me, holding up a small package. Nipple clamps!

"Don't they hurt?" I reply.

"I don't know, *bubala*. *Ve're* going to try them out tonight. Surprise your boyfriend."

She takes off while I continue to explore the various accessories. Rhinestone-studded cuffs with a leash? I have to admit I'm as aroused as I'm awed. Kinky eye candy.

My inquisitive mind wonders—what kind of toys does Brandon use? In my wildest fantasies, I've never imagined him using any. But now in my mind's eye, I picture him totally naked, wielding a whip. Handcuffed to a bed, I'm on all fours, wearing nothing but the skimpiest leather thong. My ass is in the air.

"You've been a naughty girl, Zoey."

*Oh have I!* I nod my head feverishly.

"And do you know what happens to naughty girls?"

I flinch and squeak out "no."

"They get punished."

On my next harsh breath, he growls and strikes the leather against the flesh of my ample ass. I wince in pain. And then another lash and yet another, not stopping until I'm screaming out with erotic sobs. Satisfied, he sits down on the edge of the bed and flips me over his knees, He caresses my fiery ass. The pain dissolves into exquisite pleasure but not for long. *Whack!* A paddle crashes down on my sore ass.

"Do you like being spanked, Zoey?"

"Oh yes!" I moan out.

*Whack!* And then another and another. I lose count. My moans morph into whimpers that get louder with each strike.

In my mind, I feel the sting, but in my core, I feel hot tingles. Fire and wetness co-mingle between my legs. I have the burning desire to touch myself, to make myself come. A hand reaches down, but just as my fingertips crawl to my hot, throbbing center, a voice sounds in my ear. My hand flies off my crotch.

"Can I help you find anything?" An androgynous, spiky-hair male in leather fetish attire faces me. A salesperson. Piercings dot his nose, lips, and ears, and tattoos glove his upper limbs.

Mortification races through me. "No, um, I'm good. I'm just here to pick something up. Where might I find my order?"

The young sales associate tells me it's probably at the cashier. Sheepishly, I turn in that direction.

The inky hair girl behind the counter could be the twin sister to that kinky sales dude. She's similarly clad in black leather with an abundance of piercings and tattoos; maybe it's The Pleasure Chest employee uniform. I ask her if she has a package for someone named John Steele. It doesn't surprise me Brandon used a pseudonym. The last thing he'd want would be for it to get out that he's some kind of pervert and frequents this place.

She smiles, revealing a tiny ring on the tip of her tongue. "Yeah. I have it right here." She reaches below the counter and produces a surprisingly small bag. I have no clue as to what might be inside. There's a part of me that wants to ask. And there's a part of me that wants to flee and leave the package behind. And tell Brandon that they misplaced whatever he ordered. Or didn't have it in stock so I can ruin his night with Katrina. But my loyalty to him and work ethic triumph over deceit.

"How much?" I ask with hesitation.

"It comes to forty-three fifty. Would you like me to charge it to Mr. Steele's account? He's on file with us."

I blink hard. Brandon has an account here? Does he know this, or is this something he's forgotten with his amnesia? Either way, the shocking news feeds into my wildest imaginings. Gah! Maybe he's like one of those men I've read about in my erotic romances who has a secret playroom where he stashes all his toys, fetishes, and gizmos. In my head, I picture a dark dungeon filled with spanking benches, ropes dangling from the ceiling, and racks of whips, paddles, and floggers. I inwardly shudder, but to say I'm not aroused would be a lie. A new tingly sensation invades my inner thighs.

Asking me again how I wish to pay, the cashier breaks into my deviant thoughts and causes me to startle. I just can't get over the possibility that Brandon is into kink.

"Cash," I stammer. Brandon was insistent I pay with cash and not use any of his credit cards. And maybe he doesn't want me to know he has an account here if, in fact, he remembers. Understandably, a mega-star like Brandon has to take extra special precautions to guard his identity at a place like this. I can only begin to imagine how far the tabloids would take a story about his secret kinkery.

At under fifty dollars, whatever he's bought here for Katrina isn't too expensive—certainly not some diamond-studded leash to latch on to her new necklace. I do a little math in my head. There's enough money for me to buy something. My mind lands on that pink vibrator with the cute rabbit ears that "Grandma" recommended. Why not? A job perk. Make that a necessity. The next time I get jealous or angry over Brandon and Katrina—or just plain horny—I'll use it and get off on myself. It beats smashing things. I may even start tonight. On the way back to his house, I'll stop off at an ATM machine and get some money to pay him back. While I'm sure he wouldn't miss the money, stealing from someone is not a value I was raised with. I can easily afford to put the charge on one of my credit cards, but just like Brandon, I don't want my name affiliated with this store in any way. In this town, word travels fast and with the Internet, even faster.

"Hold on, I'll be right back. I want to get one more thing," I tell the cashier. I dash back to the aisle with the toys and make a beeline for the vibrator. Just one left! I grab it and then run back to her. She's patiently waited for me despite the long line of vexed customers.

"Thanks for waiting. I want this too, but please put it in a separate bag."

"Sure. Good choice. You're going to love it."

*Not as much as I love him.*

She rings me up again. The total now comes to a little under a hundred dollars. Wow! That vibrator was expensive; it better work wonders. With a shopping bag in each hand, I head back to my car, in a much better mood and eager to find out what Brandon bought for Katrina. I'm *so* bad. The minute I get into my Mini, I look inside the bag. I don't know what I was expecting, but it wasn't this.

A dozen packages of mega-size condoms and a little toy. The Magic Cock Ring. Taking the toy out from the bag, I read the label on the package: "Guaranteed to make your erection bigger, stronger, and last longer." God, knowing the size of Brandon's cock, I don't think it can get any bigger. And for sure, he doesn't have a problem getting it up. But I'm shocked at the possibility that he needs help in the endurance department. Are he and Katrina having problems? My mind flashes back to that deep tissue massage I gave him. He hinted at ED. Maybe Katrina's birthday won't be so happy. Whoo hoo! With renewed optimism, I take one more look-see at my new toy. I love it and can't wait to try it out. While they're struggling, I'll be coming. I insert my car key into the ignition and whip out of the parking lot.

All this fantasizing has worked up my appetite. I'm starving. And I know what I'm craving. A big fat hot dog. God, that's phallic! Screw my diet! I can't wait to wrap my mouth around one. And I know just the place to get one of the best ones in town.

Located off Fairfax Avenue, The Farmer's Market is an iconic Los Angeles food court that's popular with locals, tourists, and even celebrities. I love it because it's so unpretentious, and it's the home of my favorite hot dog stand. Fritzi Dog.

After finding a spot in the jammed parking lot, I head into the busy open-air market. As I get close to my destination, the tantalizing smell of hot dogs grilling wafts up my nose, making me even more ravenous. Not only do they have beef hot dogs, but you can also order pork, duck, and even carrot ones. The line is long, but it moves quickly. While I should order the low-calorie carrot one, nothing but the beef one on a toasted bun will do. I force myself to pass on the potato tots and additionally order a Diet Coke. Holding a tray with my order, I wander through the market in search of a place to sit. While there are hundreds of tables scattered throughout the vast space, it's always super crowded no matter what time of day.

As I turn into another packed aisle, I see Brandon's manager Scott seated at a table, talking to a stranger whose back is to me. Scott's ruddy face is pinched—it looks like some angry words are being passed back and forth—and then he slams his fist on the table. Maybe I should just leave. Seeing him twice in one day is more than I can handle. I detest Scott, and he knows it. He's rude and uncouth. A total slimebucket. But my hunger trumps my second thoughts. I amble toward the only table available—the one behind Scott's. I'll just say hello and face away. I've brought along my Kindle.

As I near the table, the man, with whom Scott is arguing, leaps up. "You fucked up once. Don't do it again," I overhear him say. His tone is gruff and threatening.

"Okay, okay," replies Scott. "I'll take care of it." His voice is a tremor, and sweat clusters on his brows. He looks like a frightened mouse.

The other man turns around. I stop dead in my tracks. All at once, my blood ices over, my body freezes, and cold sweat pours from every crevice of my being. His venomous gaze meets mine. It's him! He doesn't recognize me, but I recognize him. Yes, he's twenty years older, but I'd recognize that face anytime, anywhere. Those dark beady eyes, pockmarked skin, and squashed nose that looks like it's been broken a thousand times.

Oh my God! It's the man who shot Mama!

The aftershock of my discovery hits my system like a thunderous bolt of lightening. I feel the sky fall from under me, and, on my next gasp, I'm crashing like a tailless plane to the ground.

BANG!

Oh the pain!

And then . . .

*FADE TO BLACK.*

**END OF BOOK 1**

## *UNFORGETTABLE 2*

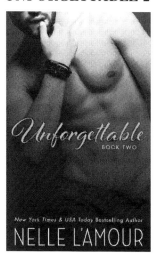

Brandon: I'd kill for her. I want to see the bastard who murdered her mother burn in hell. No other woman has made me feel so much. My heart aches for her more than my cock does. I want her to be mine. I want to own every ounce of her body and her soul. But I'm trapped by another who's holding a gun to my balls

Zoey: Who am I kidding? I'm helplessly and hopelessly in love with my boss, Hollywood heartthrob, Brandon Taylor. Our pasts are entwined just like our hearts. He makes me feel things in places I've never known before. But I don't stand a chance against America's It Girl, Katrina Moore. Forget it. There won't be a happily ever after for me.

As his memory returns, Brandon's need to dominate and possess his curvy assistant in every way consumes him while Zoey finds herself succumbing to his magnetic charm. Unexpected events and a fluffy little dog bring the twosome closer to their destiny, but an evil force threatens to end their journey. Fate's a bitch, right?

*THAT MAN*

INTERNATIONAL BESTSELLING SERIES
WITH OVER 1000 5-STAR REVIEWS!

In the meantime, if you want to find out what really happened between scorchin' hot Blake Burns and crazy Katrina, check out my THAT MAN series. Available FREE for Kindle Unlimited subscribers for the first time ever! Be prepared to laugh, cry, and swoon!

# Note from Nelle

Dearest Reader~

I want to thank my fab team of beta readers—Gemma Cocker, Kellie Fox, Kashunnah Fly, Kim Pinard Knewsome, Jennifer Martinez, Shannon Meadows Hayward, Janice Levin, Sheena Reid, Jenn Moshe, Karen Silverstein, Jeanette Sinfield, Mary Jo Toth, and Joanna Warren along with fellow writers, Arianne Richmonde and Adriane Leigh. Each of these incredible women has made a difference, and I feel blessed to have them in my life.

I also want to give special thanks to my amazing personal assistant, Gloria Herrera, for getting me through this launch. I don't know how I've lived without her!

And now, a big shout out to all of you for reading *Unforgettable 1*. If you enjoyed it (fingers crossed!), I hope you will spread the word among your friends and Facebook reader groups as well as leave a review. Positive reviews, regardless of length, help others decide to read my books and mean the world to me.

Please don't hesitate to contact me. I love to hear from my readers. And be sure to sign up for my newsletter: http://eepurl.com/N3AXb. I can't wait to bring you *Unforgettable 2* and *3*. Expect plenty of twists and turns and lots of steam! Thank you again from the bottom of my heart for your love and support.

MWAH!~Nelle ♥

# *About the Author*

Nelle L'Amour is a *NEW YORK TIMES* and *USA TODAY* bestselling author who lives in Los Angeles with her Prince Charming-ish husband, twin teenage princesses, and a bevy of royal pain-in-the-butt pets. A former executive in the entertainment and toy industries with a prestigious Humanitus Award to her credit, she gave up playing with Barbies a long time ago but still enjoys playing with toys with her husband. While she writes in her PJs, she loves to get dressed up and pretend she's Hollywood royalty. She writes juicy stories with characters that will make you both laugh and cry and stay in your heart forever.

Nelle loves to hear from her readers. Connect to her via:

Email:
nellelamour@gmail.com

Twitter:
www.twitter.com/nellelamour

Newsletter:
http://eepurl.com/N3AXb

Facebook:
www.facebook.com/NelleLamourAuthor

Amazon:
amazon.com/Nelle-LAmour/e/B00ATHR0LQ

Website (coming soon):
www.nellelamour.com

# Books by Nelle L'Amour

## Unforgettable

*Unforgettable Book 1*

*Unforgettable Book 2*

*Unforgettable Book 3*

## Seduced by the Park Avenue Billionaire

*Strangers on a Train*

*Derailed*

*Final Destination*

*Seduced by the Billionaire Boxed Set*

## An Erotic Love Story

*Undying Love*

## Gloria

*Gloria's Secret*

*Gloria's Revenge*

*Gloria's Forever*

*Gloria's Secret: The Trilogy*

## THAT MAN Series

*THAT MAN 1*

*THAT MAN 2*

*THAT MAN 3*

*THAT MAN 4*

*THAT MAN 5*

## Writing under E.L. Sarnoff

*Dewitched: The Untold Story of the Evil Queen*

*Unhitched: The Untold Story of the Evil Queen*

21995205R00203

Printed in Great Britain
by Amazon